What people are saying about …

Wolves Among Us

"Ginger Garrett's new novel, *Wolves Among Us,* transported me to sixteenth-century Europe from the very first page with its stunningly beautiful language and masterful use of sensory material. The novel uncovers an important, thought-provoking topic. Quite a few times I wanted to stop and ponder a point made in the book, relating it to life today; I could not stop, however, as the novel itself compelled me to read on."

Sandra Byrd, author of *To Die For,* a novel of Anne Boleyn

"A palpable suspense keeps the pages turning in this tragic chapter of history where innocent women were condemned, false prophets reigned with fear and superstition, and those who fought to get the Word to the masses risked their very lives. More disturbing is that such wolves still lurk among us, but thanks to the sacrifices of saints before us, we readily have the Word to expose them."

Linda Windsor, author of *Healer,* Book One in the Brides of Alba series

"With heartrending characters caught in a battle between good and evil and a plot interwoven with false religion, deception, and a hunger for the truth, *Wolves Among Us* is a gripping novel with eternal implications that had me thinking about the current state of Christianity and my own heart long after the final page."

MaryLu Tyndall, Christy Award
finalist and best-selling author of the
Legacy of the King's Pirates series

"A spellbinding journey into the heart of a village and the heart of a woman seeking truth. Garrett's lovely storytelling binds us to our fellow women of the turbulent sixteenth century and reminds us that, even today, only the Ultimate Truth can set us free."

T. L. Higley, author of *Pompeii: City On Fire*

"*Wolves Among Us* is a story that lingers in the heart, a story about the mysteries of the spiritual realm and the power of God to shine light on the darkness around us. Ginger Garrett is an excellent novelist."

Hannah Alexander, author of the
Hideaway series and *A Killing Frost*

"In *Wolves Among Us,* Ginger Garrett has created intriguing, true-to-life characters who face struggles that challenge their faith."

Margaret Daley, award-winning
author of seventy-five books

Wolves Among Us

a novel

Ginger Garrett

David C Cook

transforming lives together

WOLVES AMONG US
Published by David C Cook
4050 Lee Vance View
Colorado Springs, CO 80918 U.S.A.

David C Cook Distribution Canada
55 Woodslee Avenue, Paris, Ontario, Canada N3L 3E5

David C Cook U.K., Kingsway Communications
Eastbourne, East Sussex BN23 6NT, England

David C Cook and the graphic circle C logo
are registered trademarks of Cook Communications Ministries.

The website addresses recommended throughout this book are offered as a
resource to you. These websites are not intended in any way to be or imply an
endorsement on the part of David C Cook, nor do we vouch for their content.

This story is a work of fiction. All characters and events are the product of the author's
imagination. Any resemblance to any person, living or dead, is coincidental.

Unless otherwise noted, all Scripture quotations are taken from the Holy
Bible, New International Version®, NIV®. Copyright © 1973, 1978, 1984 by
Biblica, Inc™. Used by permission of Zondervan. All rights reserved worldwide.
www.zondervan.com. Scripture quotations marked MSG are taken from *THE
MESSAGE*. Copyright © by Eugene H. Peterson 1993, 1994, 1995, 1996,
2000, 2001, 2002. Used by permission of NavPress Publishing Group. John
10:10–13 in chapter 23 is adapted from William Tyndale's gospel of John.

LCCN 2011920857
ISBN 978-0-7814-4885-7
eISBN 978-1-4347-0374-3

© 2011 Ginger Garrett
The author is represented by MacGregor Literary.

The Team: Terry Behimer, Nicci Hubert, Amy Kiechlin,
Sarah Schultz, Caitlyn York, Karen Athen
Cover Design: Kirk DouPonce, DogEared Design
Cover Photos: shutterstock_26035945;
iStock_000000313735; iStock_000007332085

Printed in the United States of America
First Edition 2011

1 2 3 4 5 6 7 8 9 10

012711

Acknowledgments

First, to the entire team at David C Cook: I owe you a debt of gratitude. The economy is rocky, the market is changing, and even when I get discouraged, you continue to believe in my books. Thank you more than I can say.

To Nicci Hubert, an editor who gave me plenty of work (or is it the other way around?): I owe you a debt of gratitude too. I had such peace about working on this book knowing you were my editor.

To Chip MacGregor, literary agent extraordinaire: Thank you for being willing to walk with Mitch and me on this road.

To my novelist friends whom I treasure: India Edghill, Siri Mitchell, Kimberly Stuart, Sandra Byrd, the girls on the bean loop, and the writers of the Silver Arrow critique group: Thank you for keeping me sane and always laughing.

To my readers: I love your emails more than I can say! Please keep them coming. I love to know what is on your minds and hearts.

And lastly, to my family—I love you all.

Watch out for false prophets. They come to you in sheep's clothing, but inwardly they are ferocious wolves.

—Jesus

Chapter One

Germany, 1538
Dinfoil Village at the southeastern edge of the Black Forest

Weeks had gone by since winter had lost her blinding white beauty. Cold gray mud at Father Stefan's feet and dull clouds above him were all that remained of her icy pageant. He waved his hand at the low clouds, willing them to be gone. The hopeful golden sun of spring was overdue. He longed for its warmth to awaken new life in his little village.

The good Lord had other plans for the morning, however. The sun remained shrouded, and the air kept its chill after a midnight rain. Father Stefan could see his breath when he exhaled, a small wonder that still fascinated him even in these, the middle years of his life.

Each wet stone on the cobblestone streets of Dinfoil was packed so close to the next that the market lane looked like the side of an enormous, glistening brown fish. The lane was as slippery as a fish too, and Father Stefan was careful as he walked. If he slipped and broke a leg, he would be of no use to anyone—not as a spiritual father or as the town physician.

The sky may have refused any promise of warmth, but the new day still brought its own comforts. Bread baking in ovens and the crisp hints of spring's first greens teased his nose as life burst out into the lanes everywhere he looked. Last night the great lashes of lightning had driven everyone inside early. Now no one wasted a moment starting the new day: Shutters were being opened as he walked, children ran through the leaves torn from trees by the winds, and merchants dashed with their carts along the bumpy stone lanes, anxious to reclaim yesterday's lost business. When winter's ice melted away, travelers appeared from many villages, eager to spend their money at the market and meet new people. Fresh tales were as coveted as fresh supplies in those first weeks of spring.

Father Stefan walked through the town square, where children played prancing ponies, skipping in wide circles. One boy slipped, catching himself on his palms. He winced and muttered a curse under his breath. When he caught Father Stefan watching him, he blushed and looked away.

Stefan suppressed a frown and looked around. The boy's mother had done penance for her coarse language not a week ago, and here her boy was, repeating her sin.

"Mothers, mind your children," he called out, hoping the village's women could hear him through their open windows. "The stones are treacherous this morning." He shook a finger at a boy. "No more of that," he said.

Father Stefan walked along, greeting his parishioners, nodding at the shopkeepers and housemaids who were still opening shutters. The wealthier the family, the closer they lived inside the square, and the more housemaids he saw at work.

As was usual for this hour, no one appeared in the windows of those expensive homes except maids and dogs. After maids opened the shutters, several dogs popped their heads into the windows, looking down with great interest at the people in the square. Father Stefan particularly liked seeing the yellow mastiff that often sat, solemn as a magistrate, in a window, his jowls set in judgment. Another dog across the lane watched with bulging eyes and a little black mouth. That dog, outraged at the activity below him, barked and yapped at each passerby.

Marie, the young daughter of a parishioner in Father Stefan's church, pranced past, chasing after her little brother. She ran into Father Stefan, knocking him onto his rear. She looked horrified.

"Father Stefan. Forgive me," she said.

He held his side with one hand and used the other to push himself back up.

"No need for forgiveness, Marie. It was an accident, after all."

Her face looked ashen. Her chin began to tremble. She was one good breath away from a loud wail. Stefan reached out and tapped her on the nose, startling her.

"How is your mother's new baby girl?" he asked, looking down to wiggle his eyebrows at the young boy who now stood at the girl's side. The boy giggled, and Marie glanced at him before she smiled too.

She had swallowed back her tears, but her eyes were still wide and watering. "The baby is well, thank you. She is at home with Mother. She doesn't smell very good, though."

Father Stefan pressed his lips together to catch a chuckle. "Yes, Marie, babies do smell. Tell your mother I will be glad to have her back with us for Mass."

"But Mother is not well, Father Stefan. She cries a lot now that she has given birth. And she is pale. I try to get my brother to play with me outside, to let her rest, but I don't think she notices."

"I see." He smiled and nodded, a signal that he was ready to be on his way.

Marie grabbed him by the hand. "Perhaps you could come see her?"

Stefan disentangled himself and stepped back. "My place is in the church. As is hers. Remind her of that. When she gets back to church, she will feel better at once." He leaned down and flicked his hands at Marie, sending her away.

Marie hesitated, then rushed at him and planted a kiss on his cheek. She turned and ran off with her brother before he could say anything else. Stefan pressed a hand against the spot she had touched, mystified.

The sun broke free for a moment, warming Stefan's arms. He pushed up the sleeves of his shirt, catching more of this sudden pleasure, the second unmerited grace of the day.

The thought prodded Stefan to turn and get on with his morning business. He couldn't just stand here smiling in the sun like a fool. *Pleasure is a fool's reward,* he thought, *a distraction that keeps good people from doing God's work.* He must buy his dried hops and be back at the church before the next Mass. As he walked the square, he greeted the sweet young parishioner Elizabeth, who shopped at the herb market. She gave a shy nod and gestured back to the church, which stood at the far end of the square. Stefan smiled and nodded his head in agreement. Yes, it was almost time for Mass. They had both reason to hurry.

He then spotted Dame Alice with her wide, soft face. She
sat on an upturned barrel at the front door of her home. Though
wealthy, she rarely busied herself with women's work, much to
Stefan's dismay. Instead she sat at her entranceway with her white
hair neatly plaited above her ears, acknowledging those who
passed.

Stefan watched as Mia, the sheriff's wife, bustled past him,
darting between the town's children, clutching her coin bag to her
stomach as she approached the butcher's shop.

"Mia!" Dame Alice called out.

Mia stopped, clearly startled.

Dame Alice gestured widely with her arms. "Come and eat,
child. I put a leg of lamb on the fire. Come and tell me of your
morning."

Mia glanced in every direction, her face turning red as others
watched the interaction. She pulled her scarf lower over her eyes and
hurried away.

"Mia!" Dame Alice shouted. "You need to eat. It's how God
made us."

Mia pretended not to hear, though Stefan knew better. Her jaw
muscles were flexing as if she was sorely tempted by Dame Alice's
invitation. But Mia was a good wife who she knew had no time
for the gossip of idle women. Stefan would have to chastise Dame
Alice once more at her next confession, though it would do no good.
She had lost both her daughters and one grandson in a plague years
before. Since then she had cared for the young women of the village
like a mother might. He worried that too much gossip was exchanged
at her kitchen table.

Stefan nodded in satisfaction as Mia ducked inside the shop. Perhaps she was too thin, but it was merely a testament to her tireless devotion to her husband and child. *A model citizen, that Mia,* he thought. *Never a moment spent in mischief with other women.*

Stefan looked up to see an unfamiliar woman with a hard, lined face staring at him from across the square. From the distance her eyes were blue flames. Her dull gray hair was long and free, hanging down to her waist. The strange woman looked up into storm clouds that were now rolling toward the village. Her eyes narrowed as her gaze returned to Stefan, accusing and cold, as if the night's storm had been his doing.

A rooster crowed from the roof of a shop, distracting him. Thunder growled as it approached from behind the clouds. He turned back and strained for a glimpse of the woman again, but with no reward. Sometimes the market brought strange customers. She was, no doubt, just another oddity in his day.

Storm winds stirred his thin robes. He pulled his sleeves further down on his arms and put his mind back to his errand.

Mia's husband, Sheriff Bjorn, had arrived on his doorstep last night. He had drunk a considerable amount of Stefan's beer before he left for home. Stefan's beer had no equal, though all the priests of his order learned the art of brewery. Wine tasted bitter and ruined many stomachs. But Stefan's beer, made with grains he selected by hand and scent, ministered to anyone who drank it. His beer, the color of an emperor's robe, was rich in nourishment and always bubbling. Even the pasty, flecked loam, leftover from the brewing yeast, proved good for ailing infants and livestock.

Bjorn, thirsty and agitated, had arrived at his doorstep, hoping for a draught. He had said he spent all night looking for the wolf that had stolen two of the sheep from the parish stock. Erick, Stefan's servant, had wanted to join the hunt, but Bjorn refused him. Bjorn was not given to companionship. Erick would learn that in time.

The wolf—a tiresome, clever enemy who had yet to be caught—taunted then all. Taking two sheep was a crime that could not be overlooked. Stefan's flock of sheep was small, only ten animals. His flock of parishioners was small too, perhaps one hundred people in total, not including those too weak or old to come to Mass. Stefan knew the wolf would be caught in time. But wolves and sinners had one thing in common: When they stole what was not theirs, their appetite for more only grew stronger. Appetite was always the doom of the unjust.

Another cloud rolled over the sun, and its shadow swept over the townspeople. A slinking darkness stole their last hope for a fine spring morning. Everyone paused, looking up and around. Shadows so early in the day meant a storm was growing in power, hiding itself at the edges of town, preparing for its first strike.

As the cloud peeled back from the sun, the shadow passed, and Stefan sighed.

A woman bumped into Stefan just then. He steadied himself and reached out to her, but she collapsed. His knees buckled under her sudden weight in his arms, and he struggled to get her to her feet. He lifted her and realized the woman was Catarina, a quiet, gentle wife from his parish. He looked up and saw Mia step from the butcher's shop, carrying a roast, stopping when she saw the accident, as did a few others.

Catarina's eyes were open, but she didn't seem to recognize anyone. She pointed at the darkened alley that ran between two lopsided rows of houses.

"What is wrong, Catarina?" he asked.

She opened her mouth to gasp for a breath she could not catch.

"Did something scare you? Is it the wolf?"

She managed a deep breath that shook her body. "I love the Lord, as you are my witness. This crime is not my doing."

Stefan saw in his peripheral vision Dame Alice, who jumped up and moved toward them.

"Do you believe me?" Catarina asked, her voice straining. "Father Stefan," she said, grasping his arms. "I'm trying to tell you he's dead."

"Who is dead?"

Dame Alice came from behind Father Stefan, pushing him aside, taking Catarina by the shoulder. "Who is dead, child? What are you talking about?"

"My husband."

Catarina kept pointing down the lane, but there was no sign of mischief. "Nonsense, dear," Dame Alice said. "Why would you say he is dead?"

"His horse is in the lane. My husband is not on it."

"You saw his horse wandering alone?" Dame Alice asked, stroking her arm. "Is that all? My dear …"

"From this one fact you have imagined your husband's death and have frightened us all?" Stefan tried to control his indignation. "He's probably drunk again, is all. Sleeping it off somewhere to get out of the rain."

Catarina should have been happy. Cronwall was not known for being a gentle husband.

Dame Alice reached for Catarina's hand. "You're so cold, child." She took off her outer cloak and wrapped it around Catarina, who did not notice.

Stefan pressed his lips together and cleared his throat. "Now, Catarina ..."

"You're going to say this is my fault." Catarina looked up at him. She dug her fingers into his arm. "The village is in danger."

Father Stefan tried to pry away her fingers. "Stop this. Cronwall is just sleeping his liquor off somewhere. He will be home soon."

She gripped his arm tighter, making her knuckles go white, then she buried her face in his robe. "You don't understand."

"Elizabeth," Stefan called out, hoping the young girl would still be about. When he saw her peering through the crowd, he nodded to her. "Bring Catarina a dried apple. She has no color in her face." The girl obediently ran off to the market.

He sighed. "And someone wake Bjorn," he called out.

Catarina shoved him away. "No."

"My request for Bjorn should please you. If what you say is true, we'll need the sheriff. He can make an arrest."

She laughed or coughed—he couldn't be sure which—and flecks of spit landed across his cheek.

When he unlatched her hand from his arm, Catarina ran off, leaving Stefan to wipe off the spit. His wet fingers were tinged with what looked like blood, but Catarina had said nothing about being hurt. The crowd that had gathered was whispering, watching him. Stefan walked between them to peer down the lane Catarina had pointed to.

Church bells rang, calling everyone to Mass. Stefan frowned at the reminder. He belonged in church, not in the street, and not down a dirty, empty lane looking for a lone horse and a dead man on the word of a confused woman. Women were prone to hysteria. He found it most discouraging. His fine morning was ruined.

He turned for the church, which was only a few doors down, but no one followed.

"Time for Mass!" he shouted. A few people glanced at each other. "Bjorn will not be here for a good hour; we all know that." At this, people followed.

Stefan glanced back at the lane just once more. Sin was his responsibility. Crime belonged to Bjorn. As for women—well, only God knew what to do with them.

Chapter Two

Stefan refused to rush the benediction. He heard the constant sounds the congregation made, the restless tapping of feet, all those fingers drumming against jiggling knees. As soon as he finished the service, the people would rush for the doors, curious to see what Bjorn had done about the morning's drama.

Wind rattled the doors, destroying the last perfect moment of peace—Stefan's favorite moment in the service. He dismissed the congregation, remaining behind as they rushed out, watching dead brown leaves blow in from the streets in their wake. The storm was edging ever closer. Stefan left the church, struggling to close the doors behind him against the winds.

Bjorn had not yet arrived. Stefan saw the crowd eyeing him again, waiting to see what he would do next. He wanted nothing more than to be done with the morning.

"Can you see him? Is he on his way?" Stefan asked them. He liked submissive church crowds that sat politely on benches, not restless, gawking throngs milling about. "We should wait."

"Why?" Dame Alice said. "You know women can't be trusted.

We're prone to imaginations; you have often said it yourself. Surely there could be no real danger there."

"There has been a wolf among us," Stefan answered. "It might not be safe to wander alone."

"Is it really the wolf you are afraid of?" Dame Alice said. "Or are you afraid Catarina was telling the truth?"

Stefan smoothed his robe and adjusted the belt. He would bring this up at her next confession. Her tone was not fitting for her sex or his station. "I see I must do this if you are to give me any peace."

He stepped into the quiet lane. For the sake of his flock, he would determine himself whether there were dangers. The houses huddled close together, each built as high as the builder could manage, to keep the upper bedchambers warm. Roofs leaned across the lane as if to gossip with other roofs, blocking the sunlight as he came around a curve. The builders of old, while coveting height for the warmth it created, had given little care to keeping the lane straight. Houses looked as if they had been dropped from the sky along the lane. Each house had a different width and was made of different materials; together they signaled a lack of foresight among the town elders. Stefan clucked his tongue, creating the only sound to be heard above the scratching rustle of leaves and straw blown against walls by the winds. The lane appeared empty; not even a cat stirred to chase its breakfast. He cleared his throat and walked further down around the next house as an unseen animal wailed in warning. *Probably only a howl made by the wind,* he thought.

Cronwall's horse ate greens out of a window box, his heavy mouth tearing entire plots free and sprinkling shreds of his breakfast all over the lane. Stefan craned his neck and looked past the old fellow. He had eaten his way all along the lane, leaving a sad trail of broken greens. The horse looked up, then went back to his breakfast. Steam billowed out of his wide black nostrils as he exhaled.

Stefan ran a hand across his forehead. The horse was alone and definitely the one who belonged to Catarina's husband, Master Cronwall. The crest on the horse's blanket made that clear. Catarina had at least been right about that. But Cronwall abandoning it did not alone signal a serious crime, although Bjorn would have to be the final judge of that.

"Cronwall?" Stefan called his name without much force. Cronwall was not in danger, but the horse was. When the wives spied their destroyed window boxes, this horse would feel the wrath of a hundred brooms.

Stefan took the horse's reins and gave a good yank. The horse refused to leave his breakfast. Stefan yanked again, and the horse swayed his head back in protest. Stefan understood. No one—not even a horse—wanted to abandon a perfectly good sin. Many believed the time to repent came only after nothing remained to be enjoyed.

Stefan swatted him hard on the flank, and the horse finally walked back to the square. He held the reins with a strong fist. The horse whinnied in his grief but followed nonetheless.

At the mouth of the lane, a crowd waited and whispered.

"There is no wolf here," Stefan announced. "Cronwall's horse is loose. That is all. He was eating the window gardens."

A woman scowled, brandishing her walking stick at the horse. Stefan stepped between her and the horse, an act of certain mercy. He searched the crowd for Catarina. She was not to be seen. Perhaps she had run home. He hoped she would have something cooking when Cronwall returned. He was nicer when he was full.

After a quarter of an hour, Bjorn met Stefan at the head of the lane. The townsfolk parted and then filled in behind him, daring to edge closer to hear the men talk. Bjorn was a big man, well suited for his profession. People feared big men. He often had only to stand up or push out his chest to quiet down a drunk or calm an enraged husband. But he had a gentle face, with soft blue eyes and a slow smile.

Bjorn shrugged when he saw the horse. "Where is Cronwall?" Bjorn asked, reaching out and patting the horse on the flank. Several townspeople leaned their heads in closer, to catch every word.

Stefan frowned at them and motioned for Bjorn to step away to afford them more privacy. Bjorn refused. "No need, Father. Gossip dies faster when they hear the facts."

"No one has seen him."

"Did you want me to arrest the horse?" Bjorn's mouth twitched as if he might smile. The townspeople snickered.

Stefan gritted his teeth before replying. "I assume Cronwall deposited himself in a cellar and slept through the storm. But Catarina was hysterical. She stirred everyone up, coming to outrageous conclusions. That is why I called you."

Bjorn rubbed his eyes with his fingertips. It took him a long while to speak again, but when he did, his voice was clear and loud. "Catarina, yes. She is prone to imaginations. She is becoming a problem."

"I want you to return the horse to her," Stefan said.

"Since there is no crime, I'll going back to bed, Stefan. You can return the horse."

Stefan leaned in. "But there's more. Her neck looked raw. Cronwall hasn't shown restraint in his discipline."

"What am I to do? He's committed no crime."

"It's not him I want you to talk with. Speak to Catarina. You're a husband. Tell her how it is. She should have been glad to be free of him for one night. Instead, she causes a public spectacle, probably cost the merchants a tidy profit. Scold her so this doesn't happen again." Stefan thought a moment. "Come. We'll run the errand together."

Dame Alice interrupted them. "What is to be done?"

Stefan turned toward her. "We will see that the horse is returned and Catarina has been calmed," Stefan replied, walking the horse forward with Bjorn by his side. They passed a house where the wife tossed grain out from her doorway. The horse craned his neck to look back at the lane, oblivious to the chickens squawking at his clumsy feet plodding through their breakfast.

At the edge of the square, Bjorn stopped and turned for home. He waved one hand over his shoulder. "Tell her I will visit after I have slept. Or after I have found Cronwall."

A chicken pecked Stefan sharply on the leg, making him squeal, to the delight of everyone who watched. He jerked the horse's reins with authority, but the horse reared back and broke away.

He watched as the horse followed its appetite back into the darkened lane, where certain punishment would follow. The horse did not seem to mind.

Stefan walked back to the church, defeated. Appetite seemed to rule his village.

Chapter Three

Mia held the spoon in front of Margarite's face. Her mother-in-law's eyes, clouded from cataracts, focused on it. Margarite's shaking hands, the fingers bent at odd angles, grasped it, and she aimed for her mouth. The pottage landed on her lips, then oozed down her chin.

Little Alma's lips smacked together. She was hungry too. Mia grinned at her daughter and held a smaller spoon of the same pottage to her. Alma grabbed it, bringing it to her cheek before sliding it into her mouth. Mia wiped both mouths—Alma's first, then Margarite's—with her apron.

At three years old, Alma should have been filling their home with laughter and songs, but instead she often fell sick, a relentless cough erupting from her chest—a cough so frightening that it made Mia's heart constrict with fear. Alma never had a month free of her sickness, but she had better days almost every week now that the hardest days of winter were over. Her coughs were worse on cold, rainy days, and the sky had been a dead gray for hours. Surely the rain today would be heavy.

Margarite shouted a garbled word.

"Shhh, mother, not so loud," Mia said. "Bjorn is in bed."

Margarite frowned, thrusting her face closer to Mia's. Mia took Margarite's face in her hands and turned it.

"Your son is asleep," she repeated directly in Margarite's ear.

Margarite nodded gravely. Mia sighed, reaching up and smoothing back Margarite's thinning white hair. It fell forward again, the ends smearing across the mess on her mouth.

Mia patted her own hair, her searching fingers pulling free the tortoise-shell comb, a wedding gift from Father Stefan. She admired its beautiful brown patterns for a moment. A lovely piece, not fitting for a housewife who never had visitors. Father Stefan had been so generous to give it to her when she was still a stranger. Bjorn had brought her here from another town years ago, and Father Stefan had been kind. This comb gave her courage to attend his Masses. The gift meant more to her than he could know.

She pushed Margarite's hair back and tucked the comb into place on her head. Letting go, she ran her fingers across Margarite's face. "There. That's better. You look lovely." Margarite grimaced and moaned.

"Is the pain worse today?" Mia asked, not expecting an answer.

Urine pooled under Margarite's chair. Mia stood to grab some straw to scatter over it, holding her back in pain from so much work. She spread the straw under the chair and sat to resume the feedings. She could try asking again if anyone in town knew of more remedies she could try, but the women were so cold to her—all but Dame Alice. Dame Alice wanted to feed her, surely only to pry her heart open and see what Mia hid. Mia did not trust herself yet. Not enough time had passed. Her memories were still open wounds. Unless she could find a salve for those—a salve that made her forget.

Mia knew the women whispered of a healing witch who lived far off in the woods, but the thought of her frightened Mia. What good was a healing if it was cursed? Mia did not want healing if it angered the Lord. Even if healings could ease Margarite's pain. Or save Alma, whose breathing became high whistles when the air turned cold. Every shriek for air, each shredding sound from her chest twisted Mia's heart, making her half mad with fear.

Alma stared at Mia, raising one tiny, soft finger to wipe a tear off Mia's cheek. Mia took her hand and blew a raspberry into it. Alma smiled and squealed, showering them both with pottage.

Bjorn stood in the doorway between the main room and the bedroom. His bedclothes were dark with sweat. Mia rose and took him by his arm, leading him to sit by the fire.

"I am sorry," she said. "We woke you."

He took the long spoon and used it to stir the ashes beneath the pot, then stood gazing at the swords hanging over their doorway and the pilgrimage badges on either side. Bjorn's family was descended from a ghost warrior who served under Arminius. The memory of the ghost warriors of Germany still left villagers cold. Soldiers would paint themselves black, waiting until the darkest hour of night to attack. Victims saw only the whites of a ghost's eyes before they died. Arminius had used them, used all the warriors Germany had, to betray his Roman master and slaughter the Roman army as they marched through the Black Forest. Ghost soldiers left a legacy of shrewd betrayals.

She watched Bjorn without speaking. There seemed to be no end to the emptiness behind his eyes. She alone knew this about him. She alone knew this secret, how empty his eyes could become. She blamed herself for being a poor wife.

Bjorn closed his eyes, his shoulders slumping forward.

"Bjorn, what is it?" she asked, a little fear pricking at her heart. Bjorn was not a weak man. He did not stumble under his burdens.

Bjorn reached for her skirts, pressing his face into her stomach.

"Bjorn." She pushed him back to look at him, her hands trembling. "What has happened?"

Bjorn watched the fire. "I am tired," he said.

"Bjorn, come," she said, putting her hands on his shoulders. "Go back to bed, husband. There will be no more mischief for now. It's daylight." She pointed to the window. He did not move.

"Unless you would wish me to come with you." She teased, trying to make him abandon this dark stupor.

He recoiled as if she had bit him. He stood up, glaring down at her.

"You don't know what you are saying," he said.

"Bjorn."

"You have a child to tend to," he said.

"Aye, and I'd like another," she murmured, stung. Other women flirted outrageously with their husbands, and they found it delightful.

"Look at her, Mia," he said, pointing to Alma. "Look at your sick daughter and say that again. What good is another child when you can't care for the one you have?" He turned his back, walking into the bedroom.

Mia sank down onto the floor, burying her face in her hands. Little Alma came to her and rested her head in her lap. Out of habit, Mia pressed a hand on her back to feel her breathing. Tiny ribs rested under her palm, each taut and sharp under the linen shift. Margarite banged her spoon, probably wanting explanation, not more pottage.

Mia kissed the top of Alma's head and set her mind on the day ahead. It would not do to weep for any of them, and if Mia stopped for one more moment like this to think on their plight, she might never get back up.

Chapter Four

The rains came in the night, without thunder or wind, soaking into the cold earth, making the morning air crisp. The next morning Mass was well attended, more for the hope of fresh gossip than for forgiveness of sins, Stefan knew.

He was hungry. He had searched the cellar below the church, but he and Erick had eaten the last of the vegetables stored from the last harvest. His stomach grumbled as he climbed the steps and locked the door for the last time this season.

Hard work would make him forget his hunger. He swept straw away from the church aisle onto the street. One of the altar boys trimmed the wicks as Erick, who was his main attendant, polished the wood altar. Erick had been abandoned in the market square years ago, just before he sprouted up into a tall, lean young man. His parents probably had not been able to afford to feed him, but he never mentioned them or spoke of his previous life. Still, he bore the shame with silent grace, even as he quietly rebuffed Father Stefan's confused attempts to help him. Erick was often a mystery to Father Stefan, who taught on forgiveness weekly but had never had to forgive a great debt himself. Erick also worked harder for the church than anyone else in his parish. Stefan liked that very much. He nodded at Erick before closing the doors and walking back down the center aisle.

"You off to check the beer?" Erick asked. Stefan eyed the stairs that led off to the right of the sanctuary. Shaking his head, he sat instead on the first bench and removed a boot. His feet were swollen, one toe cracked and bleeding. Stretching his leg out, he groaned.

Erick came closer to sit next to him. Stefan grabbed his broom and shooed him away.

"You haven't earned a rest."

Erick sat anyway, one corner of his mouth turning up. "You've had everyone working all morning. Is Jesus returning today?"

Stefan swatted his legs with the broom, and Erick laughed, turning his body away.

"Women have their children, and men have their work, Erick. That's what life is."

"This isn't work, Father. This is cleaning. I should have a real job. You know you can trust me with one. I'm much stronger than you by now."

"For his sake and mine," Stefan said to the saints immortalized in the frescoes around him, "grant him humility."

"I may not be humble, but I am honest." Erick grinned, but Stefan sensed no real mischief in it. "Father, listen to me. You need to rest more. Let me do the hard work. I'd like to pay you back."

"For what?" Stefan frowned.

"Giving me a place to live."

Stefan turned to look up at him. "Is that all the church is to you? A place to live?"

"Father Stefan?"

The woman's voice made Stefan and Erick stand and turn. Mia stood there, clutching her hands together. Stefan sat back down with a grunt and wrestled his boot on, avoiding another look at Erick.

"Father Stefan," Mia said, "I came later than usual today, but I did hear Mass. I would like to confess."

Stefan gestured toward the confessional, and she followed in obedience. He glanced back at Erick, jabbing a finger back at the altar. Erick nodded and got back to work.

Ushering Mia into the confessional, Stefan settled his back against the wood wall of the dark chamber. He slid open the lattice window frame that separated them and stretched out his legs, wiggling his toes.

"Forgive me, Father," she began, "I have sinned. I have provoked my husband to anger again. I did not mean to. I promise I will try harder. I know what is required to be a good wife. I always fall short, Father. That is my sin. But I will try harder. I want to please the Lord."

Stefan groaned and reached down to take the boot off again.

"Did you just groan?"

Stefan winced. "I did not groan because of you. I am sorry."

"It's all right, Father. Your feet hurt. You're a man, after all, and men work hard. It's nothing to apologize for."

"How is Alma?"

She had no reply.

"She is not well, is she? The cough still grabs her? Is that the real reason you came?"

"I've done everything you've asked. She is no better. Neither of us sleeps much anymore. She coughs worse at night. Sometimes she turns blue, and I know you will say I am imagining it, but I am not. It's getting worse."

"But you said you provoked Bjorn; you were confessing to that."

"Yes."

"But not for the sake of your marriage, I suppose. Are you searching for the reason God will not heal your child?"

Mia did not reply.

"Mia, my child, do you trust me?"

"Yes, Father."

"And you know nothing I say is intended to hurt you?"

"Yes."

"Mia, this has gone on too long. I will speak plainly now. You are guilty of the sin of pride. Does God not have the right to do with your child as He will? Many mothers have sick children, and they do not complain to me as often as you do. Every week you speak to me as if God has forgotten Alma. As for Bjorn, stay out from underfoot. Content yourself with what affection he offers. Never has there been a man who could satisfy a woman."

"Yes, Father."

"Do not ask more for yourself than women are due to receive. Repent of the sin of pride. Content yourself with what you have, for these are the words of the apostle Paul."

"Forgive me, Father," she replied. "I will try harder to please God."

"Try harder to please Bjorn, too. His work is difficult. Just try harder to please him, and he will be pleased with you. A man needs to know his wife will not peck him to death before he will come home to roost."

"Why?"

"Because you need to eat."

"You don't know what I need. Go back to your business."

Dame Alice's shoulders slumped forward, her face pained. "Mia," she breathed, "you need a friend."

Mia turned for home.

ﻋﻠﻰ

Mia had a dream that the wolf was circling her house, burning Alma with yellow eyes, waiting to devour her with moon white teeth. Each paw had sharp claws that sank into the wet earth. Mia saw deep indentations between each rib and dry, withered teats that hung with no milk. *The wolf has found us,* she thought in her dream. *The wolf smells the weak.*

Pushing herself up from the floor in front of the fireplace, she rubbed her eyes. She needed a few moments to blink and clear away the dream as she caught her breath. Alma slept on her straw pallet against the wall and seemed well. Bjorn's mother slept in the chair by the fire. Mia reached out and touched her feet. They were warm, but to be safe, Mia covered them with the edge of Margarite's long cloak. It hung too big for her now that she had shrunk with age and disease, but Mia did not want to alter the cloak. Margarite loved it. Any change would remind her of how much time had taken from her. The truth would be one more screaming wound in this world, a world without remedies.

Bjorn had not returned while she'd slept, Mia decided, judging from the iron pot left undisturbed over the fire. There were hot coals glowing white beneath it but no flames. Looking around in the moonlit shadows, Mia could not guess the hour. She would listen for church bells now that she sat awake. She began contemplating whether to keep dinner warm or begin to think of breakfast for Bjorn. Her mouth watered.

Bjorn had spent many nights gone since Alma's birth three years ago. Better to police the town at night, he said, when the drunks kept business hours. Mia agreed, saying she knew nothing of men's work. She would not doubt him. She did know that since the recent drama with that man Cronwall, Bjorn had to tamp down the wicked gossip that had infected the town. Some thought Cronwall was dead, even murdered. Some said he had abandoned Catarina for reasons best whispered in the ear. Not that anyone whispered in Mia's. What news she heard in the market fell to her by accident, when women gossiped with their backs to her, unaware. Mia had good ears.

The white coals were fading to black. With a grunt, Mia pushed herself to stand. She would fetch another piece of wood from outside and then freshen herself for Bjorn's return. Some heated water would be good too. She probably looked a horror.

"I'll give you one last chance." The man's voice came from outside her door. The voice was clotted with rage. She did not recognize it.

Mia froze. She heard weeping, then a woman's muffled cry, as if someone held a hand over her mouth. Her heart fluttering, Mia ducked down to the floor. Whoever they were might see her through the window. Had she let the fire burn too low? Would they think no one home and come inside? She wanted none of their trouble.

She heard the voices arguing and then a dragging sound. Something crawled toward the front door.

The woman spoke. "If you cannot stop yourself, then I will stop you."

A low popping sound came next. The crawling, scraping noise stopped. Mia held her breath. She had one candle box by the door. The flame in it burned low, not even a thumb's width high—probably too low to be seen from outside. But Mia crawled to it, picking up each knee with silent effort, and managed to snuff it out without making a sound. She breathed in shallow bursts, listening for the voices.

She heard the man speaking in ragged whispers. Silently, Mia crawled as fast as she could toward Alma, grabbing her blanket and covering her face completely. If they came in, the pallet might look tumbled but empty. She could do nothing about Margarite. Mia saw her kitchen blade and crawled to it next. She had to shuffle under the window to get to it, praying God would not let her make a mistake that alerted the couple to her movements. The shutters hung open, but she could not shut them from the inside. Whoever stood out there could simply stick his head right into her home and see her. Mia forced herself to breathe and think.

"I have not kept your secrets," the woman said, weeping.

"Who? Who did you tell?"

Mia's hand closed around the blade as she stretched for it. She blessed the weight of the blade in her hand, the glistening edge of the knife. Slowly pressing her back against the door, bone by bone, she sat and listened, willing her heart to slow down, breathing through pursed lips. The woman's voice drifted softer now, as if she had moved farther away. The man's voice changed to a plea, but Mia could no longer make out the details of their conversation. Mia heard a sharp crack, and she started.

She scooted along the wall a little closer to the window, twisting at the waist as she pulled up just enough to see out of the corner. A man stood silhouetted against the moon, his heavy boot on the back of someone on the ground. Mia stared at the shape lying motionless, wide, and flat. *It's the woman,* she realized, *with her skirts spread out around her.*

Mia ducked back down.

The woman had tried to get to her front door. Why? She must have known the sheriff lived here. Clearly she needed his help. Mia bit her lip. What had she done, hiding like this? But no, she couldn't have helped the woman. Not with that man upon her and Bjorn away on duty. She wished this woman hadn't come here, hadn't involved Mia in her trouble.

Mia heard a rasping sound and pushed her face back up to steal another look. The man dragged the woman by her feet, and the woman did not resist. The two passed under a strong shaft of moonlight as the man heaved the woman by the feet over a fallen log. In the moonlight, Mia saw the woman's head flop to the side as she went over the log, dead.

Mia gasped as the whites of the dead woman's eyes reflected the moonlight. The man dragging her stopped, his shadowed face directed at the window. Mia ducked down, forcing her fingers into her mouth for something to bite down on. Had he seen her? He might come for her next. He might kill her—Alma and Margarite, too.

She lurched across the floor to the door, pressing her back into it with all her strength, the wood making tiny scratches all over her back. She bit down onto her fingers until she could no longer taste the salt on her skin, until she tasted blood from the little thin red indentations along her fingers. She licked them clean and made a fist instead, pressing it onto her lips. Any minute Bjorn could return. Any minute they would be safe. Any minute.

Alma turned, still asleep, as was Margarite. *Please, blessed mother of Jesus,* Mia prayed silently. *Do not let them wake.* She sat, pressing with her back and then her legs, pressing until her muscles cramped. She would bar the door. Nothing she could do about the window. She was probably a fool for barring the door when he could come in through the window, but she had to try. If he came in through the window, she had her blade.

She did not know how long she sat, pushing against the door. Darkness deceived, changing the shadows all around her so that she could not fix with certainty upon a time. At last she heard church bells, twelve in all, as rain pummeled the roof and ran in through the window. Mia watched it run down her wall and across her clean floor in unpredictable rivers, stirring up mud and ruining all her work. Her clothes stuck to her body, sweat drying in patches but leaving her sticky and sour.

She heard the torrent grow harder. Rain would wash everything away before the new morning. Everyone in town would be waking in a few hours, stirring the pots, tearing off hunks of bread and cheese to set out for breakfast. Children would be fetching new wood or eggs. Only Mia would remember what had happened in the night. There would be no footsteps, no trace of the murder. What would she say to Bjorn? Bjorn would think Mia had nightmares. He would tell her to work more, that he could protect her from everything except her own imagination. But tired bodies were not prone to bad dreams, and so he would urge her to work more.

Mia saw Alma kick off the blanket, flopping over onto her stomach, her thumb in her mouth, her hair flayed in wild directions all around her head. Mia did not like it. The girl should be hidden until Bjorn came home, until they were safe.

Please, Mia thought, *please let Bjorn come home soon. Please let me hear his footsteps. Please. Bjorn will make us safe.*

Mia jerked awake. How long had she slept? She heard Bjorn's footfall stirring the dead, wet leaves along the path. She checked from the window's corner to be sure. Bjorn had returned.

Mia threw open the front door, racing for him, calling his name. He caught her by the waist.

"What is it, Mia? What is it?"

"A man came. He killed a woman, right on our very own path, right in front of the door."

"What?"

"I wanted you to come home so badly. I thought he might kill us, too."

Bjorn pulled her in closer, one hand still around her waist, the other going to her cheek. He looked all around at the ground, wet with puddles and washed clean of any footsteps. He frowned.

"I know, Bjorn, there is no evidence. But you have to believe me."

He softly brushed her hair out of her face. "It has been a hard winter for you. Could you have been dreaming?"

"No. No, it was no dream. The rain washed the footprints away. But they were here."

"Why would they come here? If you think clearly, you will see that it must have been a dream. Who would come to the sheriff's home to commit murder?"

"I don't know. And I couldn't understand what they said. But I did see it happen. Someone died."

He felt her forehead. "You're warm. Do you feel well?"

"Bjorn—"

"I do not know what you saw, Mia, but there's no evidence here. No one in town is even stirring. I just returned from there." He looked thoughtful. "Are you sick? Do you want me to call Father Stefan?"

"I know what I saw," she said, pushing against him.

He took her in again. "Shhh. I will ask the innkeeper if she has hosted anyone who would cause trouble. If it happened as you said, I will arrest him and have him hanged by dusk. Does that please you?"

She nodded, knowing he would feel her nod against his chest. She did not want to speak.

He pulled her hand up to his face, looking closely at the reddened teeth marks visible across her hand, frowning.

"What did you do to yourself?"

Mia tucked her hand in the folds of her shift.

Bjorn hesitated before speaking, as if judging whether she was able to discuss his work in her condition. "The town has been buzzing with gossip since Cronwall abandoned his wife. I have been called on to settle fistfights between men who think Catarina caused it and men who think Cronwall found another woman in a faraway city. There have been wives scolding their husbands for not stopping Cronwall from leaving, and a few bawds even blame me."

"I am sorry."

"Please do not add to my burdens. I will find the man, if there is one. If he was real, he's probably a trader. Already gone by now."

"But what about the woman?"

He sighed, closing his eyes. Mia tried to soften her demand.

"There would be a body. If it happened." Mia added the last bit out of obedience. She did not need to be right. Not if it added to his burdens. Not if her sex was prone to imaginations. "Do you want me to go back out and look?" he murmured, sounding so tired. "I will do it, if it will give you peace."

Alma stirred inside the house. She would want to eat soon. Bjorn was surely hungry too. Mia straightened herself at once, standing back from Bjorn. She needed to do better for everyone's sake. She had slept, and she could not prove the events had been real. It might have been imagination, the most universal of women's sins. Father Stefan would be angry with her.

The sun would be on the horizon within the hour. It would be a beautiful spring morning.

Stefan's fist hit the door again and again. He would go on hitting it, splintering it if he had to, until Bjorn answered. He could apologize later.

Mia appeared.

"Mia, get Bjorn. Immediately," Stefan said. She looked terrible, as if she'd had no sleep. Stefan wished she would take better care of herself. Bjorn said other women flirted with him daily, but Bjorn always remained faithful. How long would he stay strong under such temptation? Still, Stefan could not warn Mia. The sacrament of confession could not be broken, even to aid a struggling soul.

Mia shook her head no. "Let him sleep for a few more hours, and then I will send him to you."

"Wake him up, Mia. Now."

"Father, please. He is exhausted. Let him sleep."

Father Stefan stuck his foot in the door, pushing it open wider. "Forgive me, Mia, but I must get Bjorn."

"What is it, Stefan?"

Bjorn appeared from the bedroom. His face sagged with exhaustion. Stefan pushed the door open all the way, going to Bjorn to whisper, keeping his back to Mia. Bjorn nodded then pointed at her.

"She heard an argument last night in the woods beyond our home. A trader, she thinks. No one she recognized. I thought it had been a dream."

Mia couldn't help it; she smiled at her husband. She had not imagined it. She had not been a poor wife to tell him.

"The merchants are going mad with speculations," Stefan said. "The rumors will ruin them all. People will go to another village to buy." Stefan had one hand on Bjorn's arm, pulling him toward the door.

"Let me get my cloak," Bjorn said, stepping back into the bedroom.

"Have you had breakfast?" Mia asked Father Stefan. He looked at her as if she spoke another language. She waved to the little table by the fire. "Breakfast?"

"No," Stefan said. "Thank you," he added. "Do you want to tell me what you saw?"

Bjorn stepped out, ready to go. "Keep the food warm, Mia. And don't go into town today. Not until I know who is among us."

"But I do not want to be alone."

"I'll send Erick to check on you," Stefan said, holding the door open for Bjorn before following behind. "He will even stay with you if you feel uneasy."

"But what should—"

They closed the door and were gone.

Mia wiped her mouth with the back of her hand, and it came away with bits of straw from the floor and mud. She pinched herself as punishment. She should have washed herself. She must have looked like a fool.

Margarite stirred. She probably needed to relieve herself before the pain returned.

Mia went back to her life.

Chapter Five

The two bodies splayed across the church steps had none of the peaceful repose Stefan was accustomed to. There was no embroidered pillow or handsome cloak. Their limbs were spread apart, splattered with mud. Stefan crossed himself, wondering again if this was a dream. Shiny fat flies buzzed around Cronwall. His face was bloated. The woman lay facedown, thrown over him as if in an embrace, her skirts exposing her slender white calves. Stefan had never seen a woman's calves, but he cleared his throat and tugged at the edge of the skirt to cover her, looking away from her body. He saw Bjorn taking in the scene with an expression of sadness and anger. A dark resolve passed across his face.

Bjorn had no other hesitation, no signs of shock. He set to work with a pursed mouth, pulling out the pockets lining the man's belt. They were filled with money. Using his foot, Bjorn rolled the woman's body off the man's, her dead eyes open to the morning sun.

Stefan shielded his eyes from the glare, craned his neck, and leaned closer in. He wanted to be mistaken. He asked God to take it back, to make it go away.

It was Catarina.

Stefan inhaled with a high-pitched, keening gasp, like a child about to burst into a wail. Bjorn gave him a withering glare. Stefan knew he shouldn't react to death this way. He saw it every month. But he wanted to point out to Bjorn that death and murder were not equal. Death was natural, to be expected even. Murder was a stunning perversion.

"What do we do?" Stefan asked.

Bjorn held the fistful of money out to the crowd. "This was not a robbery. Did anyone see anything? Does anyone want to speak?"

No one in the growing crowd moved.

"Why would both bodies be left on my steps?" Stefan asked.

Bjorn watched the crowd. "This is a message." He watched the crowd, his eyes moving back and forth, searching for something Stefan did not understand.

Bjorn turned back, shaking his head, and handed the money to Stefan. "Keep this."

Erick came out of the church with a blanket, offering it to Bjorn.

"Set it there. I'll cover them when I'm done," Bjorn said.

Erick did what he was told. He looked as if he, too, was wandering about in a dream, lost and confused.

"Erick? Check on Mia and her home. She will worry if she hears news of this and is alone," Stefan said. The young man nodded and disappeared into the crowd.

Bjorn turned and knelt by Catarina's body, ran his fingers along her neck, then pushed against her cheek. Her head twisted as far as he pushed it. "Broken," Bjorn said. The words carried to the back of the crowd with great urgency by the onlookers.

"Those are new bruises, Bjorn," Stefan whispered. "They're not the same bruises I saw on her last week after Cronwall disappeared."

"Do not add to her shame," Bjorn whispered. "Say nothing of those injuries."

Bjorn spoke rightly, Stefan thought. Catarina had been so modest. She should not have her marriage picked over in plain view of the village. Stefan's heart pinched a little. Why did Bjorn always know what to do and he did not?

"Bring a horse and cart here," Bjorn said to him before turning to the crowd. "Who among you loved Catarina?"

The astronomer's wife, Ducinda, stepped forward. She kept a palm flat on her face, her eyes red with grief.

Bjorn put his arm around her, leading her between Stefan and himself. He spoke down to her, keeping one arm around her shoulders, his hand rubbing her other shoulder. She calmed somewhat, swallowing down great sobs.

"Ducinda, you say Catarina was your friend?"

She nodded yes.

"Then you must know who would have done this."

Ducinda looked up at him with wide eyes. "I surely do not know, sir. She was a lamb. No one would want to hurt her."

"She said nothing to you? Nothing at all? No hints of trouble?"

Ducinda shook her head no.

Bjorn closed his eyes and exhaled. "A shame. Now, Ducinda, will you do something for your friend?"

"Anything for her, sir. And for you, of course."

"I'll remove the bodies to the church. Father Stefan will give you access to them. See to it they are prepared for a burial by tomorrow morning. Stefan will make sure you are reimbursed for all your expenses. But Ducinda, please," he added, "no gossip. Gossip dishonors your friend and muddies the waters I am to fish in. Do you understand?"

Ducinda looked back at the crowd doubtfully. She pressed her arms closer into her body. "But who did this?"

"I will find out." Bjorn rested his hand on her shoulder. "Ducinda, your job is to see that your friend is well cared for now."

Stefan approached Bjorn. "Surely you must have an idea."

"Look at the bodies. Cronwall has been dead for a while. Catarina is still fresh. What do you think this means?"

Stefan's cheeks flushed, and he cleared his throat, looking at the crowd. They were of no help, looking away as soon as he met their eyes. Stefan saw all the directions they looked instead—at their feet, at the clouds, or at their hands, which were picking at dead lice clinging to their wool cloaks.

Bjorn nudged him for an answer. "All right, then," Bjorn said, shaking his head. "Tell me this: Where was God? If God is good, why didn't He stop this?"

"We can't always understand His will."

Bjorn laced his fingers together, resting them against his chin. "Let me tell you what I understand: Prayer changed nothing here." He sighed, dropping his hands, preparing to lift Catarina's body. He turned around, avoiding Stefan's face and addressing the crowd. "This is what I suspect: Catarina was unfaithful. That is why Cronwall left in the middle of the storm: to confront her lover. We all knew him to be a proud man. As for her, she paid for her sin—at the hands of her lover, I am sure."

His last words could barely be heard over the crowd.

"Why dump them here?" Stefan asked. "Why would he not conceal his crime?"

Bjorn looked at Stefan, his eyes narrowing, as if willing him to understand. "Who committed the greatest crime? Catarina cuckolded two men."

"But why would he murder Cronwall?" Stefan said. He wished he knew more of why lovers came together and what drove them apart. He wouldn't feel so stupid in the face of their senseless crimes.

"Cronwall must have attacked the man. The man struck back in self-defense," Bjorn suggested. Stefan noticed that many in the crowd were still listening to Bjorn. "My wife saw the whole thing last night," he said, looking at the crowd. "You don't see her here, do you? She knows justice has been done."

The crowd erupted into whispers. One of the younger girls, Iris, noticed Bjorn staring at her and tucked her chin down with a blush. Stefan understood very little of women. Older women had cold hatred in their eyes, even as their mouths worked furiously, chattering to each other. He shook his head in wonder. A scandal worthy of Avignon had come to his quiet town, and Mia had seen the whole thing, though she had smiled at him this morning and offered him breakfast.

Bjorn trotted down the church steps, parting the crowd to get through. Stefan ran to catch up to him.

"Are you angry with me?" Bjorn asked. Stefan waved him off, embarrassed. Bjorn knew him well. "I am just curious. What should be done next?"

"You could try praying."

"Don't mock me." Stefan looked at Bjorn to see if his friend teased.

"I'm not. I'm mocking prayer."

Bjorn ducked into a doorway with room only for Stefan to follow, giving them privacy.

"I know you do not understand what goes on between a man and a woman," Bjorn said. "But the murders are God's failure, not mine. I am out here every night. I answer every cry for help that I hear."

"That's not fair. We can't know the mind of God. That does not mean He does not hear our cries."

"Are you sure? That makes Him a devil, doesn't it? That He hears and does not act?"

"You do not mean that."

Bjorn opened his mouth to say something else, then sighed. "I'm sorry. I can't escape these questions."

Stefan patted him on the back. "Your profession is to blame, not you." He gestured back toward the square. "The merchants are afraid of losing the best weeks of the market. What are you going to do?"

"A tart stirred up two men and paid for it. It doesn't involve the merchants."

"Two bodies left on the steps of the church? You have to arrest the man. It's a scandal."

Bjorn laughed, stepping out of the doorway. Stefan caught him by the arm. "You do not understand my meaning."

"What would you have me do? Ask politely at every door, 'Are you the man who was seduced by Cronwall's wife and murdered them? Would you mind coming with me so I can hang you?'"

"The women are superstitious and fearful. If you do not make an arrest, they'll travel in another direction to go to market. The first weeks of market are critical while we wait for the crops to ripen. We need the money. The church needs the money."

"What is the reason you are so frightened? Is it the money or the scandal?"

Stefan held a finger up to stop Bjorn from saying anything more. Bjorn was failing him. But there might be a solution that saved them all. "There is an Inquisitor in nearby Eichschan," Stefan said as the idea surfaced. "The bishop has said the Inquisitor is highly regarded by the pope, even commissioned in Nuremberg."

"What are you saying?"

"Hear me out."

"But this is not witchcraft. Just wickedness."

Stefan swallowed, rubbing his hands together before weaving them through the air, as if to stir Bjorn's imagination. "Wickedness is the Devil's work. These circumstances are unusual for Dinfoil, and I think they merit a visit from such a man. A man of higher learning will have answers for you and the merchants. If it goes well, other villages will be talking about it too. We'll have more visitors. More money. The prince would be pleased. Perhaps he would even mention us to the emperor." Stefan had never argued with Bjorn. He did not know what to do after speaking, so he dropped his hands and waited.

"No. Do not bring a stranger into this. We do not want every other village hearing of our troubles."

"Try to imagine it. I will bring in the Inquisitor and let him find the guilty man. Then he will declare the town free of all evil influences, and the markets will thrive. It will be over in a fortnight. You won't have to do anything. No one will care if you don't make an arrest. But we will all gain recognition. God could very well be in this tragedy for our good."

"No," Bjorn said in a tone meant to end the conversation. "No outsiders. Don't speak of it again."

"Bjorn," Stefan said, his face turning red. "Have you seen the way they look at me? Everyone in town looks at me as if I allowed this. Even you accuse me, in your way. I'm not stupid."

"Then don't act it. An Inquisitor will come here looking for the Devil, and he may very well find one. How will you look then?"

"You're wrong," Stefan said.

"Look at your feet, my friend."

Stefan looked down. The edges of his robe were a bit dirty, but his feet were clean, despite the mud and chaos of spring.

"Do you see the ground you're standing on?"

Stefan looked up. "Yes."

Bjorn pointed a finger at him. "That's the only thing you know for certain. You hear what people want to tell you, only the sins they feel guilt for. The difference between you and me? I see what they do when they leave your church. I see the sins they commit without guilt or shame."

Stefan watched him walk away, standing there in the dirt with chaos not far away. A red fleck caught his eye, a cardinal in a barren tree. The branches were just beginning to build up at the ends, preparing for spring, and the bird glistened, a trembling ruby startling in its perfection, in its dazzling, unrepentant red. Stefan stared at it until the sun caught its feathers just right, and for a moment he saw his whole village blinded with red. Beyond the barren tree, behind the houses with dark smoke curling from their chimneys, a wolf howled.

Cold wind stung his cheeks, and he shook free of the moment, pulling his arms in with a shiver. Winter had not finished with them yet.

Chapter Six

Mia was startled awake when she heard a spoon bang against the wall. Margarite was anxious for supper.

"Coming, Margarite," Mia yelled. Yelling made her sound angry, but Margarite could not help being deaf.

Margarite groaned and hit the spoon against the wall once more. The busyness of meals, of interacting with Mia, made Margarite forget the pain, Mia suspected. Food became something they could still do together, one last link. Mia did not know if the woman even tasted the food or just wanted Mia to touch her and look at her. When old ones stopped eating, they died. Everyone knew that, including Margarite. She wasn't ready to die.

The old woman held on even though her body failed more every day and the pain in her bones grew steadily worse. Her wasting disease showed no remorse, daily marching her closer to death. Mia did not understood why Margarite held on. She, too, once had a will to live, even through times when nothing existed to live for. But then she had been young, and there had been hope. For Margarite, what hope was there but death? Death would relieve Margarite's suffering, so why did she resist it?

Mia sighed, walking to the pottage, waving a hand at Margarite to signal that the meal was on the way. She stirred the pottage, careful to scrape along the bottom where most of the meat had sunk. Margarite should put some more weight on her frail frame. She might feel better if she had more cushion, more softness around her bones.

Mia hoped Margarite's sense of smell was still intact. The sage, already good for picking this early in the season, blended well with the rosemary. Sage lent a lovely green undertone in their tiny home that always smelled of sharp, sweet rosemary. Rosemary stayed green and lush through the final frost of spring and needed no care from Mia. She loved it for being so dependable. She loved it for not needing her.

Ladling the pottage into a wooden bowl, Mia pushed a chair close to Margarite's and took the spoon from her. Margarite stared at her with a closed mouth, nodding in the direction of Alma, who played with a kitten. The kitten's mother had depended on Mia for scraps in the winter, and Mia regarded the kitten as a welcome visitor. She would have to shoo it outside before Bjorn got home. But it was not the kitten that agitated Margarite.

Little Alma had those dark red circles under her eyes again, looking as if she had been beaten overnight.

Mia looked back at Margarite, her own stomach churning. Margarite nodded. Though deaf and not always lucid, this one thing she understood: Alma remained very sick, and Mia remained helpless. A rare moment of understanding passed between the women, a generous miracle. Another woman saw her struggle and did not judge. Mia would spoon a thousand mouthfuls of pottage for that one blessing.

Since her first true friend, Rose, had abruptly deserted her two years ago without reason, refusing to have anything to do with her, Mia had not known the comfort of another woman's reassurance. Mia's heart pinched at the thought of Rose's strange, silent betrayal. Mia had poured herself, for the first time, into friendship with another woman, nursing Rose along after her husband died, when she had nearly died herself from grief. Mia reminded herself she could not think on it any longer. It only caused confusion, and Mia had plenty of confusion already. Even if she scraped the bottom of that old pot, what would she find but more trouble? She didn't have to know the truth. Truth wouldn't make it hurt less. She remembered what truth did to those who were not ready for it. What Mia needed was answered prayer for Alma. If God ever heard her prayers and healed Alma, Mia would not ask for anything else again. She swore this to Him, but it had not prompted Him to act.

Bjorn slammed the wooden door wide open, making the wood crack along the bottom. Mia jumped, stifling a groan of complaint. The cold night breezes must be kept out, away from Alma.

She forced a smile and cleared her throat.

Bjorn heard her stifled groan; she could tell by the way he sat at the table staring at her with an angry face. He looked tired and likely to start a quarrel. Mia kept spooning the pottage into the mouth of Margarite, who stared in the distance.

"What happened with Stefan yesterday morning?" she asked. Bjorn had left with Stefan early and then had come home drunk last night, angry and unsteady. Mia had lain in bed, stiff with dread, trying not to move until his breathing became deep and steady.

"Is there a reason you let Alma bring an animal in the house?" he asked.

"It keeps her happy while I feed Margarite," Mia said, keeping her voice even.

"I don't like it," he said.

"I know, husband, and I meant to put it out before you came home. You returned early today."

"Is that all that happens while I am away, Mia? Or are there other betrayals?"

She glanced at him, a darting look to judge his expression. "What did you say?"

He folded his arms. "I'm hungry."

Mia wiped Margarite's mouth and settled the blanket up higher on her lap. She pointed to the window, where the sun made its marvelous exit from the afternoon. Margarite liked watching the sunsets.

Alma had walked, in halting, heavy steps, to the door, her breath bubbling, the squawking kitten tucked under her arm. Mia nodded for them to go, knowing Alma would stay near the door until Mia had the warm evening milk ready for the kitten.

She ladled pottage into another bowl and set it before Bjorn, trying not to meet his eye. She had done nothing wrong. She did not want to be flayed for someone else's sins. Not today. She had spent her dawn hours holding Alma, who had to force each breath through a tightened chest, sweating from the exertion of just surviving the night.

Mia had prayed in the name of every saint she could think of, but no help came. She stood condemned in their eyes of some unnamed sin. Any hope she had of a miracle for Alma became more distant with every passing season. Alma should have been much taller and stronger. If she did not gain in strength this spring, Mia knew the next winter would be waiting for her. Winter was never satisfied here, taking new children every week. It had waited three times for Alma. It would not wait again next year, Mia knew. She knew the saints heard her pleas for her child, but the battle would be determined by who fought for Alma with greater force: the bitter winter or the vanished saints.

Bjorn looked at the pottage but did not eat.

"May I get you something, husband?" Mia asked, sweeping the filthy straw on the floor into a corner so he would not smell it tonight as he slept.

"Bread?"

"Oh. I did not make bread today. I'm sorry. I stayed up with Alma and fell asleep this afternoon."

"You are either a good wife or you are not." He slammed his fist down on the table, making the pottage slosh out of the bowl. "What do you do while I work? Why can I not trust you?"

"Bjorn." Mia scolded. She didn't mean to.

"You raise your voice to me in my own home?" He dumped his pottage on the floor. "That will give you something to do," he said, walking to the bedroom. "Keep you at home."

Mia felt the rage shooting up through her veins, taking control of every last ounce of common sense and decency. She had no control, her exhaustion eating through the last of her self-control.

"I am kept at home! I am busy! I have a sick child! And I feed and wash your mother who cannot even thank me. Other wives would roll her down the hill and straight into the river. Then they'd be free to make your bread. Is that what you want?"

He was on her before she blinked, his hand around her throat.

"You were nothing but a filthy cow when I married you."

"Is that why you don't love me anymore? Am I too dirty for you?"

"You know what you are." His grip grew tighter. "Say it."

"What am I today? Shrew? Cow? Nag? What does that make you?"

"A fool."

He dropped his hold on her, grabbing his cloak as he walked out. "You will regret talking to me like this. When you cannot stop Alma from coughing and you are on your knees saying your rosary, begging God to hear you, you'll remember what you said to me in my own home. You'll know why God won't answer your prayers."

Chapter Seven

Stefan polished the altar until his arms burned, not knowing when his secret rebellion would be made known. He saw that Erick had already spread fresh straw and polished the wood doors and had done a fine job. After Stefan checked that his robes were clean and his hair combed, he sat on the first bench, staring at the altar with the picture of Christ hung above it. The air in the church rested still and cold, faint scents of straw and incense tempting him to close his eyes, just for a moment, and savor a brief, secret rest.

Instead he stood, walking back up to the altar, turning to look down at the pews. Everything must look perfect before the Inquisitor's arrival. He mentally noted where he would like to see certain people seated for the next Mass. He wanted his esteemed guest to have a stunning first impression. He rubbed his chin, considering what else must be done.

He remembered an errand he had to run in the square, so he walked down the church steps. He turned around to look at his church and took it in with a grin. It had never looked better. Everyone would be impressed, even those who usually slept through Mass. But that would not happen again. Never again, once his guest arrived.

Opening the church doors, little Marie squealed to see him, rushing to grab his hand. She had been on her way in.

"Come and see, Father Stefan! The sheriff caught the wolf last night! He was enormous!"

A wolf's limp body hung from a stake in front of the church, visible to all in the market. Shepherds who killed predators would hang the carcass near their flock as warning to other animals. Stefan wondered why Bjorn chose this spot; his flock was behind the church, farther out where the pleasant grazing was.

Stefan had never seen a dead wolf, and he approached it with cautious steps. It held a strange beauty. Stefan stood under it, fascinated as he reached up to touch its paw with a deep sigh. He had not realized that he had been holding his breath, and the sudden gasping exhalation left him light-headed. The wolf was so beautiful. Had he been wrong to have it killed? How could an animal of such majesty and beauty be evil?

Stefan ran his hand over the ridges of his paws, through the soft sable perfection of his fur. He ran his hand next over the velvet muzzle and saw a flash of red wipe across his palm. Lifting one side of its thick black lip up, he saw the flesh of one of his own lambs shredded between the sharp teeth of the wolf. Stefan dropped his hand and stumbled backward. *Appearances deceive,* he reminded himself. *Nothing is as it seems in a fallen world.*

"What will you do with him?" Marie chirped. He looked down, realizing she was at his side. She was unafraid of the dead wolf. She seemed more fascinated by Stefan. He wondered how he must appear to her, how the young saw the old. He probably seemed like a living relic.

"I will have Bjorn take it down and carry it into the woods to dispose of it. He has made his point to the village."

Marie nodded and saw something of interest in the market. She motioned for him to lean down, as if to whisper a secret, then pecked him on the cheek before dashing away. He shook his head. Mysteries abounded in the world.

Turning for the market as well, he concentrated on steady breathing, clasping his hands behind his back to maintain his dignity. He saw little work being done and very few sales being made. Yet he saw many people, mostly villagers, standing close to each other, mincing tender details among themselves, lurid speculations about poor Catarina and who her lover might have been.

"What are you doing?" Stefan said, tapping the villager Paulus on the shoulder. The man was standing in a circle of gossipers. "If we feed on the details of sin, we'll stir up our own appetites. I suggest you direct your energies toward finer pursuits. Make ready your stalls; put out your finest merchandise."

Paulus, red in the face now to be caught at a woman's game of gossip, nodded and attended to his stall at once.

Stefan had preached on the destructive nature of gossip not long ago. Little good it had done. Bjorn would have appreciated the irony. Parishioners agonized over whether God heard their prayers, but priests agonized over whether the parishioners heard a word God said.

"We must present our best, our bravest faces today," Stefan said to the remaining villagers in the circle. "What do we want to be known for? A terrible crime? Or that we ran evil out of this village—that we are the bravest, most devout people in all the land?"

They all probably thought him mad. He hoped they trusted him anyway.

He had made excellent arrangements for the Inquisitor. He cocked one ear to the wind, listening for the sound of hoofbeats, the sound of approaching deliverance.

$$\sim\!\stackrel{\bullet}{\mathcal{L}}\!\sim$$

Stefan noted with satisfaction that every pew was filled, except the very first ones. Only Mia sat on one of those. Soon, when neighboring villages heard, even the first pews would be coveted. Mia sat alone, seemingly unaware of anyone else, with her red face and puffy eyes, saying her rosary under her breath, her fingers flying over each of the beads. *She probably does not even consider the words,* Stefan thought. *She doesn't linger over them long enough to let them do their work in her.*

She probably had disappointed Bjorn again and was feeling guilty. Stefan could tell. She would expect him to sit through a long confession, and in the end, she would not be a better wife to Bjorn. She only wanted Alma healed. She did not want to work harder. Stefan frowned. He could offer God's forgiveness, but could he change God's mind? Alma was as she was created. Mia was as she was created. Stefan could do nothing, really, except exhort Mia, once again, to rise above her own nature and learn to trust God. Much work needed to be done with Mia. Others surely knew that too, as they avoided sitting with her, filling in the pews just behind her.

Rose, the widow from the village whose husband had died early in her marriage, sat behind Mia. Though the women claimed the same age and Stefan had seen them once growing as close as sisters, it was clear that they were not friends anymore. Rose stared at the back of Mia's head.

Women's jealousy proved a strong sin to contend against. That's what Stefan figured was Rose's conflict with Mia. After all, Mia had a husband and a child, albeit a sickly one. Rose had nothing. Her husband, who had long been ailing, had died two weeks after their marriage. He had died working with the townsmen digging a new well, clutching his chest and falling over dead before anyone could call for help. Stefan had always said it was a blessing that the couple had not conceived, but now he doubted himself. A child would have made Rose happy in these years. Stefan did not know why Rose had turned nervous and withdrawn, more so recently, except that grief had caught up to her and overwhelmed her completely.

Stefan turned his attention away from the women. He had never seen this many souls in his church at once. Everyone stared at him as he prepared to begin. He concentrated on his posture, biting his cheeks for a solemn look. More money might come in today than all of last month. All the secret sin that Catarina hid, the final tragedy, and then the lingering gossip—that was what had filled his church. But his plans, yet to be revealed, would fill the church past standing room. Good would come from evil. That was the work of God.

Stefan licked his lips, beginning the Mass. All fell silent as his voice hovered above them. The empty, strident echo that had mocked him all these years evaporated today with almost every bench filled. "Lord," he said under his breath as their upturned faces waited for his words, "whatever You must do through me, do. I am Your servant. I am *their* servant."

A startling thought jarred his composure, one that did not seem like his own. Why had God called him to the priesthood? Stefan did not know. He'd never asked. *Perhaps later,* he thought, shaking his head. He smoothed his robe and took a breath, lifting his arms wide open so the gestures would not be missed.

"Blessed be God in heaven," Stefan said. "May we be reminded of our sins as we sit in silence, that we may confess and be forgiven. I will begin our service."

Heads pointed down now, everyone staring straight into their laps. Stefan continued with the Mass for several minutes, intoning the Latin perfectly.

He became distracted as he thought of Bjorn and the wolf.

Bjorn did not understand the burdens of a priest. A priest had to give answers, had to explain it all—unanswered prayers and death and misfortune. Of course no one ever questioned Stefan about good health and fine houses. He never had to worry about finding answers for those any more than Bjorn had to worry about being invaded by peaceful citizens and obedient women.

Bjorn had the easier job. He could arrest and punish. He could go home and sleep with his wife and watch his child play. Stefan would have liked to arrest and punish, would like to return to a warm home and not a cold room with no one to prepare his meals. Still, he did not regret the priesthood. He simply regretted that so many made outrageous demands of him.

He began the benediction, surprised to be ending the Mass already. He spoke faster, probably because he was so excited, he guessed.

In the silence of prayer he could hear feet scuffing the floor, people shifting their positions on the stern wood benches, the soft breathing of the elderly ones who had fallen asleep, and a sound he loved: the quiet gentle pause after a prayer is finished. People always hesitated in that moment to look at each other, or at him. He sensed God most in that moment.

Outside, wood wheels dug into the path, sending pebbles shooting out from under the heavy turning. The horse clopped along slowly and steadily, the steps of an animal with only one long journey, never a home. His footfalls did not quicken as he neared the town.

The people rushed to finish their own prayers, their hands flying across their chests as they made the sign of the cross. The quiet grace Stefan loved lifted away, back into the rafters; every face turned to the doors. Outside, the horse's steps stopped.

Both doors swung open together, and strong sunlight swept in, causing the people to wince and squint. All could see only the darkest outline of a man standing in the doorway, his cape swirling around his calves. The man carried an enormous bag. When he dropped it on the floor, the noise exploded across the church. Everyone lurched in fear as a cloud of dust and dirt swirled around the man, obscuring him further. Stefan knew with certainty the man's identity. His stomach churned.

The man stepped out of the doorway, and Stefan got his first good glimpse of him. He had light brown hair that hung in curls down past his ears and a dark brown beard neatly groomed; there wasn't even a hint of silver in his hair. Stefan hoped this man was not younger than himself. The man had spring blue eyes and perfect teeth that flashed beneath his mustache as he smiled. He walked down the aisle, turning to look straight at each person as he passed, his serene eyes noting each upturned face. He nodded as if he understood everything they had come here to whisper to God. Extending his hands, he began to touch the shoulders of those who sat on the edge of each pew, nodding with mercy. Stefan marveled at his demeanor. The man preached a sermon simply by the way he walked down an aisle. Stefan cleared his throat to break the spell.

"Welcome, brother," Stefan said. "I have concluded our Mass, but I have yet to finish the benediction."

The man clasped his hands as if to pray.

"Forgive me, Brother Stefan," he said. "I have interrupted, haven't I?"

Stefan finished the benediction, allowing himself a deep breath before the end, not knowing what would come next. He had called for this man, the Inquisitor Bastion. Stefan watched the faces of his villagers, who were shocked by the sight of this new man in richly done clothes, a cape over his shoulders that would cost any of them a year's labor. The villagers did not glance back at Stefan.

"Go in peace," Stefan said with a sense that he had just released something, something that would fly away, never to return. That could not be.

The people always began their exodus with great speed, but this time no one left. Instead, they sat in their pews, waiting. Only Dame Alice stood to leave, her mouth a tight, thin line. When she looked at Stefan, he thought she looked disappointed in him.

Bastion had sat for the benediction but now rose, extending his arms to Stefan first. Stefan walked down the altar steps into the embrace. He glanced at the women in the pews. They seemed to find him attractive. Stefan positioned himself to block Bastion from their view.

"Well done, my brother," Bastion said. "You have a good voice."

Moving away from Stefan, he turned to the people and addressed them.

"You have in Father Stefan a good and constant shepherd. He alone has recognized the evil that is at work among you. He alone has called for the church's assistance. For this reason, I have come."

He moved to the bottom step of the altar, making it easier for all to see and hear.

"My name is Father Bastion, and I am an Inquisitor. I have heard of your troubles. I have come to give you assistance. You must not regard me as a priest, for I have no interest in ordinary sins. You must not regard me as an enemy, for I have no interest in persecuting the innocent. I am called for one reason alone: to find evidence of witchcraft, and if witches are found, to free you of their influence."

Stefan positioned himself in front of Bastion, though he stood below Bastion on the steps. He saw Dame Alice standing at the back of the church, her arms folded. Curiosity had gotten to her, he surmised.

"Most of you would agree that it is better to know for certain that we are safe rather than wait for further proofs of evil," Stefan said. "We live in dangerous times. The church is under assault from heretics across the empire, under assault from scholars who claim to be outside her authority, under assault from princes and rulers who desire power over principle. I will not let danger come to our village. Bjorn has hunted and killed his wolf; now I must hunt mine." Stefan exhaled and pursed his lips as he stepped aside. He had not rehearsed any more than that.

"Tell me, my friends," Bastion said, "what could compel a woman such as your very own Catarina to cuckold her husband? Was she not a good woman? Was he not a good man?"

"She seemed the best of us," Stefan answered, looking at his people for agreement. "We were shocked to discover she lived a secret life of sin."

"You should hope sin is all I find." Bastion said. "Sin has a remedy. Christ has given us means to atone. But heresy, witchcraft, the trampling of the sacred Host wafers from Communion and fornicating with devils—there is no remedy we can apply to such actions. We can only purge the evil and trust God's punishment will be enough. Father Stefan cannot conduct this investigation alone. It is a civil matter as much as it is a religious concern. My job is to secure your village, purge the evil I find, and assure you that you will suffer no more."

Soft murmurs floated past, but no one spoke up.

"Men," Bastion continued, "how can you trust your wives? Who among you will be next to discover that his faithful wife is a bawd and his children bastards? Women, why did Catarina hide herself from you? Why did she not trust any of you enough to reveal her true face, her secret adulteries? Were you to be her next victim? Or her next recruit? Who else hides among you?"

Any movement would seem an admission of conscience. Stefan saw his flock frozen in their shoes; not even their chests moved as they breathed.

"Prepare yourselves," Bastion said. "Tonight we begin."

Erick moved out from the shadows and walked toward Bastion. Dame Alice reached for him, trying to grab his arm, but Erick did not seem to notice.

"Can I stable your horse for you?" Erick asked. Stefan pressed his lips together to discourage a grin. Erick had no stable. But given the command to stable a visiting dignitary's horse, he would convince one of the wealthy families to assist. Everyone loved Erick, who always shoveled snow from widows' doorways in the winter and supplied the poorest with fresh firewood and a few hens when babies were born.

"Whose son is this?" Bastion asked.

No one moved. Erick's face went red, his eyes looking only at the floor.

Stefan realized he should speak up, but Erick spoke first. "I have no mother or father. I serve the church."

Bastion stared at him, his eyes wide. Stefan could not tell if Bastion might be ready to yell or laugh; he had the unreadable face of a feral cat.

He broke into a wide grin. "Well done," he said. "Well done indeed. Yes, stable my horse. Then take my bag...."

Bastion stared at Stefan.

"Oh!" Stefan caught on. "Yes, I've prepared a bed for you in our dormitory. Erick knows where it is."

"Then, Erick, my son, take my bag to the dormitory. And for you, my good people, go in peace. Meet me in front of the church steps tonight when the sun sets."

Erick walked to open the doors for the people, bending down to lift the bag. He needed a second attempt to lift it. Stefan wondered what could be so heavy. A traveling man often brought an extra cloak but rarely anything more.

Some of the people wove around Erick, slipping out at once, while most stood around, eager for something else to happen. Dame

Alice crossed to Mia, her head cocked as if to ask a question. Mia saw her coming and hurried down the aisle and out the door. Stefan watched her flee and caught sight of another woman in dark robes, her long gray hair blown back by the wind. She stood beneath the wolf, stroking his fur, then turned and caught sight of Stefan, her ice blue eyes glaring at him in fury. She crooked one finger at Stefan, her lips pulling back over her teeth in a snarl.

Stefan stepped back into the shadows of the church, his heart thundering in his ears.

Chapter Eight

Bastion paced in front of a covered cart as the bonfire grew higher. Stefan watched him through the flames, standing in front of the congregation of villagers. Bastion's eyes glittered in the flames as his gaze swept side to side over the people, searching their faces. He seemed hungry, but it was an appetite Stefan did not recognize. Smoke between Stefan and Bastion rose in waves, a thin veil separating priest from prophet.

The people moved closer and closer to Bastion, edging Stefan out. Only a few lingered on the periphery of the crowd, perhaps too intimidated to come closer.

Bastion stopped and signaled for Stefan to cross over. Stefan approached, unsure what would happen. Bastion kept his words soft as he grasped Stefan's hands.

"You were wise to call for me," Bastion said. "A man must admit when he is outnumbered by his enemy. Only if he has courage will he live."

Stefan shook his head in confusion. "I am not outnumbered, sir. We seek one person here, one murderer."

"You have a sheriff to rid your town of murderers. Should I leave?"

"No." Stefan was humbled. "I need an answer. The mystery is how a woman such as Catarina could stray so far without any of us noticing."

"And you think that is a mystery? Do you know nothing of women? Or of witches?"

Stefan looked away before answering. "We so rarely have crimes, Inquisitor. It's a quiet village."

"A quiet village with bloodstains on the steps of the church."

"We might have one witch here; I don't know. But no more than one, I'm sure. It would explain why a good woman was caught up in this."

Bastion set a hand on his shoulder. "You called for an Inquisitor. Trust your instincts. One man cannot fight one witch. They are powerful; so must we be. I know priests who died fighting their witches before anyone thought to call an Inquisitor."

Stefan opened his mouth to say more, then shut it. What knowledge did he have of witches? Who would call in an Inquisitor and then be so bold as to argue with him?

"My friends," Bastion called, circling the fire to either side. The heat distorted his face. "Can a good woman be forced to commit adultery? Would a good woman welcome the Devil into her home, destroy her marriage, provoke her husband's murder?"

Stefan saw looks exchanged among his people. What the looks meant he did not know. His people had their own language, just as he had his Latin, he supposed.

"Catarina was no good woman. She was the witch," Bastion declared.

Heads in the crowd swiveled, words were murmured as hands clutched onto arms, and children put their hands to their mouths.

Stefan caught sight of Dame Alice, arms folded, jaw set. She did not
believe Bastion. She turned to look at Stefan, shaking her head at
him.

"Does the news shock you? In the Spanish royal court, we saw
many of these cases. But I will prove it easily. How did the husband
die?"

Stefan spoke for the village. "Stabbed in the side."

"The wounds of Christ." Bastion smiled to himself. "Stabbed
in the side, just like our Lord and Savior. Betrayed with a kiss, no
doubt, just as our Lord and Savior. A righteous man dying an unjust
death. Do you see it, the mockery of what you hold sacred?"

The people nodded. But Stefan didn't see it, certainly didn't see
the Savior in Cronwall, not with Cronwall's drinking and temper.

"And the witch, the woman you call Catarina, how did she die?"
Bastion called.

"A broken neck," someone replied from the crowd. "There were
bruises, too."

Ducinda pressed her face into her shawl, weeping. Stefan
instinctively reached for her but stopped himself when he noticed
the villagers watching him. What would it mean to comfort Ducinda
if her friend was a witch? He took a step back from her, returning his
attention to Bastion, willing the people to do the same, to turn away
from his momentary indiscretion.

Bastion smirked, eyes closed. "Our enemy is predictable.
Dangerous, yes, but entirely predictable. My friends, I have chased
your enemy, the Devil, over sea and land, across borders and kingdoms, and yet I tell you the truth: Never once has he surprised me.
His work is always the same. Only the women's names change."

Stefan nodded in agreement with Bastion, cutting his eyes side to side to see if anyone still watched him.

"The Devil often breaks the necks of his witches. In my travels, when I have caught a witch and she is to burn, I often find her dead in her cell by morning, most often by hanging. Her neck is always broken. Witches who desire confession, who desire to turn from their errors, are troublesome to the Devil's work. He silences them the only way any woman can be silenced: through death. Sometimes there is a struggle, if the woman had been a good soul before she gave herself to him. Oh, beware, my friends: The Devil is indeed among you. But he cannot harm you without human assistance. For how can the spiritual world enter into the physical world except by human host? The Devil is powerless among you until he inhabits one of you. Bring me Catarina's body."

Erick pulled a cart with the casket upon it toward Bastion. Erick's shoulders strained under the linen shirt Stefan had supplied last year. Erick had outgrown yet another set of clothes. He had become an impressive man in many ways. Stefan wondered if Erick would remain with him much longer, especially now that Bastion had arrived.

"Thank you, my son," Bastion said. Erick seemed taken aback. Bastion called him a son for the second time today. He had only just met him. Stefan frowned.

"What fellowship does light have with darkness?" Bastion asked the people, who remained silent. Stefan glared at them and huffed. They should know the proper response. "What have you taught them, Father?"

Stefan froze with no answer.

Bastion ran his hand over the coffin. Ducinda had paid for a lovely coffin, carved with spring flowers and vines. Bastion shoved the lid onto the dirt and tilted the coffin away from himself. Catarina's body tumbled out, her broken neck making her head land at a grotesque angle.

Children screamed and ducked underneath their mothers' shawls. Men looked away, twisting their mouths. Stefan found he could not close his mouth, his shock freezing his will.

Bastion pointed at him. "You would give a Christian burial to a witch?"

Stefan was nervous. "I … I asked a woman, Ducinda here, to help with her burial, and this is what she chose." He didn't mean to turn against Ducinda, but it was the truth. He wanted this over quickly.

Faces turned to Ducinda, who lowered her shawl from her tear-streaked face in horror. "I did not know. Father Stefan told me nothing."

"A witch must be burned and her ashes dumped into a river," Bastion said to the crowd. No one moved. Erick stepped forward to protest, but Bastion whipped toward him with a pointed finger, holding him back.

"Did you hear me? Does anyone among you fear the Lord? An enemy of Christ is before you. Throw her body into the fire! Show me that you fear your Lord."

In obedience, Stefan made a move toward the body, but other men grabbed her first. One took her by the ankles, the other by her hands, carrying her to the bonfire. Erick threw his arm over his eyes, turning away. Stefan looked away too, into the dark edges of the night. These men once hoped to court gentle Catarina. He had heard their confessions; he knew the thoughts they had of her in those days. Now he heard them grunt as they lifted and threw her into the flames. A shadow caught his eye, and he thought he saw a woman running into the forest beyond them, her silver hair catching the moonlight.

"Praise God," a man muttered. "Let us be done with evil." Other voices carried over the pops and cracks of the burning wood. A stench foreign to Stefan, foreign to them all, spoiled the air, seared into the night and memory, sneaked past them by the smoke, soaking into their clothes, their hair, their village.

"I always knew she wasn't right." Another voice Stefan did not recognize. He did not know this side of his people. He caught sight of little Marie looking at him as if he was a monster. She did not understand. She was still too young to know right from wrong.

"A fine girl Catarina was," he heard someone saying, "until the day she came to market with bruises round her wrists. Her husband away on a journey, said she hurt herself carrying water buckets. Never the same after that."

"Her eyes were cold. No life in them anymore."

Stefan saw Bjorn on the other side of the crowd, observing it all from a distance. Bjorn caught Stefan watching him and nodded without expression. Bjorn crossed his arms, his body settling into place as if ready to hear Bastion turn the village upside down. Stefan turned away, telling himself his cheeks were flushed from the bonfire's heat. Bastion paced in front of the fire, his eyes wide with excitement as the corpse burned. People circled and leaned in, waiting for his next word.

God burned Sodom and Gomorrah. Stefan reminded himself of that, for strength. God's work was sometimes done with fire.

They wanted to hear what he said. And what he asked would be done immediately. *They aren't the sort of people who respond so well,* Stefan thought. At least not to him. Now he could see they were exactly that sort of people. Stefan did not want to look at Bjorn again, but he did anyway. What had he taught his people, indeed? Bjorn's criticism had been right. Tonight he knew this with grim certainty: His congregants hid from him, in plain sight, sitting through all those Masses and prayers and penitence with no intention of changing. If Bjorn asked again why his prayers went unanswered, Stefan would tell him this.

Bjorn had pushed his way to the front of the crowd, close enough to grab Bastion if he wanted. Stefan couldn't reach him without calling attention to himself. He was stranded in this crowd of unrepentant sinners and a woman's burning body, her beauty turning into a vision black and unrecognizable before their eyes.

Stefan's shoulders slumped. He must apologize to Bjorn later. Bjorn had been right. Bastion would not stay longer than two or three days at most. Stefan would learn how to lead the people, how Bastion called up their obedience and hunger for righteousness with only words. Stefan would be Bastion's most devoted student, and his people would prosper. That was what a good priest must do.

Bastion ducked his head, whispering something to Erick. Erick looked with great sorrow at Stefan before disappearing. He returned, wheeling a cage straight to the crowd. The people pushed into each other, making room for Erick, none wanting to touch the cage.

Catarina's burning body made the air smell foul. Villagers lifted hems and sleeves to their faces, blocking the smell. A worse smell, almost inhuman, seeped from the cage Erick drew near. No one wanted to know what could be inside the cage, covered by a thick wool blanket, but no one could turn away. They pressed their clothes harder against their mouths and noses so that only their eyes remained visible on their faces. Stefan could not tell them apart.

Bastion stepped in front of the cage, giving the people something to focus on, an excuse to look away from Catarina's lovely blonde hair rising up to the moon as it caught fire.

"Search your hearts. Think on Catarina, a seducing witch who caused an innocent man's death. Consider what evil hides among you. Witches are real, my friends. The Bible teaches their existence and says we must not suffer a witch to live. These witches, what do they want from you? Do you know? Have you guessed? A witch craves what is forbidden, and what is forbidden but carnal knowledge? Witches will drive a good man to do terrible things. And their power in this village may be great."

"But what of the cage?" Erick asked. "What is inside?"

"No, I can see I have told you all too much tonight. Go home and rest."

Stefan moved beside Erick. "Where shall I put the cage?" He would secure it somewhere out of sight. Bastion would probably sleep in tomorrow, and everyone would be anxious to attend the first Mass of the day. Stefan would use his most thunderous voice to speak the old Latin words. The people would find great comfort in Stefan—the way a child runs to his mother after a frightful dream in the night.

"Put the cage where it can be secured at all hours, near the church," Bastion answered. He said it loud enough for several men in the front row to hear. "No one must be allowed near it for fear of their very salvation."

"What is it?" Stefan asked, ready to kick himself as the words left his mouth. He sounded as eager as Erick.

"I think it's an animal," Erick whispered to him. "Smell it."

Bastion sighed as if exasperated. "Let me relieve your impatience," he said, then took hold of the corner of the wool blanket. With a violent snap it ripped away. A beast crouched in the corner, thick, tangled hair hanging down past its spreading haunches. It was covered in filth. A handful of yellow teeth broke the dark opening of its mouth; underneath, its eyes were covered with crusts of mucus. As the crowd watched, it picked at a scab.

Stefan studied the beast with the slow realization that it was a woman. Erick ran to the edge of the woods and vomited.

"She, too, once had a name, a home. But the Devil came to her window one night, and she beckoned him in. How handsome he must have looked to her in the moonlight, a seducing serpent. Look upon her, ladies. This is what becomes of the woman who abides with the Devil. See what has become of her beauty. Look upon her and know what it means to be abandoned by mercy. Behold, a witch!"

No woman found the strength to look at her. Their heads were bowed, and they cried into their shawls. Stefan heard little whispers of prayers, as if they could repent right then of every wrong they had done if it would save them from this woman's fate.

"Go now! Go and pray to be spared!" Bastion called as the people fled into darkness in all directions, through gardens and past homes, trampling the tender green growths of the fresh and innocent spring that had overcome winter.

Chapter Nine

Mia kept her eyes on the ladle, careful to scoop from the sides to get the hottest portion of the stew to please Bjorn. She ladled it into his bowl then pushed the ladle deep into the center of the pot, touching bottom, scraping up thick chunks of the best meat and depositing them in his bowl. She picked a soft leaf of sage from the plate on the table and tore at its edges, dropping the bits in a neat cluster in the center of the stew. Her mouth watered at the thought of her own bowl, and she fantasized about a chance to sit and rest as she ate it. But she would wait.

Alma gnawed her bread, taking bites then holding it out for inspection, fascinated by the marks her teeth made. She bit the bread at a new angle, delighted at the new shape she crafted. Margarite sat forlorn, her hands folded in her lap. She stared at her bowl as if it had been responsible for some great sorrow. Mia left her to her quiet thoughts. Not all sadness needed an immediate remedy. Mia had learned to sit with her own sorrows on many nights and had discovered that very few sorrows needed anything at all from her. They came and settled in her soul while Mia tended to her work, like quiet companions, like birds in the town square. They came and settled in, right in the middle of life, with no hope of scattering off into the winds.

Bjorn watched her, his hands clasped together, one finger raised and laid over his mouth. "What is the gossip? What do the women say?"

She set the bowl before him and began tearing free a thick chunk of bread to serve him. Their earlier argument still pierced her heart. He would say nothing more of it, she knew, and he would not allow her to bring it up. She put the entire loaf before him and sat, feeling the pain of blood rushing into her feet as they left the floor. She was exhausted from her soles to her head.

"Well?"

When Mia had exhaled, letting the pain pass, she answered. "I've heard no gossip."

"Really?"

"None."

"I will tell you what I have heard, then. The Inquisitor, this man named Bastion, said Catarina was a witch. That she bewitched another man, luring him to sin, that it is her own fault she died. He says the Devil murdered her."

Mia's body went numb. Her mouth dropped open, and she took small, hot breaths.

He waved a hand at her as he ate. "Is this what the women say?"

Mia reached down, rubbing her calves. "I have no idea. But it sounds more tale than truth."

"You went to the market today, did you not? There's meat in the stew, I see. I want to know what people are saying. I want to know if they believe the Inquisitor."

"I went to market," Mia admitted. "I bought the meat and came home after Mass." She gave great attention to stretching her legs, keeping her head bent low so he would not read her expression. She told him the truth, but not all of it. Women had been whispering, and she had heard some of what they'd said, but she had not listened well. She had interrupted them, asking if anyone knew of a new remedy to try for precious Alma. She'd said that Alma had kept Bjorn awake again, and that would not do. Husbands can be so ill-tempered if they don't sleep. She meant it as a joke, but the stone faces around her just stared, immobile. She apologized, letting her shawl cover her face, running away, not stopping when she heard Dame Alice calling after her.

Bjorn chewed, nodding. "No matter. I heard him myself last night. Father Stefan hired him, did you know that? I told Stefan not to. But I could be wrong. There might be truth in his words."

Mia wished she had served herself stew. Her feet hurt too much to get up again now that she had sat down, never mind her back. Too many nights without sleep lately, too many errands and chores; her body could not recuperate from one day to the next. The aroma tortured her. *Just as well that I hurt,* she thought. She could not eat in front of Bjorn. He might think she took too much from him, wasted his money, forgot that he alone saved her and held them all together. Hunger shamed her.

"I am glad you are not angry with Stefan," Mia said. Stefan might blame her for that, too.

"I only went to make sure he kept order. I didn't plan to listen to this man Bastion. I had hoped to arrest him, in fact. If the people became agitated."

"I'll do a better job of listening for you. When I go to market."

"It doesn't matter." He grinned at her, and this second shock, this sudden burst of pleasure, shot through her like a new pain. "Perhaps nothing that happened is as we thought. But you should hear Bastion. He said women are prone to the Devil's temptation, that the Devil woos a woman like a man might."

Mia laughed; she couldn't help it. If the Devil wooed women, then he, too, had avoided Mia entirely. A woman like Mia waited her whole life for someone to notice her. If the Devil had courted her, she would not have missed it.

Bjorn watched her, then pushed back from the table and let his head fall back as he laughed. Perhaps he would not scowl if she ate just a small bowl of stew. She edged toward the bowl.

"You, of course, have never been tempted by the Devil because you are a good woman." He leaned across the table, catching her by the hand. "You *are* a good woman. I am harsh sometimes, when you test me, and I say harsh things. I do not mean for you to remember. You don't remember them, do you?"

"No," she lied. She wanted it to be true. But his words were as unpredictable as his moods, and she could not forget how he had wounded her without reason on so many nights. He always apologized, and she always lied, saying no harm had been done. One day she hoped to understand what called up those dark rages in his soul.

"There is no such thing as an unanswered prayer of the believer. Deliverance always comes if we do not give up hope. Do you believe that to be true?"

She pushed his hand away. What did he know of unanswered prayer? "Where did you hear that?"

"I do not say Stefan is a bad priest ..." he said, standing to refill his bowl before sitting back down.

She nodded, acknowledging his kindness in serving himself.

"... only that he has not taught us many things, important things. He has not taught us of the Devil, of his ways among men."

"I would not care to dwell on that even if he had."

"That is why your prayers are not answered. You do not know the truth. How can you pray if you do not know the truth? Come with me tonight, to hear the Inquisitor."

She flinched, turning away so he wouldn't see tears spring to her eyes. He was wrong. She did know truth, she wanted to scream, and she knew what truth did to people. Truth did not always bring peace and healing; sometimes it set the world on fire and took loved ones away to the place where the living could not follow.

But what if Bjorn was right about her prayers? "Put Alma to bed and see to it that Mother is well covered with a blanket," Bjorn said. "This man, Bastion—you must hear him. What he teaches is powerful truth."

"And if it is not?"

He dropped his spoon and stared at her like she had taken God's own name in vain. "If it is not," he said, choosing his words slowly, "then we will leave this village and never return. The dangers are too great."

Chapter Ten

The witch crawled to the bars, pressing her face against them so that red lines looked as though they had been burned onto her cheeks. The clean whites of her eyes sparkled, but every other visible inch of her body was thatched with filth. She reeked of waste, the straw in her cage used both as toilet and a bed.

Mia turned away in horror, pushing her face into Bjorn's leather vest. His arm went around her, holding her there. She held her breath, willing his arm to stay there. He rarely touched her.

Why did he want her to hear Bastion or look upon this witch? What could any woman do to deserve this living death? While everyone around her pressed closer, hungry for details of this woman's crimes, Mia turned her thoughts to her home. She wanted to run home, not stand here. She did not want to hear such details.

Mia's stomach growled. She had not eaten. After everyone slept tonight, perhaps, she would eat. Stefan had sat with her and Rose once, long ago when Mia had been round with child. Stefan told them of the fasting women of God. *Anorexia mirabilis,* the miracle of no hunger. These blessed women ate nothing, not even a crust, as a sign of their favor from God. Holy women were not hungry women.

Pilgrims made long journeys to see them, touch them, to listen to their intimacies. Miraculous healings were said to occur through the touch and prayers of such holy women, these miraculous maids, as Stefan called them.

Mia had no favor from God. She was often hungry. Stefan had patted her shoulder that day, telling her she should eat plenty while pregnant. Then she would deliver a strong child, a sign of his blessing. Mia had failed to secure that blessing too.

Now, as she stood in front of the cage, she ached from the day's work done in patched, worn shoes. She tried rolling her weight from side to side, trying to ease up on the painful, swollen pads. The pain made her frown and purse her mouth, and Dame Alice stole a glance at her sour face. No wonder all the women shied away from Mia and gossiped about her. Her face probably shouted that she had a shrew's heart. Dame Alice nodded as if she understood. But Mia knew; Dame Alice understood nothing. The old widow would regret it if Mia stopped to eat one day. Mia imagined she would sit and eat, and eat, and never leave her table. She would eat until food fell out her ears and she would die, full of food and relief, right there in Dame Alice's kitchen. That would give the village something to talk about.

Mia heard a voice parting the crowd, causing the whispers to stop. She could hear the bodies shifting, faces turning to hear him more clearly. She had seen him enter the church just two days ago. He had held their attention, even then, just by being new. Now he held them rapt and hungry. Mia marveled that a person could charm a village in two days. But he fascinated her, too, his face hard and clever, his eyes moving rapidly across the crowd. He seemed to be making secret judgments. Mia straightened her back, turning her face away from Bjorn's chest. She forced up a pleasant expression.

"Friends of my Savior, welcome in the name of the Father, the Son, and the Holy Ghost."

She lifted her head for a better view of Bastion, tilting it to keep the witch out of her field of vision. Mia took little comfort in the cage. She did not know what powers a witch had. The witch might look into her and know everything from Mia's past. She would know that good Christians were burning all over Europe, and Mia herself had helped light the fire long ago. A witch would know why other women here avoided Mia suddenly, why whispers started as soon as she was three paces gone. Mia did not know for certain, but she had a guess. She guessed she was filthy in her heart, just like the witch. Nothing lovely grew there, just shame that she never knew how to clean herself like the others did. She never knew how to present herself or do anything other than fail and watch as the ones she loved died. A witch might know that God was allowing Alma to die, to punish Mia.

The witch might look at her and know everything. The witch raised a bent finger caked with dirt, pointing right at Mia, and screamed. Mia's eyes went wide in fear.

"Hail Mary, full of grace, the Lord is with thee," Bastion began, his eyes settling on Mia. "Blessed art thou among women, and blessed is the fruit of thy womb, Jesus. Holy Mary, mother of God, pray for us sinners, now, and at the hour of our death."

Mia mouthed the first words of the rosary along with the others.

Bastion held his hands out to the people, and they waited. Tears formed in his eyes, and he forced them out with a slow blink. He held his arms out above them until they began to shake. Erick ran to catch hold of them and lift them up, causing Bastion to weep without shame.

"Bless the strong youths here tonight. Bless those who use their strength for service to others. Bless those who uphold the cause of righteousness and seek to banish the oppressor."

A tiny drop hit the back of her hair. Looking up at Bjorn, she saw a tear run away down his face. He caught her looking up at him and did not look away. She reached up to touch his face, but he caught her hand with a gentle touch, pushing it back down. Whatever Bastion had taught last night, Bjorn's heart had opened. It would never matter to her if it was truth.

What mattered was his touch. She had lived for years without comforting touch, ever since she saw her father murdered and walked to a new city, where she lived unknown and unloved, a child of the streets. A seasoned grifter named Thomas had found her, treating her as a valuable find among the refuse of the street. But he did not touch her. He did not hold her or hear her sorrow. He spoke to her when he needed money, and sometimes not then; he rattled his wood cup at her and threw it in the street.

He spent his days drinking beer in the town square, watching with narrowed eyes as customers purchased rags from his table in the market. They cheated him, he once yelled at the sky. Nothing but cheats and liars, he yelled, and he'd be a fool to stand on his feet all day while they cheated him. He'd rather sit with a beer, so the day wouldn't be wasted.

She had been lucky to have him.

After the deadly raid, her father's death, the screams, and pecking birds, finding Thomas had been a stroke of rare good fortune.

Mia had been just shy of eleven, afraid to enter church again alone. A priest might ask questions. He would ask what Mia had done, what her father had done. She couldn't lie. She didn't want to sin and make God angry again. She did not want to tell anyone her name or why she fended for food alone. Let them all think she had been abandoned through some fault of her own. It might even be true.

God had spared her life, but He hadn't saved her. That was her work to do in this life. Her penance.

So for three years she stayed by Thomas's side, scavenging for firewood and rags and begging for alms on his behalf. She could usually get a goodly number of alms after Mass. She watched for the church doors to open. Those doors meant salvation—until she began changing, her body filling out in new ways, her monthly courses beginning. After that, when she begged after a Mass, women scowled at her and pushed their husbands along. They must have seen she was broken, the kind of broken that begins inside, marking the heart and the face.

She worked harder then, scavenging, learning to eat less and ignore the pains in her stomach. It had been a fall day, winter fast approaching, when her life ended for a second time.

Thomas would not rise one morning though she shook him— which she never dared to do—and told him that she had enough to buy dinner, plus enough firewood to last through at least two days. He looked beyond her, unblinking.

When she touched his cheek, she wondered if it had always been so cold. She pressed her hand to her own warm cheek. She put her hand to his again. Dead. The priest came to close his eyes, and a man with a foul, stained wooden cart came and picked up his body, throwing it in with others.

As she thought on this, Bjorn exhaled heavily as he continued following along with Bastion's prayers. Bjorn had found her shortly after Thomas died. He spied her stealing bread, and when he grabbed her to arrest her, she pushed herself into his arms, not caring if he put her in the jail. He would have to hang her if he wanted to be free of her.

Bjorn threatened to at first. But soon he realized how many things she could do and that she never complained at his treatment, and never complained when he stayed out late, and never demanded newer clothes or a fancier house with mirrors to catch the fleeting sun in winter.

He could continue his life just as before, she promised, only now he would have someone to keep him fed and warm.

"The wise man is the one who builds his home upon the rock," Bastion proclaimed, bringing her back to the moment. "When the storms came, his house stood. My friends, a storm has come to this town. Can you feel the wind rising? Yes. A storm has come, and the wise man's house will stand."

When he smiled, something sweet crinkled around the edges of his eyes, something that made her want to encourage him further. He might be overcome with this kindness.

But the hard blue stones that were his eyes flashed and cut through the crowd, refusing to acknowledge her again. He spoke, using his hands as teachers do, waving them through the air to emphasize some emotions, using a single finger to jab a word straight at one person. Mia thought he looked like a sculptor, his hands working with some invisible material, shaping it before their unseeing eyes, creating and building, stacking words upon words, so that when he finished, there would be something unseen but finished between them.

"Eve stood in the garden. Though she walked with the Almighty God Himself, though she had the love of a perfect man, though she had paradise stretched before her, Eve took of the apple and ate," Bastion said.

Mia licked her lips without meaning to, hoping it didn't make her look foolish. She glanced at the other women transfixed by Bastion. None seemed concerned with her. She knew of Eve, she knew of the apple, but she had never understood. This had the sound of truth.

"Eve, the first woman, the woman who experienced complete paradise and knew nothing of sorrow, or starvation, or death—Eve could not be satisfied. What evil is in the heart of a woman, my friends! God offered her everything He has, and she wanted still more. What man, then, could ever satisfy a woman? Women want more than they are due."

Mia put a hand to her stomach, willing it to be quiet. Just like Eve, she wanted more than what she had.

"The good brothers in Christ have, in response to the Holy Father's proclamation that all witchcraft be rooted out and destroyed in God's kingdom, completed a book called the *Malleus Maleficarum*. It is in this book that I find my work, my law. I do nothing except that which the church has commanded and the civil authorities require. Before I pursue God's good pleasure among you, tell me: Do I have your permission to perform a great deliverance here?"

Some called out the word *yes*. Others nodded. Mia's heart lurched. Deliverance might be for Alma, too. Bjorn squeezed her shoulder, calling out, "Yes!" He was surely thinking of Alma.

"Then understand the word of God: Eve had a carnal heart, which led her to damn all men for eternity. And now this same evil has caused great mischief among you. I have been brought here to deliver you from these women, to save those of you whose foundations are not upon the rock."

The crowd murmured. Mia strained to hear their words but couldn't. She heard only the name of Catarina. Bjorn gripped her hand so tightly she winced.

"Friends, for what reason did Satan visit paradise? Did he come to talk with God?"

"No," the crowd answered.

"Did Satan come to tempt Adam?"

"No."

"Satan came to paradise because a woman walked there. A woman's weakness, her carnal lust, called the Evil One to the very gates of paradise, and she alone bade him enter."

Bastion raised his hands above his head, listening.

"Satan," Bastion called, "you cannot enter here. I am watching these gates. I will protect this flock." Bastion looked back at the people, his finger a little dagger that he thrust at them one by one. "And when I discover a witch, when I find her black heart dead beneath a woman's sweet face, I will tear it out and burn it so Satan will cry out in despair and see this town is lost to him forever."

"Death!" the woman in the cage screamed with a voice that sounded like a shrill cry of an animal. As she did, she tore out a clump of hair and spit at the crowd.

He dropped his voice and took a step closer to the crowd. They huddled together, pressing back, away from the woman's cage. Mia did not trust herself; had she understood him? Catarina was dead, but there was yet another witch?

"I must warn you: There may be more than one. Like snakes, when you find one, you find a nest. The work will be dangerous, and some of you may suffer the wrath of these witches as I work. But build your house upon the rock, my friends."

"How will we know?" Bjorn called out. Mia pulled back to look on him, shocked he had spoken. She saw Stefan at the edge of the crowd too, his face frozen after seeing Bjorn ask a question like this.

"How will we know the work of a witch?" Bjorn asked again.

"Do children fall ill for no reason? Do they often die?" Bastion asked. Mia's heart rose in her chest, her throat tightening. *No,* she thought. *Alma's illness could never be the work of another woman.*

Bastion saw her react, and he paused, his eyes resting on her. Mia looked away.

"And men, what about you? Do good men find themselves unable to bear the temptations of a woman who is not their wife? Do good men ruin themselves with carnal lust? Is the marriage bed kept pure, or is it defiled? All these, plus rotting crops, injuries that will not heal, accidents and misfortunes, all these are signs of a witch among you. Go, then, to your homes, and tonight pray that your eyes may be opened. Think on sadness and trials you cannot find explanation for. And men, you must consider what evils you may have done, even if only in your heart, for these may be the work of witches. Go then, and tomorrow night return, for my work must begin with great earnest."

Mia glanced back up. Bastion studied her as he spoke one last time.

"I will save the innocent and set the sinners free. Your time for deliverance has come. Do not be afraid."

The woman in the cage stood up as far as she could, with straight legs and a bent back, and snapped her teeth at anyone who stared too long. She urinated as she did this, letting the urine flow down her leg, creating a path through the dirt that clung to her legs. She caught Mia's eye and gnashed her yellow teeth at her. Mia screamed, burying her head in Bjorn's vest again.

"Do not be afraid, my child."

Mia looked up. Bastion stood in front of Bjorn, Bastion's hand resting on her shoulder like that of a god. His power buzzed through the fabric of her sleeve, the warmth of his palm spreading across her body. His cold eyes met hers, and goose bumps rose on her flesh.

Bastion spoke to Bjorn, leaning his head at an angle as if to keep his words private.

"From your question, my friend, I am guessing that you are perhaps afflicted?"

Bjorn could not answer. Mia felt his body freeze.

"Our daughter is often sick," Mia said. "But I attend Mass every day and love God. I try to please Him."

Bastion nodded, not looking at her. He removed his hand from her shoulder and laid it instead on Bjorn's. Mia's shoulder turned cold, colder than before, all warmth lost.

Bjorn took a deep breath. "Is it true? A witch can do these things? I've never heard this before."

Bastion grinned. "Hearing does not make a thing true. Even our belief does not make a thing true. Truth is actually quite indifferent to us. She cares little for what we think, and even less for what we think we know."

Mia wanted to speak but pressed her lips together. Bjorn knew how sick Alma was. He could get this man to help her if he wanted to. She had to make him want to. She had to be a good wife right now.

"A witch can make a good man fall?" Bjorn asked. "She can make him suffer and sin, do things against his pure Christian will?"

"That is precisely their method, my friend."

"Alma," Mia whispered to Bjorn. "Ask him."

"Alma? This is your daughter, yes?" Bastion seemed concerned.

Mia opened her mouth to explain, but Bjorn shushed her. "You say the Devil is responsible for Catarina's murder, and her husband's?"

Bastion watched Mia, frowning. "We should not discuss this in front of your sweet wife. Let us meet tonight at the church, with Father Stefan. We will take refreshment, and I will teach you what I know. My friend, if you have been troubled, you will be troubled no more."

Mia's stomach growled, catching Bastion's attention. He betrayed nothing in his expression; she was not shamed. Mia smiled at him, and a slow smile spread across his face in response.

Chapter Eleven

The caged witch stared at Stefan, her lips wet from her tongue licking them repeatedly. His stomach turned as she stared at him. He couldn't smell her from the porch of the church, but she made him sick just as if she were pressed up against his nose.

Bastion had left him and sent Bjorn home hours ago, just before 3:00 a.m. He said he was eager to brush out his cloak and wash his face. He was asleep in the dormitory that stood across the church garden. Stefan stayed behind to attend to make preparations for noon Mass, though the bell had not tolled 6:00 a.m. yet. Stefan's head swam with Bastion's words. Bjorn had stayed and sat with Stefan and Bastion, with a rare smile to let Stefan know he had been forgiven. Stefan wondered at the change coming over Bjorn, his sudden hope in the ways of God, as if hearing the truth for the first time. That wasn't right—hadn't Stefan's Masses been enough for Bjorn to learn the truths of God?

Bastion had spoken of many things as both men listened. Women often became witches, he said, and witches did the work of the Devil.

"Satan spirits them away to celebrate the Sabbath," Bastion had said, "by fornicating, and spitting on the bread of the Eucharist, and drinking the blood of children."

"You're saying witches can fly?" Stefan had asked, his eyebrows arched. He would not be made a fool, especially by a guest he had invited.

"I'm saying their master can carry them off wherever he wishes. As a priest, I am surprised you do not know this. Remember that the Devil spirited Jesus away to the top of a hill in the great temptation?"

True, Stefan nodded. He had been told that could be found in the Bible.

"Men, Scripture is clear: Witches exist. Like their master, the Devil, they can go anywhere at any time. And God demands we rid the earth of them. To deny any of these essentials is to deny Scripture, to deny God. Only a heretic denies God."

Stefan replayed the words, finding no fault in them, only zeal. He stretched, picking up a rotted peel from the church steps. The church would be full in the afternoon, filled with everyone from the village who had heard Bastion last night and those who only heard his words repeated. They would be flowing out of the nave, pressing him further back into the choir, anxious for the wafers of the Host to be elevated and the bells to ring out announcing the presence of Christ through Communion as the morning sun pierced through the single rose window.

Stefan kept his mouth shut and took shallow breaths through his nose, desperate to keep the witch's smell from sickening him. He should walk back in. But he had never seen such complete pollution, a woman living in death. She embodied every sin, every condemnation brought to life. He touched the cross at his neck, and fury flashed through her eyes. She howled, throwing back her head so the sound rose above them both into the black hours. Goose bumps raised on Stefan's arms. A movement at the edge of the square caught his attention. He stared into the darkness but saw nothing. Someone had stood there watching him; he was sure of it.

He refused to look at her again. She had no cause to torment him. He set back to work, sweeping the church steps.

"Father."

She made it sound like a joke.

He forced himself to do it, walking straight to her, his eyes only on the ground. He grabbed the edge of the wool blanket and slung one end over the cage, running around to take the other end and pull it down, covering her from sight. Her hand shot out from between the bars, flailing in the darkness.

"Father. Father. Father." Her sour, gritty voice chanting his name. "Hear me. I want to make confession."

Stefan looked around for Bastion but saw no one. She was either very clever or pitiful and sincere. He could not refuse her, since he was a servant of God. She might ask for mercy. She might want to be delivered. Or she might be blaspheming. He edged closer to her hand, her fingers clawing at the air.

"I know you're there," she whispered. "I hear you breathing. You are afraid."

"I am here."

"I want to confess. I want to be clean."

The witch belonged to Bastion. Bastion should know what she said, that she called for confession. Bastion should be there. Bastion would know what to do, handle it all effortlessly, probably rolling his eyes at this rural priest who could not even handle a confession.

Stefan held his breath. He would do it. Bastion would sleep through it all. Stefan would deliver this woman in the name of the Lord and present her to the people the next morning. Their awe at the power of God, through Stefan's hands, would be immeasurable. What Bastion could stir up, Stefan could stir up. Word would spread.

"God help me," Stefan prayed. "Help me to free this woman at last. Deliver her through me."

He grasped her hand, ignoring the grit beneath his fingertips. He whispered Latin words like a lullaby, waiting to hear of her deep and unthinkable shame.

He thought of Bastion's face, what it would look like when he saw that Stefan had delivered this hardened witch. And he was still picturing Bastion's face as the witch yanked him toward the bars, as her teeth sank into his ear, ripping off a piece of his flesh. Her grip was stronger than any man's, the fury of the Devil himself digging her fingers into his flesh as she bit into him again.

Only in later hours would Stefan remember the moment clearly and swear silently to himself that he had heard the distant sound of laughter.

Chapter Twelve

Bjorn walked Mia home in silence, deep in thought.

"You sat and waited? The whole time I sat with Stefan and Bastion?"

"Is that all right? You wanted me to come, didn't you?"

He nodded, saying nothing more.

She flexed her toes with each step, trying to get blood back in them, to keep the remaining toes from turning gray and hard. She said nothing, though. He did not need to hear of her troubles or discover a new flaw.

He kept his hand at her back much of the way, except when he had to help her climb over a fallen tree, or step over a narrow turn in the creek. She wanted to thank him, or praise him for his kindness, but she did not know if other wives did that. It might call too much attention to her, make her seem insincere. She tried to copy the speech of other wives in town, but it always sounded false.

The dark path provided welcome distractions. She loved the changing scent as they walked, weaving through the trees back to their home. Sparse areas had clean, quiet air, but deeper in, the moss scrambled and the trees rioted together, creating a denser air. Smells of decay and dirt and hidden dens mixed with the smell of crushed ferns and warm sap. Already there were flowers coming up. Mia wondered what else had grown underneath her, and all around her, during the long winter. She watched where she stepped.

Mia paused for a moment to inhale a long draught of air, trying to fill her belly and keep herself moving. Her home sat away from the town square, away from other farms and families. Bjorn didn't like noise or other people. He said he got enough of both in his work.

Mia wanted to fill the house with more children, but Bjorn had resisted. Whether he did not want more children or just didn't want Mia anymore, she never dared ask. She couldn't even ask herself in the quiet at night, those long nights when he was working or having beer with townsmen. She worked to please him. She had pledged herself to him, bursting with so much gratitude she would have done anything for him, had he asked it.

Still, sometimes being his wife wasn't enough to sustain her. She had wanted marriage so badly once, dreamed of nothing better than a home and husband and a child to love. She had those things, but the awful ache, the dark loneliness, still hid inside.

Mia tripped on a stone. Bjorn paused, waiting for her to regain her composure. Mia spoke to turn his attention off her clumsy fall.

"You were moved by Bastion's words tonight."

She tested the air with a long exhalation. She could barely see her breath. Spring worked to reclaim the world. Winter staggered back, almost finished.

Bjorn broke his silence. "He said so many new things that my head is aching."

"I think perhaps he can help us."

"Us?"

"With Alma."

Bjorn paused, as if trying to clear his mind. "Yes."

"Do you know what's odd?" Mia hated the way her voice sounded when she prattled on like this. "Dame Alice calls to me when I go to market. She says she wants to feed me. Isn't that odd?"

"Are you testing me?"

"What?"

He studied her face but seemed to find nothing. He released her and they continued home.

"I do not want you to speak to Dame Alice. Keep to yourself."

They reached the final clearing. She decided not to speak any more tonight. Nothing she said came out right. She could sit by the fire alone, warming her feet while everyone slept.

She looked up at the night sky, seeing the bright star that followed the moon this time of year. She wondered why the stars changed, why they did not stay fixed in the heavens. She would like a world where the stars were constant and nothing could be moved, a world she could orient herself in.

Bjorn gestured to her with an open palm. "Suppose the Devil overpowers a woman. She gives in, becomes a witch. But the Devil does not want her. What use is that woman? No, the Devil wants the man. Just like the serpent wanted the fall of Adam, a man made in God's image."

"Yes?"

"Suppose the witch overpowers the man's good nature by the Devil's power. Who should be punished? The man or the woman?"

None of this had to do with Alma. Mia had no idea what she should say. Bjorn often brooded, but he did not like her to comment.

"I asked a question," Bjorn said.

"I have no training in the church."

"Did God make me a woman?" he asked, surprising her with a smile. "Bastion spoke of women, how they cause all suffering, but I have not heard that before. You being a woman, you must know."

Her feet hurt, her stomach burned, and she didn't like Bjorn asking these questions, wanting to hear her thoughts. That's not why they married.

"Say something so I know your mouth at least works."

"I only know that most of my sorrows have lately come from women. They are cold to me and whisper about me. If they have remedies for Alma, I have to plead for them to share what they know."

"But if Bastion speaks the truth, they have no reason to help Alma."

"Because they cause her suffering? No, that is too awful a thing to believe."

"But my question. Who should be punished?"

"Let me think. Only God can punish the Devil, so then we cannot. The man fell under a spell, against his will, so his sin does not come from his heart. It is the witch who must be punished. She offered herself to Satan. The evil began with her. Although Satan is the cause of all their suffering, she has brought it all to pass."

"Stefan never told us these things. Why? Why would he keep these truths from us? Did he not know?"

She could see home.

The door, a series of boards banded together, well oiled by Mia, slammed open, and Margarite fell out onto the ground. Bjorn took off at a run, Mia running behind. Margarite moaned, her hands stretched out to Bjorn, her mouth open wide in a horrible grimace as she tried to make words. One arm rested at a sickening angle. *She must have used it to catch herself in the fall and it snapped,* Mia thought.

"What is it?" he yelled, reaching her and lifting her. Mia, only a few steps behind, pushed past them both. A woman, even an old woman with so little mind left like Margarite, would only do something so dangerous for one reason.

Alma.

"Alma!" Mia screamed, rushing to Alma's mat, scooping her hot, red body into her arms. Alma's head rolled off Mia's forearm, flopping toward the ground. Mia yanked at Alma's nightshirt and saw her skin retracting between each rib, her little gaunt stomach sucking in hard with each breath.

"Oh God. Oh God," Mia prayed. Bjorn stood in the doorway, his arm around his mother's side, helping her back in. He froze when he saw Alma's body.

"Go!" Mia pleaded. "Get Father Stefan. Bring whatever medicine he has."

Bjorn's movements in the house were a blur. Mia cradled Alma and kissed her, over and over on her forehead, praying God would not be angry with her for begging Him to save Alma one more time.

As Bjorn sat Margarite in the chair, Mia heard what he said under his breath.

"What have I brought upon us?"

Chapter Thirteen

"Was it jealousy?" Bastion asked, dipping the rag into a bowl of water.

Stefan wasn't sure he had any of his ear left. The witch had bitten hard, jerking her head back when she clamped down. He assumed his ear had come clean off.

"You thought if you could deliver her, people would be enthralled with you instead of me. Don't be embarrassed. Admit it."

Stefan's face grew hot. "When someone calls for God, I answer."

"Everyone was talking last night, excited, frightened. Not for me, but because of her. She enthralls them, Father Stefan, not I. No need for jealousy."

Stefan rubbed his temples, wincing as the skin near the bite moved. Bastion pushed his hand away, trying to study the wound, see what else needed to be done for it.

"That's why I bring her," Bastion continued, dipping the cloth again into the water, now red. "People listen. She stirs their blood. But she is a witch, and a witch wants one thing: destruction of moral order. She has been to enough towns with me to know that the priest is always the best, first target."

"I'm a fool."

"Not at all. You are a good man but an uneducated priest. Submit to my instruction. That's all I ask. No more mistakes."

"I'll try."

"She wants to kill you. Are you going to give her the chance?"

"Bastion," Stefan said, turning to look at him for the first time in the conversation, "I called for you because a good woman, or a woman we called good, was murdered, as was her husband. I thought we needed help rooting out one person. Bjorn didn't think it important; the incident was over. A lover's quarrel of sorts, he said. I thought if you came, rumors would stop. One person committed the crime, one person punished, only a few days lost. Now you arrive, and the whole village is infested with witches?"

"You don't believe me because there is evidence of only one crime."

"It is a lot to believe."

"It stretches your faith."

"Not just my faith. When you speak, my whole head hurts. I have never heard all this, what you swear is God's truth."

Bastion set the cloth down, moving his chair to sit in front of Stefan. "I've served the Lord a long time. Have you?"

"Yes."

"Then you understand. I have known the trials of Saint Paul. Abused, shipwrecked, beaten … compelled to travel on, shouting the truth to a deaf and dying world. Not everyone accepted his testimony, Stefan. Not everyone accepts ours."

"Why do you do it?"

"The same reason you are a priest. God's truth compels us. It's lonely work, isn't it?"

"I did not mean to say I doubted your word."

Bastion patted his leg. "You have not been taught. That's not a crime I hold you responsible for. I will teach you. When I leave, you will teach others."

"You seem so confident."

"You have many questions. Ask one."

Stefan wiped his neck. A little trickle of blood had run down into the crevices of his skin, making him wince. "The witch you travel with, your words … it frightens people. I never thought God's work could be so dark. How can you be sure it pleases God?"

"Excellent question. You will make a fine student."

"What proofs do you have from Him?"

"Has He given us, above all other creatures, the gift of reasoning?"

"Yes."

"Does God want us to apply our minds, this gift, to the understanding of His will and His ways?"

"Of course."

"So, let us begin. Can we see God?"

"No."

"Can we see Him walking around this village?"

"No."

"Then there can be no better way to know God than to study His opposite, which we do see. We do see His opposite in the world, in flesh and blood, do we not?"

"Yes."

"And so we study this witch as a particular example. Everything this witch is, God is not. That woman out there can show God to this town."

"All she is showing them is filth."

"Precisely. You follow me well in this. Now I will ask you a question: What was Satan guilty of? Why was the serpent cast down from heaven?"

Stefan chewed his lip. It would match his ragged ear if he didn't stop. "Pride," he ventured.

"Excellent. And what is pride? What did Satan want?"

"To be like God."

"What is God like? What does He do?"

"Gives laws," Stefan offered.

"And demands obedience to them. Asks us to worship Him. Provides prophecy. Demands sacrifices. Raises up a church, spread throughout the world, that seeks to please Him and carry out His will on earth."

Stefan suspected Bastion had had this conversation with other priests. He sounded rehearsed.

"So our enemy, Satan, is all these things in opposite," Bastion continued. "He gives law, demands obedience, asks for sacrifices, raises up faithful believers. But where God creates life, Satan destroys it."

"You travel with this witch so people will see and understand evil? And by seeing evil, they will see God?"

Bastion nodded and opened his mouth to say something else. Stefan cut him off. "But if we are commanded by God to destroy witches, you cannot permit her to live. You should kill her."

The door slammed back on its hinges so hard it fell off at an angle. Bjorn burst into the room, and Bastion stood, grabbing a satchel. Stefan could not comprehend the sudden explosion of noise and words. Bjorn shook him by the shoulders.

"Alma is dying."

Mia rocked Alma's limp body, keening her prayers. Her breathless words drained away into the night, blending into the darkness outside their door.

"Take Alma outside," Bastion ordered her. "Stefan, bring a bucket of water."

Mia hesitated as Stefan rushed to obey.

"It's cold tonight," she said, looking to Bjorn. Night air couldn't be good for Alma, especially now.

"Do it," Bjorn told her.

Mia stood, still cradling Alma, and went outside, not bothering with a cloak for herself. Her mind knew it was cold. Her body felt nothing but fear. Holding Alma like a fragile infant, Mia swayed side to side in the starlight, trying to keep her frightened voice strong enough to coax Alma back. Alma's eyes remained closed, her lips blue and swollen.

"Do you hear the birds, Alma?" Mia coaxed. "How noisy is spring, even at this hour! How we've missed our friends, the birds! Come back, Alma. Come back, and we'll feed them at our window."

Mia could hear the men inside and stepped closer to the window to listen. How could they cure Alma if Alma stayed out here? The child's rabbit-fast breathing had slowed, but Mia could still see every rib between each breath. Alma's heart slowed, growing tired from the effort. It would not be long now.

Mia rubbed Alma's chest with one hand, leaving it red. "Do not give up. They'll know what to do."

"These signs trouble me," Bastion said. His voice sounded strong, cutting through the shrill songs around her. She knew his voice apart from Bjorn's. Bjorn's voice was deep and rough at the edges. Bastion had the smooth, certain tones of a man who had spent years at a university. "Who among the women would curse you?" Bastion asked.

She heard no reply.

"Bjorn, you must not let a kind heart blind you to the truth. A woman is out there who has caused this. Either name her, right now, or your child will die."

Mia closed her eyes.

She heard Bjorn mutter.

"I do not care. Name the woman who hates you."

She heard the tone of Bjorn's voice but not the words.

Mia waited there, cradling Alma until her arms ached. At last, the door opened, and Bastion motioned for her to come in. He had a hard, accusing look on his face. Fear boiled again in Mia's stomach.

Bastion rested a hand on Mia's arm as he spoke. "I took water and put it in your kettle over the fire with some rosemary leaves you had about. Keep Alma near the steam."

Bastion lifted his hand, and Mia's arm went cold again. Something left her each time he touched her. She looked away.

He laid his hands on Alma to pray. "Most Holy Father, hear the prayer of your servant. Break every curse upon this child, and release her from Satan's power. Grant me the power of Elijah, that I may return this child, so near death, to its mother. Amen."

Alma stirred a little, just a fluttering of her eyelids and movement of her head. Mia hugged her tighter and wept.

"Please, God," she added. "Hear his prayer. Whatever I have done, forgive me. Please forgive me."

Bastion stared at her, flames from the fire reflected in his eyes. He looked like a prophet of old, she thought, one capable of great deliverances.

Bjorn did not look at her. "Let's go."

Bastion looked about and grabbed a chair from the table, dragging it over to the fire. "Sit down. Your arms must be so weak by now. Would you like a blanket?"

"No, thank you. The fire is warm."

"Your husband and I have work to do, Mia. When Stefan returns, use the water he brings you to keep that steam constant. And say your rosary. Do not stop saying your rosary until you see Alma open her eyes and return to you. Do you understand?"

Mia nodded.

Bjorn left without looking at her.

Bastion paused at her side as he left.

"Mia, God has heard your prayers. I will save her."

Chapter Fourteen

All of Stefan's head throbbed, his ragged ear a relentless pain that tore through his body. He could not even bear to raise his arm as if to touch it. He had tried only once, and nearly fainted from the agony. His fingers had come away with something foul. He suspected the site might be putrefying from the witch's bite. A witch's bite could be more dangerous than any animal's.

He had delivered the water to Mia last night only to find the men had already left on their mission. Mia said Bastion had pressed Bjorn to name a woman. She had not heard the name, but Bjorn would not look at her afterward. She said she felt glad Stefan had returned, hopeful he would have more answers. Alma had slept in Mia's arms, a little color back in her cheeks. Not much.

He had been sent on a woman's errand, and now the men, the real men of the town, had gone to do the men's work. Stefan used all of his self-control to keep from kicking the bucket of water.

Mia had not wanted to speak about anything else. She rocked Alma and went back to her rosary. Stefan left, promising to send Erick back to check on her, and wandered through the town, hoping to catch sight of Bastion and Bjorn. He had no luck. The sun rose as he gave up and returned to the church, walking past the sheep in the back already bleating for breakfast. Erick filled a bucket with grain for them, pushing them back as they nudged his legs. Erick had the patience to feed them despite their constant bleating demands.

Stefan walked past him, saying nothing, attempting to put a hand over his wounded ear.

Stefan spied Bastion and ducked behind the corner to the dormitory entrance to avoid being seen. Bastion stood near the caged witch, pressing his body through the bars as she kissed him on the cheeks. The pink sunrise illuminated her thin frame and the wide bars of the cage. Bastion looked like a pilgrim worshipping at a shrine, kneeling before a saint.

She fell to her knees and took his hands in hers. She kissed them, then pressed them against her cheek. She had a look of ecstasy that made Stefan blush. No woman in his congregation had ever looked at him like that. He would not want them to. Why would Bastion allow it?

Bastion pulled free, bending down and lifting a plate of food to her. She jerked the food off the plate and ate with ferocious speed. Bastion just watched her, his face a mix of pleasure and regret. She finished, letting the bones from the meat she had eaten fall onto the straw around her, the same straw she would relieve herself on, the same straw she would sleep on tonight.

"When will you do it?" she asked. Stefan strained forward to be sure he heard the words right.

"Soon."

"Please," she pleaded, thrusting her arm through the bars, trying to catch hold of Bastion. He stepped out of her reach.

"Please," she called. "Haven't I done everything you asked?"

Stefan ducked back and walked into the dormitory. Gray clouds hung low in the sky above him.

He needed to tend to his wound. He needed time to think.

Mia's voice grew hoarse from praying out loud for hours through her tears. Her head kept dropping down, startling her back awake, shamed she could sleep when her daughter's life depended on her prayers. If Alma died, it would be her fault.

I am a wretch, she thought. *What Bastion preaches about women's weakness is so true. Why did they leave me here alone with Alma dying? Didn't they see I would fail?*

"I can't do it, Lord," she whispered. "If miracles come by force of prayer, and great persistence, then I cannot have one. I am not strong enough to force You to do anything for me. Either heal or let us both die."

Mia went back to the first bead on her rosary and took a deep breath. She had to keep trying until Alma awoke whole and healed or they died sitting here. She swallowed hard, trying to ignore the pain in her throat. She pushed the words out, no longer hearing or meaning them. She just wanted God's attention, and if this worked, she would say her rosary until she dropped dead of exhaustion.

"By morning we will know," she whispered to Alma. "We will know who this God is that we have prayed to all this time."

The sun began its rise off to the east. She saw its light peeking in under her door, and dazzling pink rays streaking in through the shutters. Today's sunrise would be glorious, but Mia and Alma would not see it.

A different light, made of thick gold, pooled under the door, pouring in across the floor. The heavy gold light rose into a shimmering veil all around them, wrapping around Alma and Mia. Lost in this golden mist, Mia's head fell forward, and she snapped it back up. "I must not sleep."

"Sleep," a voice whispered. It could have been a voice in her head. Her whole body ached, so tired she couldn't tell if she was already dreaming. Or if she was already dying, departing this life with Alma in her arms, this strange peace swaddling them and carrying them together to God.

Hot tears rolled down her face as unseen hands slid under Alma's body, lifting her. Mia slipped back into the veil as she heard the whisper again.

"She is my child too."

                                   ❧

Mia dreamed of a river. She had been sleeping on its banks under a tree covered in fresh green leaves the size of her palm. The spring sun shone all around. A man stood beyond the tree. She shielded her eyes from the light coming from him. She could see only his outline and the bottom edge of his robes.

"Why can I not see your face?" she asked.

He walked to her, but the light became too strong, forcing Mia to look away. He extended a hand.

"This is what you fear," he said.

She reached for his hand, but saw it clearly, broken and bleeding, a horrid open wound torn through it, flesh splayed out in all directions. It stank. Mia remembered the stench of her first fall into darkness, that fearsome well, reeking of burning wood and oil, inks and ashes. Looking into His dark, deep wound, she saw all the horrors of her life, driven into this one man.

He laid her hand on top of the wound and turned His hand over to show her. His hand became whole. The well she feared lived in this wound, those dark secrets that destroyed flesh and life. But when she put her hand in His, she no longer saw the wound sin made. She saw healing, the hope of miracles. His wounds could bring healing, but she had to put her hand into His first.

She heard His laugh, and then woke from the dream.

ﮯ

Bjorn's mouth pressed against Mia's cheek, whiskers scratching her skin.

"Good news." He was laughing. "Wake up."

Mia yawned and tried to lift her eyelids. She didn't want to return to this life.

"Alma," she cried, sitting up as the night's full memory came back to her.

Bjorn laughed again, trying to catch her with one arm. In his other arm he cradled Alma to his chest. Alma popped her fingers into her mouth, staring at Mia.

"Alma?" Mia whispered, reaching out to stroke her hair. Alma smiled and reached for Mia. Tears came to Mia. "Her cheeks are pink. I've never seen them pink. Alma, can you breathe? Show Mama. Take a deep breath."

Alma giggled and hid her face in Mia's shift. She had been healed. She looked fresh and rested, whole. Mia looked at her own hands, trying to remember the dream.

"I did not do this," she said to Bjorn. "I tried to, but I did not have enough strength."

She realized how it all looked. "I am sorry, husband. I did not mean to sleep." How had Alma been healed? Mia had slept; she'd had no part in it.

"Everything will be better now, Mia," Bjorn said.

"How long have you been here?" Mia asked. "Did you see what happened? Do you think God did this? Is this a miracle?"

"While you were here with Alma, we found the witch that cursed us. Bastion knew her to be a witch at once. She refused the first hour to confess, but Bastion knew well a book, one called the *Malleus Maleficarum,* a book that describes how witches may be brought to the truth and to repentance. He is a marvelous man, Mia. He has set us free."

"Did he come back here while I slept?" Mia shuddered, remembering her dream. "Did he touch Alma? Is that how she was healed?"

"You don't need to fear him. A woman like you has nothing to fear."

"No, I am not afraid. Look at Alma. She is healed. How did it happen?"

Bjorn shrugged. "I came home, found her playing with the kitten. I suppose the witch's confession set her free."

"How can that be? Why would any woman curse her? She's done no one any harm."

Bjorn looked out the window; its open shutters let in the strong morning sun. "I think I'll shut those," he said.

"No. I like the light. Bjorn? Are you hiding something from me?"

He stopped, his back to her. She could see Alma peeking over his shoulder at her.

"Bjorn, if there is a witch, if she cursed us, am I to blame? Did I do something?"

He sat Alma down. "Go outside, Alma. I saw your yarn doll under the beech tree over there. Run and play with her."

Alma walked outside and squinted up at the sky, cocking her head as if listening. Mia's heart skipped a beat, and she wanted to hold her. But she had to know.

"If I am to blame, if I have done something, I have to know. Alma is healed, but what if I fail again? How can I keep Alma safe? I need an answer."

Bjorn came and knelt before Mia.

"Just remember who you are."

"Who am I?"

"My wife. I bear the responsibility for this house, not you. Keep to yourself for now while Bastion and I work. Don't ask for help from the women in the village."

"But if this is my fault, I have a right to know...."

"You have no rights! You have duties. And your duty is to keep your mouth shut and trust me. If you can't do that, then trust Bastion. Pester him with your little fears if you must."

She didn't know Bastion. How could she open her wounded heart, where her fears lived, where they pierced her, to him? Mia's mind flashed to the woman she had seen around the village. She was not of the village, however. She was said to be a healer, to have powers, to know what hid in the hearts and minds of people. *Perhaps she would have answers,* Mia thought, *and I would not bother Bjorn again, or fail Alma.* But healers like that woman were dangerous, Father Stefan had said, enemies of the church, heretics who offered salvation from herbs and spells, not God. Even thinking of her might be a sin. Mia pinched herself to stay true.

He looked up at her, taking hold of her hands. "Don't do that. I am not angry with you."

"I will try harder to please you."

"It was never you, Mia. But I will say no more. Everything has changed," he whispered in her ear as he pulled away from her and stood. "Bastion has brought salvation to this town."

Her empty stomach growled, and she pressed a hand over it to silence her hunger.

Outside, Alma stared at them both. Mia saw a dark shadow pass over the child's face, a strange, fierce anger. Mia turned her head, giving Alma a quizzical look, and Alma went back to staring up at the sky.

Chapter Fifteen

Stefan's neck hurt from wrenching it at odd angles to get a good look at his ear. He only had a small, chipped mirror to use.

"I have to stop this," he said, setting the mirror down. "Worry won't move God to heal it any faster." His fingers went back to his ear, feeling the wound's edges as he looked around at the empty dormitory.

Bastion had not come in yet, though he had been out all night. How could a man work so hard and not need rest? Stefan had sneaked in here to sleep for just an hour, to clear his mind, perhaps strengthen himself again. All of it for naught, though. Sleep had eluded him.

He groaned, pulling his shoes back on. Bastion's bag that Erick had brought in, the bag that made such thunder in the church when it had first dropped, sat in the corner. Stefan glanced around, his heart kicking up. Edging toward the bag and listening for steps outside the chamber, Stefan took hold of it and gave it a tug. It barely moved. Whatever hid in there, it was not an extra cloak for Bastion. Something heavy and unyielding waited in the dark folds of this bag.

"Stefan! Wake up."

Erick burst through the door. Stefan sat upright, spinning around to conceal the bag.

"That's *Father* Stefan," he corrected Erick, who pulled his chin down, frowning.

"Were you looking in the bag, *Father?*"

"Of course not."

"What's in it?"

"I didn't look."

"Well, time for you to be up. And you'd best attend to the women before prayers."

"What's that?"

"Bastion's got everyone stirred up, especially the women. Dame Alice nearly pulled my arm off, trying to drag me into her house. The women are all gathered around in there, gossiping. Asking me all kinds of questions. Thought you would want to come talk to them."

"Where is Bastion?"

Bad enough to be sent for water in front of Mia last night. Bastion might be off doing something important right now, some ritual or ceremony, Stefan thought.

"I don't know. I didn't go looking for him."

"Is that supposed to mean something?"

"Just go. Please."

Erick shook his head, holding the door open as Stefan exited.

Erick didn't follow him. "I have to get the church ready," he said.

Stefan paused, then decided against waiting for him. "Don't touch the bag."

The church stood along their right, past the opening to the gardens and the kitchen. Stefan did not see anyone on the church steps. The town square only now began to come alive for the day, with mules dragging loads of goods toward the market. Shutters were still drawn, trying to keep out the cold night air. Inside, most people were just waking, careful to avoid tumbling out of their high beds. Unlike Stefan, they had beds raised high, as high as a bed could be without collapsing. It made the bed warmer in the winter months. Warmth drove every design, all construction.

Stefan rubbed his arms and exhaled to watch the frost. Hard to believe women were already gathered at Dame Alice's, nervous as hens.

"Is she beautiful?" a voice hissed.

Stefan jumped. He had kept his eyes on the market as he walked, inspecting the day's beginning. He had not meant to come near the cage, though the dirty thick blanket still covered it.

"Is she?" she asked.

"Is who beautiful?" Stefan replied.

"The witch Bastion caught last night. Tell me of her."

Stefan grabbed one end of the blanket and tugged. He held his breath as dirt and lice flew through the air.

"Bastion caught a witch? Is she from this town?" he asked her, careful to stay at a safe distance.

The witch stared at him, her head swaying from side to side. She did not reply.

"Where is Bastion now?" he asked.

She began sweeping her hands through the straw, looking for something. Her hands closed around something, and she pulled it to her chest.

"Do you want to see?" she asked. "I was beautiful."

"No. Where is Bastion? What do you know of this witch?"

"I was beautiful, Father. But I do not cry about that anymore. I'm going to die."

She thrust her hand through the bars. Stefan jumped back, startled, then saw she held out a tiny portrait to him, painted on a metal pendant. Someone would have worn this. A man—a husband, perhaps.

He did not reach for it, so she threw it at his feet. "Look at it."

"I just want to know where Bastion is."

"Look at it and I'll tell you."

He picked it up, keeping his eyes focused on her, his body tensing to spring back if she moved. She didn't. He picked it up, turning it over to look at the portrait. It showed a woman with long gloss-black hair left free and flowing down across her shoulders. She had the skin of a newborn, smooth and perfect in tone, just a little pink in her cheeks and lips, an exquisite face—a woman of such beauty that he had no words to say, no comments he could make that would be proper. He did not know how a woman so beautiful could be brought so low. Only perversion would cage such a beauty. She had first become a monster, surely. How gravely she must have offended the Lord. Stefan tossed the pendant back between the bars and stepped back. He wanted nothing to do with this.

"I looked at it. Where is Bastion?"

"Did you look closely?"

"Where is Bastion?"

"I think that is your sin. You do not look closely at anyone."

Stefan turned to walk off.

"He went off with the young daughter of the miller. Look closely at her, Father. She is beautiful too."

"What would he want with Iris?" Stefan asked. Iris had reached all of fifteen years, but she never missed a Mass.

The witch grinned, and Stefan saw she had a perfectly straight set of teeth, which shocked him. They were yellow, but they were all there.

"Do you look closely at anyone? Do you know the mind of men?"

"What does he want with Iris? What has she done?" he asked.

"Nothing yet. But she will. Bastion will convince her to. She will sin because that is who she is, but Bastion will save her."

"That's blasphemy."

"No, Father, Bastion can do it. He is going to save me."

"You are condemned as a witch living in a filthy cage. You have not been saved."

"But I will be," she answered.

"So he taught you of Christ? He promises to lead you to Him?"

"Nay, he taught me of Satan. I will burn one day, and Satan will be expelled from my body. My sins will be atoned for, and I will be free."

"Burning will not make you free."

"A curse on you! Bastion warned me of your kind. Examine your soul, Father, before Satan devours you."

Bastion appeared with Iris on his arm, her father and mother trotting after him, joyful expressions on their faces. Bastion released Iris back to her parents and bowed low to them before turning for the church.

When he saw Stefan talking with the witch, his hand went to his side. Stefan's stomach lurched as Bastion pulled out a long, thin whip from his belt. The witch cried out, rushing to one corner of her cage, scooping up the straw, attempting to cover herself in it, hiding herself from view.

"Talking with the witch, Stefan?" Bastion called. "You should know better than to put your soul in danger. You already lost an ear to her."

"She tells interesting tales," Stefan replied, willing his legs to stay planted and firm.

"Aye, as do all women," Bastion laughed. "You must excuse me now, Father. There is a punishment for talking to others, and she knows it well."

Stefan didn't move.

"I cannot allow it," he said. "Not on church grounds." That last part sounded like a concession.

"I am too lazy to move her," Bastion said, replacing the whip after a moment's thought. "I will show you mercy," he said to her, "though you deserve none. Pray to God that He will make you worthy of it."

Bastion put his arm around Stefan and began walking toward the dormitory. "Come, brother," Bastion said. "We both had long nights. We must sleep while we can, for tonight God will do an amazing work among these people."

"You speak as if you know God's mind."

Bastion laughed. "My friend, when you have served God as long as I have, you can anticipate His movements."

Stefan chewed the inside of his lip, ignoring the growing sore. He didn't follow. Bastion was not like the Inquisitor he had envisioned. Bastion kept walking. Stefan watched him disappear inside, then looked back. No one paid attention. Stefan jogged to catch up to him.

"Who is the witch you caught?" Stefan asked. Inside the dormitory, they faced each other alone.

Bastion grabbed him by his robes and jerked Stefan's face closer to his.

"Do not ever challenge me again in front of others or I will have you sent to a parish so poor the people will skip communion and want to eat *you*."

Stefan swatted at Bastion's hands. Bastion released him and yawned. "You interfered with my work, but I have forgiven you."

"I thought you did God's work."

"Is there a difference?" Bastion sighed, kicking off his boots. "Do not question my authority, Father. It is not good for your mind."

"What's in the bag?"

Bastion glanced at the bag, shrugging. "If you're curious, open it."

"I'm not curious."

Bastion laughed. "You're really moody this morning. I'd say your faith is wavering. Get some sleep and you'll feel better." He stood and walked to the bag, untying it. The mouth of the bag flopped open, revealing a tangle of metal contraptions.

Bastion pulled back the cover on his bed and stretched out, crossing his legs at the ankle, tucking his hands behind his head.

Stefan gave in. He went over to the bag and reached in a hand, grabbing a hard, cold object, shaking it loose from the pile. He pulled it out and held it up. It appeared to be a vise, made of two metal planks no bigger than a man's hand, with thick, rusted screws driven down between the planks.

"What is it?" Stefan ran a finger along the rust. He held his finger up to wipe it clean across his pant leg.

"It's a thumb screw." Bastion sounded sleepy.

The stain on Stefan's hand, and now his pants, was blood. Dried blood covered the device. Stefan dropped it, stumbling back.

"Show some respect!" Bastion grumbled, snatching it off the floor, thrusting it back in the bag.

"What else is in there?" Stefan threw the bag open again and began pulling out every device his hand fell to.

Bastion turned on his side this time on the bed, his eyelids getting heavier. He named the objects as Stefan held them up, like Adam naming the animals.

A helmet of metal with screws to tighten the band.

"Skull crusher."

A mask that clamped round the jaws, with an iron pig's nose.

"Scold's bridle."

A metal stake no bigger than a small dagger, with a blunted end.

"Fire poker. If Satan gives a woman a mole or freckle as a sign of their pact, I burn it off."

Tongs.

"Good for holding a tongue when you need to cleanse it with fire."

Bastion fell asleep before Stefan got through the bag.

One of the village boys rang the church bells, calling him, and the village, to morning Mass. Stefan walked to the window in a stupor, his hands shaking, seeing his people leaving their homes and the market stalls, more people than he had ever seen awake, ready to worship at this hour. Their faces looked anxious for Stefan's words. Stefan had once thought crowds were a sure sign God blessed him. When the people came in great numbers, God was blessing the work. God should be credited.

God and no one else, Stefan thought. *Unless, perhaps, God could not be found in this at all.*

Chapter Sixteen

In the late afternoon, waiting for Bjorn to return from an errand in the village, Mia watched Alma napping with the kitten tucked into her side. Mia sat, hands folded in her lap, watching the steady rise and fall of both chests, the serene curves of their closed eyes. Behind her, Margarite sat in a chair near the fireplace, her chin almost touching her chest. She snored softly, her injured arm held close. Outside, a woodpecker tapped against a tree.

Mia stood, keeping her movements slow and quiet. She walked to the door, picking up her garden trowel from the basket near the door. The ground would still be hard and too cold for planting the seeds she harvested last fall. Swinging the door on its hinges only a breath at a time, she eased it open and stepped outside. After pacing in every direction, surveying the path that led to her home, and the woods around her, she chose a spot. Using one hand, she swept away leaf litter and pulled up dead vines, getting to the bare earth. Using her trowel, she began digging. She didn't need a big hole, just a deep one, a well to swallow up her sin.

The hole completed, she sneaked back into the house. Her body felt weak. Fear drained her strength. She should eat, just for strength.

But her appetite had fled. Maybe that was how the miraculous maids resisted food. Maybe they were afraid too.

No one had stirred inside, although the kitten opened its round eyes and blinked once, watching her without interest before returning to its nap.

Mia slid the delicately tooled chest from the dark, unused corner of her home. Alma sometimes used the chest, with its heavy frame and strong lid, as a stool. Mia should not have allowed that, she thought now.

She took a deep breath and opened the lid. Inside hid linens and pearls, gold thread and fine needles. They sparkled, even in the dim yellow light of the fire. Mia pushed them aside. She had used this chest only once, four years ago when she made a christening cloth, anticipating her first birth. Alma had been born in distress, and Mia lost much blood.

"Have her keep the christening cloth," Father Stefan had told Bjorn at the christening. "We'll bury the child in it."

Bjorn became cold, unwilling to have another child, loath to touch either of them.

"You look so sad," Dame Alice had said to her as Mia passed by her home on the way to the market. "Come inside, dear."

"No, the baby is unwell today. I need to get her home."

"Don't you trust me, Mia? I've had children too."

Yes, but they died, Mia thought. "Perhaps later."

And then other women began to turn a cold shoulder to her, as if she had offended them. She had sought advice sometimes, working up the courage to speak to another new mother, only to be rebuffed.

"Have I done something?" Mia asked Rose. They had both reached for a summer apple at the same time. Rose jerked her hand away as if burned and turned to walk away.

"Please tell me," Mia called after her.

"Perhaps later."

Alma survived that first stone-cold winter. Mia had spent all her energy keeping Alma warm, willing her to breathe.

"There was no time later," Mia said to herself, thinking of Rose. To drive the thoughts away, Mia moved her hand under the sewing goods and clutched a metal square, drawing it up into the light, turning herself from the door so she could not be seen with it.

She traced the outline of the perfect letter M. Her father had given it to her when she was just a few years older than Alma. Mia glanced back at the door again. She had to bury it forever. Her stomach burned. Her knees were shaking as the memories came back to her.

She had been so happy, peeking around her father's legs, making him swat at her with feigned impatience. He held his impossibly strong arms—the arms of a printer—straight out, grasping the handle, pulling it to him until the press shook with terrible creaks and snaps.

Releasing the handle, he nodded to Mia, who pulled the paper free with her small, gentle hands, walking somberly with the sheet as though she held the emperor's crown. She took it to the sad man who sat so often by the window.

She knew him as Master Hutchins. It was not his real name. He would not tell her his real name. Only later did she learn it, when it was too late to save her father. Or herself.

Master Hutchins took the paper and studied it. She saw how his eyes moved over it, from one side to the other, starting at the top and working down to the last line of type. One day he did not hand the paper back to her. Instead, his eyes peered back over the top, looking down at her, his thick eyebrows wiggling.

Mia laughed and held out her hands for the paper.

"'Tis fine," Master Hutchins called to her father. "We have money for ten tonight. Best to work fast and eat later."

Then he returned his attention to Mia. "You have no brothers, do you?"

Mia hung her head.

"No, no. I did not say it to shame you, my dear. Indeed, it could be a blessing. Look how fine your hands are, how delicate and careful your every movement with them. You have made a fine puller."

Mia tucked her hands behind her skirts.

"I can see that you like to work. But tell me, Mia, do you like to learn?"

Mia bit her lip and looked back toward her father. He pressed the paper. She should fetch it. That was her job as puller.

"You will outgrow that task, probably by winter's end. You could be worth more than ten sons to him, if you are willing to learn."

Mia ran away from him. She took the paper from the press, her hands trembling, and laid it with the others, listening to her father argue with Hutchins.

"You surprise me, William."

"Are you quite mad? When she's married," her father continued, "what use will she have for letters and words?"

"Oh, she might marry a printer, a man like yourself."

"I pray not. One cannot make a living in publishing."

"She's a bright girl but lonely. You cannot give her brothers or sisters."

Mia had hung her head again then. Her mother had died giving birth to her.

"But you can give her truth."

Her father lunged at the man, the man she would later learn was called by the name of William Tyndale. Her father knocked him to the floor. Mia hid her face in her hands. She heard punches and grunts. When she looked back up, her father stood over Master Hutchins, who had blood pouring from his nose. Mia tore across the room, ripping at her cloak, pressing it against Master Hutchins' wounds.

"Father, no! He is my friend!"

"He's going to get us all killed."

"All we have is each other. You said that yourself!"

"You are not a parent, Mia. You can't understand."

"I want to know this truth he speaks of. I want to know."

Father shook his head at Master Hutchins. "She is my only child."

Master Hutchins made no reply. Father scowled at Mia. "Learn the letters if you want. But hear me: Letters become words, words become books, and you will become an unfit wife. It won't matter that you know the truth. Is that what you want?"

Mia nodded her head yes with great vigor.

Her father had laughed without joy, extending a hand to Master Hutchins, lifting him off the floor.

Mia sighed as she remembered days that were no more, and men she had loved. Those loves were long dead now.

Carrying the silver piece of type with the letter M, she went back to the hole she had dug and dropped it in. Getting down on her knees as if to say a prayer over it, she leaned over the hole. "I am sorry." She sat back on her heels and began pushing dirt into the hole, tamping it down, piling leaves and dead vines over the spot. With any luck, spring would cause something green to grow up over the spot.

Going back inside, Mia set her mind on the life she had now. She sat next to the box with great relief, waiting for strength to return. She smoothed the linens and christening cloth back into place inside the chest. Catching a hint of smoke, she pulled out the christening cloth and held it to her nose. It smelled like smoke and needed a good airing. She set it in her lap and fished in the chest for her sack of pearls.

"Burial cloth, indeed. Those days are gone, Father," she said, though she knew she sat alone. "But you'll see. I'll sew my pearls onto this, and she will wear it at her wedding someday."

The pearls were gone.

"How could that be?" Mia asked, dragging the chest closer in between her feet and searching again with trembling fingers. The pearls were small but not so small that they could go missing in this chest. They were held together on a simple string, tied together like a necklace with a silver clasp in the center. The clasp, a poor-quality one, had marks on it from the smith's tools. Even so, that crude clasp proved strong enough to hold the little pearls secure. The pearls had been her mother's, meant to be sewn onto Mia's own bridal veil.

Hairs raised along Mia's forearms. Tears started to build, making her throat burn as she swallowed and tried to stop them. No one even knew she had the pearls, save for Margarite and Bjorn. Why would anyone steal from her? She was neither rich nor proud.

Mia threw a hand to her mouth. A witch had stolen these pearls intended for a happier day.

"I have to ask Bastion. Why would a witch steal them? Are more curses still to come?"

The home remained silent, save for Margarite's soft snoring. Alma stirred, opened her eyes, and smiled at Mia. She sat up in her bed, pulling herself up to the window. She loved to watch the squirrels scampering all around the house. Spring meant squirrels jumping from tree to tree, and turtles lumbering though the leaves, and birds singing at all hours. Alma slapped her palms against the window frame, cheering.

Bjorn opened the door, leaning in. Mia jumped, startled.

"Bastion will begin the burning soon. Will you come with me?" he asked.

"I am not sure," she said. "I should stay here, keep watch over the house. And Margarite."

Bjorn held out a hand to her. "Mother is asleep. She's fine. Come with me. You need to know who the witch is. I don't want to be the one to tell you."

The fire popped and sent sparks in all directions, threatening to set them all ablaze. Mia realized Bastion had used fresh, uncured wood.

Alma slept against Bjorn's chest. She looked like a yarn doll in his arms. She had fallen asleep in Mia's arms, but she had grown so heavy. Mia could not hold her all night.

"If she wakes, I'll take her back," Mia promised.

A woman stood tied to a post near the fire, a leather face mask drawn tight around her and cinched at the neck. Mia could not recognize her by her clothes. Bastion's caged witch sat a good twenty paces away. She would not be the center of attention tonight. Mia wondered if witches felt jealousy.

Mia pinched herself. Witches could not have human emotions. Thinking those thoughts, making them human, was a sin. Witches probably thought of nothing but curses and sacrilege.

The townspeople all pushed each other to get the best possible view, craning their necks, moving slightly this way or that, all wanting to be sure they did not miss anything Bastion might do tonight.

Bastion allowed the small children to sit up front, and he had a large semicircle of little faces watching him. He passed out sweets to them, little dried raisins that they gobbled up and begged for again, clapping.

Mia watched as Father Stefan stood to the right of Bastion, his hands behind his back, chewing his lower lip. Mia expected him, as their Father, to have something grave or comforting to add to Bastion's words, but Father Stefan looked as if he wanted to run away. Behind them all, in the darkness near the edge of the forest, Mia saw a shimmer in the moonlight, like a horse's mane. She bent her head forward and squinted.

Not a mane, she realized, but hair. The woman who watched them all, the healer herself, with her long, loose silver hair, was standing at the edge of the forest, watching them. A gray wolf circled round her legs, his head low as if spying his prey somewhere in the crowd. A shrill cry pierced the night and drew Mia's attention away from the pair. The children screamed and clapped their hands over their ears, grimacing.

"A rabbit," Father Stefan said, patting his hands against the air as if to calm them. "Probably just a rabbit. Something is hunting it."

Dame Alice caught Mia's eye and motioned for her to come near. Mia jerked her face away, pretending to study Alma's bare calf dangling from Bjorn's arms.

Bastion raised his hands for silence.

"Tonight I will show you the truth of all I say. A witch has been identified and caught and has confessed. I present her to you tonight so that her evil may be ended and you good people freed."

There were murmurs of approval. Mia thought that, taken together, the crowd sounded like cows.

Bastion smiled, stroking his chin and nodding before continuing.

"In some villages people must seek out a savior who can free them of a witch's power. Not so for you. It is not Father Stefan's desire, nor mine, that you be exploited in such a way. It reminds me, in fact, of a town I was called to by the bishop. The noblemen had set up a tollbooth, and all who were bewitched in their own persons or in their possessions had to pay a penny before they could visit the Inquisitor and be cured. And the noblemen made a substantial profit. Have I asked you for anything?"

The people shook their heads.

"That is right. Like Paul, I do not wish to be a burden on you. I want you to understand that my motives are pure. Can you imagine a man who would profit by another's misfortune? And yet one man's trouble is often the means of another man's wealth.

"My friends, especially in these days, when souls are beset with so many dangers, we must take measures to dispel all ignorance, and we must always have before our eyes that severe judgment that will be passed upon us if we do not use, everyone according to his proper ability, the one talent that has been given.

"And what is your talent, friends? Is it not sober judgment and clear thinking? Are you not called upon in this hour to sacrifice your comforts, your inclinations to mercy, and strike a blow against the Devil himself? Or would you leave that work to your children?"

Bastion motioned to the children seated round his feet. The crowd grew anxious; Mia could see it on their faces and in the way they shook their heads, in their clasped hands, the women rocking on their heels.

"I am not surprised that a witch lived among you. In these days witches are everywhere about. Here is what surprises me: that a witch could cast her spells for so long without detection. I fear you are good people but ignorant. Though it gives me no pleasure to describe the evil a woman may do under the power of the Devil, if I do not do it, what will become of you? Witches will return and bring many more spirits with them. That is biblical, is it not, Father Stefan?"

Father Stefan opened his eyes wide in surprise. "Uh, oh, yes, the parable of the man delivered of one demon, and did not take precautions, yes, many more came and possessed him."

"Mothers, if you do not wish your children to hear of carnal matters, it is now time to remove them," Bastion said. "Return home, and your husbands can instruct you on my message later tonight."

Mia searched the crowd for little Marie but did not see her, to her relief. Marie loved Father Stefan with plain devotion. But she had a sick mother at home, and no child would travel alone near these woods at night. Strange blessings, Mia thought, but blessings for Marie tonight all the same. Mia saw that among the people present, not a soul moved. The children who were present hunched down, giggling, hoping for a scare.

"Very well," Bastion said. "Strange events have plagued this town, but events that have not been spoken of. And yet the women know, don't they? The women have gossiped about these events, having no sense to suspect a witch.

"Let us suppose a man be tempted, though he has a beautiful and honest wife. Suppose his good judgment is so chained up that by no blows or words or deeds, or even by shame, can he be made to desist from that lust.

"Suppose he cannot contain himself, but that he is at times unexpectedly, in spite of the roughness of the journey, forced to be carried through great distances by day and by night, risking body and soul to have the object of his lust.

"This man is not himself evil, but under the influence of evil, of the Devil himself. This man has been bewitched. And there is only one remedy. Only one cure for witches, just as there is but one penalty for sin. Witches must burn."

Mia was entranced by Bastion's wisdom. She looked at her husband, holding her beautiful daughter, and felt no fear, only a sense of justice.

"Who among you desires to be free? Who among you has struggled with lusts and temptations? Who among you would see this evil rooted out and Christ reign once again in your town and in your hearts?"

"Yes, yes!" the people replied.

"Away with her!" Mia shouted.

Some turned to stare at her in surprise. Mia raised her chin, not looking at them. She called out again. "Away with the witch. Let Bastion have his way!"

Bjorn put his arm around Mia. No one stared again.

Bastion extended a hand to Bjorn and another to Stefan, making himself look like Christ at the final moment.

"Come, Sheriff. Come, Father Stefan. I can bear my burden alone no more."

Bjorn handed Alma back to Mia and went to stand with Bastion. Mia saw his hands shaking, his face a gray color. Stefan looked no better.

The woman under the mask moaned, shifting her weight from foot to foot.

Mia understood. The witch might still cast her spells, though her time was almost gone. Only when she had been punished would the spells end. Mia wanted her gone. She should be punished and sent away. The sooner she left, the better. Mia had a good life to make for herself now.

Bastion put his arms around Bjorn and Stefan, drawing them to a tight circle. Stefan threw his arms straight up, breaking Bastion's hold, shaking his head in anger.

Bjorn grabbed Stefan by the arm, speaking in an urgent, pleading manner. Mia could not understand his words.

"My friends," Bastion said, "you have a fine man for a priest. A fine man with a soft heart."

Everyone around Mia nodded. A few clapped. Stefan held up his hands to silence them.

"We must punish this witch. God commands it," Bastion said. "But Stefan has not the heart to scourge a woman. I cannot blame you, Stefan, for you are a simple parish priest. You have not seen the evils I have. And yet it must be done. Good men and women depend on us."

Stefan opened his mouth to speak, then closed it. He looked at Mia as if expecting her to say something. She frowned.

"Father Stefan," Bjorn said, "you have heard tell of many evils a witch is capable of. You have seen two of the worst, two of your own flock dead and tossed out with the chamber pots on the streets of this town. You must do this. For them. For Christ, Father Stefan. Do it for Christ."

"I cannot scourge a woman."

"I will do it. If you give me leave," Bjorn said.

"Wait! How do you know scourging will have the desired affect?" Stefan asked. "Show me your proof."

"Proof?" Bastion's snicker was sardonic. "An odd word for a priest. But let me reassure you, reassure you all, that faith is always best served by reason. We must pair faith and reason. So let us reason this together: God uses discipline to change our desires, yes? Just as we discipline our children for their own good."

People nodded. Stefan said nothing.

"Scourging is a severe discipline. Scourging will make sure she has no desire to bewitch anyone in this town, ever again. Scourging will turn her heart back to God," Bastion promised. He looked at Mia, and she felt it in her knees, in a sharp stabbing pleasure through her abdomen. "Discipline of one serves the whole community. If there is sickness among you, if prayer is ineffective, if there is alienation where affection should live, these curses a scourging can break."

Please. Mia mouthed the word to Father Stefan. *Please God,* she prayed silently, *give Stefan the strength to do what is right.*

Stefan nodded, his eyes focusing on little Alma, his face a mask of sorrow. "Bjorn may scourge her."

Bastion jumped, clapping his hands. "Yes. Justice is upon us." He ripped the leather mask off the witch and then turned her and ripped her shift down the back. He forced her to face the crowd.

The widow Rose blinked and shook her head, dust from the hood settling in her eyes as she faced them all.

"No," Mia murmured. Rose squinted at her, confused, as if seeing her through stained glass.

Rose's shift slipped off her shoulders, sliding down her chest, stopping just before it revealed her nakedness. She squirmed but could not adjust it with her hands tied. Mia followed the shape of the shift, the way it hung over Rose's bulging belly. She was with child.

"What have you done? Rose!" Mia yelled her name, but got no response. No life remained in Rose's eyes. Rose lifted her face in Mia's direction, not seeing her, looking beyond her, beyond them all, at the horizon, as if waiting.

Bjorn took a whip offered to him by Bastion and swung his arm up behind his head. Mia cried out, hiding her face.

Bastion held one hand to delay him. "Bjorn will cleanse her of the malice she held toward you all." Bastion looked right at her as he said it. "I promised you freedom and healing, did I not?"

His attention turned to the crowd. "I need men, strong men, to raise a wooden pole with plenty of kindling at the base."

"Wait!" Father Stefan stood between Rose and Bastion. "You said you needed only to punish her; a cleansing. You said nothing of a burning."

"My brother, we are only men. We can punish her for the spells she cast, for her heart inclined to evil, but we cannot save her soul. Even you cannot do that. Can you?"

"You did not say we would burn her," Stefan answered.

"She is going to die. If not by my hand, then someday. Would you want her to go to Christ with these sins clinging to her? Would not God's wrath be so much greater than mine?"

Stefan did not answer. Mia tried not to breathe. Bastion addressed the crowd.

"Solomon himself would have trouble with this great dilemma, my friends. Do not judge Father Stefan for his hesitation. Do not be surprised if you are troubled too. Only listen to reason before you render your decision. Who knows the parable of the good Samaritan? One man lay dying in plain sight. Many righteous men walked past him and did nothing. One man saved him, at great personal expense. And this was the man Jesus praised, is he not?"

All nodded. Stefan did not look happy.

"This witch is dying, consumed with evil. Though it will cost us, in peace and in good dreams, we must save her. We cannot leave her to die in her sins. We must purge her of the evil she has done and release her to God. To do anything else is to comfort ourselves at her expense. Father Stefan, as our priest, your job is to show mercy to sinners, is it not?"

Stefan did not answer. Mia prayed for him to say something. There had never been a burning in this village. Mia thought she had escaped the burning days. Never did she think there could be a burning here, and never that Rose would die in one. Mia stared at Father Stefan, trying to catch his eye. She was tormented. How could Rose be the witch? Mia desired justice—without pause, she desired for a clean home and good and righteous life—but Rose had been her friend. How could she support burning the widow?

Mia could tell that Father Stefan avoided looking at Mia or Alma. "Yes, that is my office," Stefan said.

"Then look upon her, Father Stefan." Bastion grabbed the widow by the chin, forcing her face up in the bonfire's light. Mia saw her eyes blinking only at strange, slow intervals. Her lip looked swollen and purple. Blood matted the hair along her forehead. Mia looked around to see if any of the women would come forward and offer to clean her

face. Rose would not want people seeing her like this. She had always
been so beautiful, so much more delicate than Mia.

Bastion spoke to Stefan in a voice the crowd could hear. "Have
mercy, Father Stefan, on this poor woman. Would you leave her in the
Devil's bosom? Would you leave her to wallow in her filth, to return
like a dog to its vomit? Is that mercy?"

Stefan shook his head.

"You may begin, Bjorn," Bastion said. Looking back at the woman,
Bastion spit. "May God have mercy on your soul."

Mia looked at the faces of her townspeople. Would they stand and
watch? Mia could not. She turned to run.

"Mia."

Rose had called her name.

Mia turned her attention back to Rose, her eyes clear and fierce as
the woman screamed at Mia.

"He'll do this to you, too. Flee. Flee tonight."

Mia saw Bjorn raise the whip as she scooped up little Alma and
ran, as best she could, finding the dark path home.

She heard Dame Alice's voice calling to her from the darkness.
"Mia, come this way! Please!" A group of women huddled around
Dame Alice, their eyes cold.

Mia ran with Alma, alone.

☙

Mia ran as far into the forest as she could with Alma, but the child
grew too heavy. Mia sat her down under a huge tree and leaned against
it to catch her breath.

"You think I am a monster."

Mia cried out in fear, whirling to find the source of the voice. Bastion stood, not far from her tree, and began walking with his hands extended in peace.

"I did not mean to frighten you, Mia. May I call you Mia? I never asked permission, and I should have. I am sorry."

"You may."

"I do not care for titles. I have several of my own and find them all a distraction."

"How did you get here so fast?"

Bastion shrugged, dropping his hands. "'Tis not hard to be fast when you do not carry a child. Would you like me to carry her for you?"

She took a step back to shield Alma from his eyes. "Leave her. She needs sleep."

"You're upset about the scourging."

"Scourging? If she was guilty, she deserved it, I suppose. But to burn her …"

"I wonder what you think of me. A gentle woman like yourself must think I am a monster."

"Why does it matter what I think?"

"Because I have so few friends. I would like to consider you a friend."

"Rose. I knew her. It doesn't seem right." She had to know what sort of man could do that before she pursued a pleasant conversation.

"You think I do not suffer on nights like this? You think I take pleasure in a death? I feel pain. I do not show it, but I feel it. My work takes a great toll on my spirit. And I have no family, no wife to comfort me when I have done the Lord's will. I am the disciple Christ wrote of, the hunted animal with nowhere to lay its head at night, loved by no one."

"You forget God."

"What?"

"You forget that God loves His servants. You are not unloved." She would not respond as perhaps he hoped. His remark sounded more like bait than true conversation.

"Listen to me, burdening a good woman with my sorrows," Bastion said with a laugh. "Yes, of course, God loves all His servants. Please forgive me. I am not always a strong man like your husband. You are a lucky woman to be so loved."

Bastion looked on the brink of tears. He had promised her healing for Alma, and Alma had been healed. If Bastion had delivered the healing, Mia should be grateful. She knew she should push her heart to open to him. Even Bjorn thought so. Mia bit her lip.

"No, please forgive me, sir. I should offer you what comforts I have."

"And what comforts are those?' he asked. Her knees felt weak as he moved closer.

"None, save my ears," Mia said, aware of what a fool she sounded like. "I can listen as well as any woman. Though I have little wisdom to make comment. But you can talk. I can offer a listening ear."

A woman's scream broke the moment, making them both turn their heads back toward the town. Howls from the forest echoed her scream all around them. Mia knew she was unsafe, but she could not be sure the wolves were the only beasts to fear.

"Bjorn has taken to my teaching quite quickly," he said. "He wasted no time setting to work. He will be tired when he returns tonight. I wonder what you will do to pass your evening?"

"If he comes home, I will tend to him like a good wife."

"A wife like you waiting on him? I would come home."

"People cause the most trouble at night, under the moon. He has a difficult job."

"All of men's work is cursed. No man has it easier than another."

"You cannot know that. You've never been a sheriff. The hours, the things he sees, it would make any man cold." Mia turned her back to him, wiping at her eyes with her fingers.

"I can't imagine any man could be cold to you."

Mia did not turn back around. "I need to get Alma home."

"May I visit you again, perhaps in the morning?"

"Why?"

"I have so often desired for a woman to speak with, one I know will not fall prey to the Devil's advances, one I know would never tempt me to sin. You are a virtuous woman, a woman of intellect. I feel safe with you."

"I am sure Bjorn will come home, but late, as you said. He will sleep late. He will need sleep."

"I have no desire to disturb Bjorn. And there are matters I should discuss with you, Mia. Matters about this witch Rose, and about Bjorn. Will you allow me to see you? I can come later in the morning."

Bjorn would say very little to her tonight. If he did come home, he'd fall into bed, exhausted. He would have no interest in talking to her, not tonight, not in the morning, not ever. She might never learn why a witch had cursed him or if a witch had indeed cursed Alma.

"I cannot agree to a visit without my husband present. A good woman would do no less, even if you are our salvation."

"You acknowledge that I alone can save this town? That your daughter has been healed? And still you will not entertain me?"

"I cannot. Not alone."

"You would risk everything to deny me this?"

Mia pushed her foot deeper into the dirt, trying to steady herself. Her legs had gone soft. She exhaled and turned around to face him. "You say a woman is corrupt in her very nature. I am trying, sir, to be righteous, despite myself. You would not fault me for this, would you? You would not take away the healing Alma has found?"

Bastion's steady gaze betrayed nothing of his thoughts. He grabbed her hand and she gasped. Lifting it to his mouth, he kissed it, a formal kiss without passion. Mia felt heat surge through her stomach.

"I've never met a woman like you."

"I should go."

"Yes. I will return to my work." He bowed his head before he went, keeping his eyes on her, making her feel like a bloom forced open.

Mia bent down to take Alma back up in her arms and return home. Alma's eyes were open wide in horror.

"You've seen too much tonight, child," Mia whispered. "It is all over now. Everything will be all right."

Alma took her thumb from her mouth and spoke her first word, though Father Stefan had said Alma would never speak.

"No," Alma said.

Chapter Seventeen

Stefan sat on the bench closest to the altar, his head in his hands. The candles burned too low, but he did not move. Nothing mattered. Bjorn's words echoed in his mind. Bastion came looking for the Devil and found one. But it had been Rose. It couldn't have been Rose. She had been so quiet, so kind to the beggars who passed through the village. Yet Stefan let them burn her.

Bjorn came in and sat behind him. "I was wrong," Bjorn said, resting a heavy hand on Stefan's shoulder. Stefan lifted his head.

"I am not a good man, Stefan. I feared an Inquisitor would see that. I thought that would bring disaster."

"What disaster?"

"It wasn't disaster. It was freedom."

"I gave you the sacrament of confession and forgiveness."

"I did not tell you some things."

"Because I am a priest? A priest and not a man like you?" Stefan heard how angry and cruel his voice sounded.

Bjorn looked up at the cross hanging above the altar. "You're a good priest. But you cannot understand all sins. Even I cannot understand all sins."

148

"God doesn't call us to understand our sin. Just to repent of it."

"Sometimes we want to be done with a sin, but the sin is not done with us."

"How can I lead you if you do not speak plainly with me? My people lie to me, hide from me, and now I have to watch them burn?"

"Words have been of no use. You tell us to pray, to cleanse our hearts, but we go on sinning. Bastion roots out the source of the evil and does away with it."

"Do you know what one of the village women told me tonight? She said the town has been in fear since Bastion came, not knowing whom the witch might be, whom she might hurt. A cat fell through her chimney, right into her ashes one night. She was afraid it might be a witch come to curse her, so she grabbed the poor thing and dunked it in a bucket of water, baptizing it in the Lord's name. She tried to deliver it from Satan."

Bjorn laughed, making Stefan twist his shoulder, throwing off Bjorn's hand.

"It's a cat, Stefan," Bjorn said. "You can laugh."

"What did Rose have to do with Catarina or Cronwall? Why would she want them dead?"

Bjorn leaned forward. Stefan could feel his breath on his neck.

"Rose is dead, Stefan. You should be in here praising God instead of questioning His ways. "

"Tonight is Bastion's last night here. He did his job, rooting out the witch who stirred up trouble among us. I'll accept that. But I will see that he is gone by tomorrow morning."

Bjorn looked confused. "You do not know?"

"What?"

"Rose confessed during her questioning. She said there are dozens more witches in our village. Witches that fly with the Devil to Sabbath meetings, where they smash the sacred Host wafers under their feet and commit evil, indecent acts with their demon lovers, or even Satan."

Stefan's stomach pushed up into his throat, making him want to vomit. He shook his head. "Do you hear yourself? This is madness. It will end tonight, and Bastion will leave in the morning."

Bjorn smiled, a kind, pitiful smile that comes with bad news. "No. Bastion has only begun."

Alma stirred in her bed, her little rump sticking up in the air, her thumb rooted in her mouth. Mia did not wake her even though the breakfast was ready. Margarite sat by the window, staring out at the spring green leaves fluttering on the trees, inhaling the sharp scent of the evergreens. Mia had sprinkled some seeds outside the window to draw the birds, seeds that had split as she dried them and were of no use to her garden. A brilliant red cardinal found them first, but he did not eat alone for long. Margarite seemed to enjoy the activity.

The morning mist had burned off early, promising them all a perfect spring day. Bjorn had not slept late after all, though. He had said no more than five words to her last night, coming home stinking of smoke and the sharp metal tang of blood, and he had nothing to say when he woke. Mia's heart ached. Rose had been the witch. Mia must have done something to make her vengeful or hurt her. Even Rose's dying words were a curse on Mia. She wondered why Rose would do that, tell Mia she would burn too. Mia was no witch. She had never even visited the old healer in the forest, not even when the other wives had told Mia about her.

"Come with us, Mia," Rose had begged her when Mia had been big with child. "She can make sure you deliver a boy."

None of the women ever spoke in public about the healer, never acknowledged her when she slunk through the market gathering herbs and oils. Mia knew that to be invited was to be welcomed into the secret sisterhood of the village, a sign Mia had passed their invisible tests. But Mia knew something they didn't. Mia knew what people did when they were frightened by new knowledge, new beliefs. Mia would get her answers from Father Stefan. God would honor that.

"No, I should get home and cook for Bjorn."

The women had rolled their eyes and gone on without her. Dame Alice had started to say something to Mia, but Rose shushed her.

Mia wanted to tell all of this to Bjorn, to lay it all out for him. He might see where she had committed her error.

Mia had held her breath when he came home last night, waiting for some sign of their new life now with the witch gone. Bjorn had slept hard and left in the dark hours of the morning with nothing to say.

Mia's thoughts were interrupted when she saw Bastion standing in her doorway.

Mia gasped in her embarrassment, being caught daydreaming when the day's work stretched out before her. Bastion only smiled and leaned against the door frame.

"May I enter?"

Alma cried out from a nightmare. "Excuse me," Mia said as she whirled around to attend to Alma. The girl was sitting up awake in her bed, pushing herself against the wall in fear. Mia patted her and turned back to Bastion. He had moved closer, standing next to her now.

"She is still recovering," Mia said, looking down. Her stomach fluttered. "She was unwell her whole first three years."

"'Tis no wonder, with the witches about. Would you walk with me outside? You would feel more comfortable, I think."

Mia nodded. It would get him out of her house before anyone could see him in here. "I'll be just beyond the door, Alma. Play with your doll for a few moments."

She stepped outside into a perfect spring morning, into a world oblivious. Had she imagined the strange and unwelcome feelings Bastion aroused? He was smiling and kind today. But on a morning such as this, anyone could be mistaken for a saint, she supposed.

Bastion offered her his arm.

She quickened her pace.

"You said 'witches'?" she asked. "You meant to say 'witch,' of course."

"Why does that alarm you? I wonder, do you wish your troubles gone or do you wish me gone?"

The words stuck on her tongue, hard to say. "Rose is gone. Alma has been much better. I do believe she was healed that night."

"The night I came to you?" He had baited her again, she suspected.

"Shouldn't we be careful to give God the thanks for the miracle?" She smiled at him, as if in innocence, to see how he would respond.

He did not reply, but his eyes narrowed. There was wariness in them, recognition that she might be a challenge.

No use trying to outpace him, she thought, stopping. She had spent too many years trying to outrace her fear and sorrow. She refused to do it any longer.

"What if it's me?" Mia blurted out. "What if I am the cause of all this trouble? I brought it with me."

"You are such a kind, godly woman. Your fear is proof of it."

"Can you just go? Now that Rose is gone, you're finished here. Can you leave us now?"

"Mia, you are a mystery. What do you think I am?"

"You said there were witches? More than one?"

"Yes, there are others. I had only to get the names from Rose."

"No. Surely I would have known."

"I doubt that. You do not seem to have many friends. And you should quit trying to find the fault with me. Do I not know my work? You have a problem, and you won't admit it."

"I have no problems."

"I'll tell you what it is if you want me to."

Mia started walking.

"You're blind, Mia. Beautiful and blind. You don't even know your own husband has been unfaithful."

Mia's mouth fell open. Bastion caught up to her, wrapping an arm around her waist as if for support.

"Bjorn has been bewitched, my child. Have you not noticed his odd hours, his preoccupations? Has he not been cold with you?"

"You do not understand Bjorn," she said in a tiny child's voice, afraid to take a deep breath, fearing her body would press further into his warm palm. "He is strong. Even if what you say is true, he could be bewitched and not sin. He could."

Bastion nodded, his mouth a tight line. "I have upset you. I can be such a fool sometimes. Not everyone is ready for the truth."

Mia shook him off. "You did not speak the truth."

"Perhaps these would be of some consolation?" He produced a string of pearls with a clasp that Mia knew at once. She frowned to see them in Bastion's hand.

"I will not tell you where I found them, so do not ask. Not today. No more truth today for you. You need rest. And comfort."

The ground went soft under her feet. Bastion caught her as she fell. He held her up, pressing her into his body.

"Why?" Mia asked. "Why is this happening?"

"No more talk of witches, I said. I will keep you safe if you will let me. I can keep you all safe." He gestured toward her home and Alma. "I am not a monster, Mia. I am a good man."

"Why would you care about me? You don't know me."

"I know you better than you can imagine. I see who you are, how you strive to be a good and faithful wife. It moves me."

He pressed his lips against her neck, moving up. "Give me a kiss to seal my pledge to you."

Mia turned her head and looked down to the side. She did not know what to do. She had no experience with bold men.

He pressed his mouth on hers, but she did not respond.

He pulled back and looked down at her, then kissed her again until she responded. She did not know what another man's lips would feel like or the taste of his skin. He tasted salty, the skin around his mouth rough, just like Bjorn's. But Bastion did not push her away.

He moved her hand, hanging at her side, and placed it around the small of his back. "It's all right," he whispered.

She left her palm there. She remembered the warmth of flesh. He pulled her to him until her belly was pressed against his. She could not tell if his stomach burned like hers. He took her other hand and brought her palm to his mouth, kissing it before he wrapped this one behind his back, too, and they stood entwined. She lost herself, not knowing his limbs from her own, not knowing where he was taking her, or if she led them there.

His mouth on hers was an education. Men had appetites too, hungers that waited and grew no matter what good women did. She rattled off her childhood lessons in her mind. Was she not modestly dressed? Had she not refused his advances? And still he desired her. Those lessons had not been wrong, but they had been incomplete. Not all appetites could be guarded against. No one ever taught that. But she suddenly saw that now. No matter how good she tried to be, how faithful and devoted to God, she lived in a broken, bitter world, a world of raging hunger. She struggled to break free.

He released her.

"I will not fail you," he said. "I am not Bjorn."

Mia looked back at the home. Alma was standing in the doorway watching them.

"Leave. Get away from me."

"You are protecting your family. You are a brave and good woman. Perhaps that is why no one trusts you. You live in a village of secrets."

Mia shook her head. There was nothing good about what she had just done. Even a fool like herself knew that.

"Mia, look at me. Do not dwell too much on your emotions, for by emotions many women are snared by the Devil. You must trust me."

Mia looked again at her house, empty save for a table and a bed, where her husband ate and slept. There was a tiny mattress nearer the fire, a child's bed that would be empty this winter if the healing did not hold. Mia looked down at her hands, at her ring of betrothal. Hope held it all together. Nothing else. Only her blind, foolish hope.

"Who am I," she asked, "that a great Inquisitor should show me any affection? What have I to offer you?"

"Any other woman would ask what I, a great Inquisitor, could offer her."

"I did not bid you to come." Her heart beat fast as she spoke, so fast that she rushed the words out before she lost nerve. "You came to me because you want something. Even a fool like me knows that. Why can you not find it among the other women?"

"A man spied a pearl in a vast field of stones, and he went and sold all he had. He purchased that field and claimed his treasure, and none could stop him."

"And Jesus said this was like the kingdom of God."

Bastion raised his eyebrows. "Do you know the Bible?"

"Not as well as I should." Mia could not hide the pain in her voice.

He bent for another kiss, but she pushed him back.

Bastion bowed and departed.

Chapter Eighteen

Stefan looked at the boys' dirty faces. Their bodies were smeared with ashes. The eldest insisted he should be paid more, as he had collected the bones. Bastion requested the bones be saved for him. He would smash them and scatter them in the river, sending Rose's—the witch's—remains out into the sea, where she would be lost forever. Stefan pressed a coin into each palm covered in ash and grime.

"Bless you, Father," one boy called, running for home. Their mothers would be filled with joy at the money. Or maybe they would pause for a shy moment before extending their palms, thinking this was blood money—blood money that Father Stefan had brought to them all.

It had been the right thing to do, calling for an Inquisitor. A murder had occurred—two murders, in fact. Left on the church steps like a dare. Bjorn could not have been counted on to understand the enormous opportunity. He had even seemed hostile to the idea of calling for an Inquisitor. Stefan heard tales of Inquisitors, always busy in more prominent towns, always doing great works that the church fathers would not soon forget. The village of Dinfoil could be remembered too. Great works could be done here. Two murders gave reason enough to call for an Inquisitor.

"I have done what was right," Stefan prayed aloud, "and yet, Lord, my soul is not at peace. Something raw lies in my heart that will not let me rest. Is it something I have done? Have I failed You somehow?"

The candles below the altar burned but did not dance. Stefan saw that nothing stirred the air. He was alone. Maybe he had always been alone in here. Or maybe God would not answer because the answer must be brought up from Stefan's heart.

Stefan cleared his throat, grateful to be alone. He was going to say something foolish. "I brought Bastion here. But the suffering he caused does not seem right to me. I cannot argue with what he says. He is smarter than I am, and better educated. All I have is a painful sense that You are not pleased. Is it me, O Lord? Do I displease You? What more do You have for me to learn?"

After a long, empty silence, he looked around, his eyes noting the seat Rose had preferred. He had known her for more than ten years, since her husband came to work the land for the baron who owned much of this village. She had arrived in winter, and Stefan had gone at once to welcome them. Rose had clutched his hand and thanked him, over and over, for such kindness. To a frightened young bride in a new village, a kind priest was a lifeline.

She had attended every service, except when her husband's recurring illnesses prevented her from leaving their home. He had declined fast after the wedding, leaving her with work and no children for comfort. After the funeral, Rose had continued to stay on in the village, a faithful, friendly face as he said Mass. Two springs had passed since she stopped attending so often, even struggling for words when she sat in the confessional. *I was a poor priest,* he thought, *to fail in giving sustaining words.* He had no idea what was wrong with her. Her faithful, friendly face turned dark and hard, sitting through Masses with an accusing eye.

Eventually he became glad when she did not attend.

But had she been a witch?

Behind the altar, in the back of the church, was a hallway. The sun came in through a single window. Stefan watched as the light illuminated particles of dust floating in the air. They swirled and flew up like sparks. Something had stirred them.

"Hello?" Stefan listened and heard nothing. "Who is there?"

He heard a scratching sound.

Stefan grunted loudly, ignoring his quivering hands, and stood, walking past the altar, approaching the hallway. The sound intensified. He stepped into the hallway, his hands curled into fists.

A cat scratched at the door at the end of the hall, wanting to be let out. Stefan's shoulders slumped down, and he laughed, scooping it up, ruffling the fur around its ears. The cat meowed in outrage. *A big female, probably just had kittens, too,* Stefan judged by her loose, flapping belly. He opened the door and placed it on the ground, letting it flee before he shut the door once more. He didn't turn around. What he really feared, the course of all his deepest dread, rested behind him.

In the forlorn hours of the night, years ago, a stranger had come to the church. Stefan had fallen asleep on a pew before the altar, too tired from his midnight prayers to walk back to the dormitory. A noise disturbed his sleep, and he woke to find a cloaked man placing something on the altar. Stefan sat up.

"What are you doing?" he had called.

The man turned, and Stefan looked into his face. He would never forget the man. The stranger had haunted eyes with dark circles underneath. His face looked gaunt, his body thin like a saint who fed on suffering. Stefan reached for his bag to offer the man a coin, but the man fled back down the aisle and out into the night. Stefan rose to examine the gift left by the stranger on the altar. It had been a book. Stefan opened the cover and looked inside, as the hairs rose along his arms. He could be excommunicated if caught with this.

Stefan considered burning it, simply walking down the aisle and throwing it into the fireplace in the dormitory. No one would ever know. The flames would destroy all evidence. He would only have memory, and memories could prove nothing.

Stefan stood, his palms pressed against the altar, staring down at the book he had been so thoroughly warned against. Tearing the empire apart even now, the book ripped apart churches and families. No one disputed that it was God's Word. But the Word became a sword flashing back and forth across all kingdoms, and people disputed God's will. Was it wise to read it? Was it best left to the educated priests?

Stefan lifted the book to carry it to the dormitory, but his legs did not move. He held it in midair, deciding.

He felt a clear and certain piercing in his soul. Truth was the one incurable wound in this world, the rip in the wineskin. If he opened the book, if he set his mind on understanding God as revealed in these words, there might be no end to the suffering in this village. Men like Bastion persecuted witches, but other men burned those who dared read this book.

Stefan carried it into the hall and hid it in an empty cupboard. Stefan had always hated that cupboard. He prayed for riches to fill it with serving pieces or relics like the other churches had. God never seemed to hear those prayers.

Remembering that night, Stefan lifted the heavy book and set it on the top of the cupboard. The table sat under a good window, and the sun allowed for perfect reading. Straightening his shoulders, he opened it. He thumbed through the pages for the first time, examining the Tyndale Bible that caused so much outrage throughout the empire. Stefan stepped back, rubbing his hands down his legs.

"I cannot believe I am doing this," he said, kneeling. "God, treat me as a child. And forgive me as such, if what I do here is wrong. I have no idea where to find what I need. I do not even know if it is in this book. But I know that Bastion's words do not seem right, yet no one can argue with him. If this is indeed Your true nature, to burn and scourge, to ask your saints to punish the sinners, then show me. But if Bastion is wrong, if You are indeed a kind and gentle God, even to the worst among us, show me that."

Stefan stood and opened the book once more. His eyes fell to a wood-block illustration, a scene of sorrow and grief. A blade had carved into soft wood to show Christ crucified, His mother mourning at the foot of the cross, His disciples staring helplessly. In the background, a triumphant rooster crowed.

Turning the page quickly, he saw another woodblock of an empty tomb. A huge stone rested against the edges of the frame. Inside the tomb a great, gaping hole slashed into the wood by the unseen artist, Stefan saw darkness. Nothing remained inside it except for grave clothes, discarded. His stomach twinged. He flipped the pages once more and saw another woodblock, an illustration of Christ, triumphant, broken hands stretched out to the people. Stefan worked to sound out the strange words, words in his own language:

"Peace be with you. As the Father has sent Me, I am sending you."

Stefan glanced over his shoulder, thinking of his village. They had no peace. Their graves remained filled. Where was Christ in this village?

Erick rang the bells for Mass. Stefan replaced the book and went back to his work. He had to tend to people, not riddles.

ﻋﻠ

The afternoon warmth faded as evening approached. Mia stepped outside to close the shutters, pulling her cloak in a bit tighter. Alma's afternoon nap stretched into the mealtime hour. Mia smiled. Alma had played hard today, chasing the kitten through the bursting green leaves, returning every few minutes with a new bloom for Mia.

She had smelled rain as she gathered wood earlier today, watching Alma. *It might rain yet,* she thought. Hard to judge from the dull gray sky, hanging low and listless above.

Bjorn came down the path. "Leave the shutters," he called. "I'll attend them."

Mia stood with her hands at her sides. Her face turned hot, so she looked down, picking her skirts up so she could see the condition of her shoes. Bjorn's work made him good at spotting a liar. He would be just as fast uncovering betrayal. They were the same thing, really.

He went to work fastening the shutters into place, then squinted up at the sky. "I smelled rain earlier today. 'Tis a shame it did not come in the afternoon and cool us off. I got soaked through with sweat."

"It was that hot today?" she asked. "I did not think so." She pressed her lips back together. "Were you working hard?"

"What goes through your mind? What else would I be doing?"

Mia flinched and stepped back.

Bjorn cleared his throat and took a deep breath. "I had a lot of work today. Last night Bastion gave me a list of inquiries to be made. He wanted me out the door early this morning, to get it all done."

"I did not mean to say I doubted you. I didn't know."

"Because I didn't say anything, I know. But Bastion asked me not to. He even asked that I not tell you of that conversation. He didn't know I would have to defend myself to you. He's not married. Probably knows nothing about women."

Mia rested her fingertips against her mouth, bringing her other hand to her throat. She said nothing.

Bjorn sighed. "Rose gave us names. I had to make arrests today, bring women to Bastion for interrogation later."

"Did you see Bastion today?"

He slammed a fist against the window frame. "Of course I saw Bastion. I am following his instructions."

"I only meant to ask of your day. I am not trying to provoke you."

A light rain began. Bjorn put a hand on her back, lightly pushing her toward the door.

Mia tried a new approach. "Last night Bastion said many new things, things I have never heard."

"Yes."

"And today? Did he say anything of interest? Anything you would want to share?" Mia paused at the doorway.

"Who cares what he said today? I arrested seven women. I worked hard."

"Of course."

"Bastion told me that you would seem skittish today. A lot happened last night. Your mind needs more time to understand it all."

He pushed past her and went in, heading for the pottage pot. Mia nodded to herself, grateful she had attended to it earlier. Her home looked perfect, swept and tidied, serene with its full pottage pot. She could not bear to be idle today; at every moment she had found work to do. She had not sat down once, save to feed Margarite and Alma.

"I wish Stefan was not so offended by this man," Bjorn said. "I would like to talk of these things with someone."

"You can talk to me," Mia said, in her quiet child's voice, though it didn't suit her anymore, she knew. A different version of her had taken over, one who hungered.

Bjorn snorted. "You can listen. But do not offer anything to me in conversation."

Mia tried not to feel the sting of his words. "I will listen, then."

"Bastion says women are a necessary evil. He is a bachelor. What does he know of my pain?" Bjorn watched Mia's face as he laughed. She kept her expression still and empty, and Bjorn settled down into his chair with a bowl of pottage, talking between bites. He didn't look at her again. "Bastion is a true man of God. His words change me. Today I learned even more. The Devil may occupy the body, but not the soul. A man may be essentially pure and good and right before God and still be driven by lust to a mistress's bed, all by the power of a witch—a witch with charms, or the Devil occupying his mind and body. 'Tis a wondrous thing. A good man who sins is not always guilty. There is a type of madness, a strange lust that does not come from his own heart, but another's. It's as if something possesses him, and in this mad fit, he does things he should not."

"I don't know if you are accusing someone or confessing to something," Mia said.

"Talking with you is a fool's errand," he muttered.

Mia's father had known this moment would come. That is why he hadn't wanted her to learn those letters, to learn how letters made words and words made a new world. Master Tyndale had taught her the letters, and she had learned how to lay them in the wooden case to make his words and sentences. Mia also printed pamphlets for the church and for profiteers, even spent weeks on one volume titled *The Good Wife's Guide*. She could read by that time, and she read that one so many times that she committed entire sections to memory.

"You'll put your father out of business," Tyndale had laughed. "You'll stand in the market and recite it all, line by line."

"Not so. I'll be married. I'll be so busy being a good wife that I'll have no more time for books."

Tyndale scowled. Mia wrinkled her nose back at him, inching closer to him so he could hear her whisper.

"Unless you would let me sell your book, along with the others in the market," she said. "You can trust me with it."

Tyndale took her by the shoulders. "I do not trust the world around you."

"'Tis not fair." Mia's eyes filled with tears.

Tyndale's tone changed into a soft, soothing comfort. "Mia, I will never have a daughter. Did you know that? I will never marry, never hold a child of my own. You are the only daughter I will ever have. I am afraid you will get hurt."

"But why?"

"Because these are dangerous times. If harm came to you, in my name, I would die in my heart, Mia. Promise me that you will tell no one you have helped print it. Keep that secret. Memorize it if you want, but tell no one what you know. Store it up in here," he said, pointing to her heart. "But trust no one."

Mia had begun to hear whispers in the streets as she fetched eggs or bought bread for her father. Those caught with Tyndale's book were burned to death like criminals, they said. But for Mia's father this book meant life, not death; bread for the table and eggs for his daughter. She forced herself to eat them, smiling, as if she did not understand the risks her father took to feed her.

"I will store it up in my heart," she said, taking Tyndale's hand. He drew her into a hug, kissing the top of her head.

"And keep me in there as well," he whispered. "Always."

"I'd like a taste of beer before I sleep."

Mia was startled back to attention, refocusing her thoughts on her husband. She fetched a wooden mug and poured some of Stefan's brew into it from a ceramic pitcher. She cocked her head to the side with a new thought. "How does Bastion interrogate the women? Surely no woman would confess to a crime if the punishment is burning."

"Bastion knows what women hide in their hearts. And he knows every trick of the Devil. It is written that the Devil forbids some women to confess, even under the most severe torture, so that they will not admit the truth. Bastion must bring some to the very moment of death before they confess."

"Could they not be innocent?"

"What do you know? You know nothing about witches or their foul sins. You've never read the *Malleus Maleficarum*."

Her chin trembled.

Bjorn's face softened. "Mia, we are near the very root of our troubles. Trust me. Bastion and I will clean this village. I will have peace, no matter what it takes."

Mia kept her voice gentle. "I want you to have peace. But I would say, although I am but a woman and know very little, that peace is a gift of God. I thought gifts were freely given."

"You do amuse me with your logic. If peace were freely given, as you say, I would be out of work tomorrow."

Mia made no reply.

"I will sleep now, at last. Try not to wake me."

Mia watched him stretch and prepare for bed.

Bjorn saw nothing in her except a dutiful, dull wife. Once that had seemed enough. It had seemed more than enough. But she had let another man kiss her. Was her heart infected with witchcraft, or was this her true nature? How could she harbor this sin in her heart, the same place she kept the sacred Word, the same place she kept the memories of her father and Tyndale? How could a good woman have such hunger?

Mia looked down, shielding her eyes with her hand. Bjorn had changed since their wedding day too. The once-friendly women of this village had changed, as had Rose. Everything had changed.

Please God, she prayed. *Give me something to hold onto, one unchangeable thing.*

"Answer me." Stefan shook the bars of the cage, but the witch would not look at him. "How do you know her to be a witch? Just answer that."

"Your midwife, Nelsa, she kills newborns and offers them to the Devil," the caged woman said.

"What? Why do you say that?"

"Bastion says it."

"How does he know? Where is his certainty?"

"You never asked me my name." She turned her back to him, sitting there on her rear, wrapping her arms around her knees.

Stefan groaned. "What is your name?"

She shook her head.

He changed his tone. "What is your name?"

"Ava."

"Ava? It's a good name."

"It's not my name."

He was so tired.

"Are you so easily discouraged? I am asking you a riddle. Now, think: How do you know Ava is my name?"

"Because you told me. I believed you."

She turned her head and grinned. "Yes! That is the answer. You believed me."

Stefan understood. "Bastion tells you these things, and you believe him. Does he have proof?" His heart beat faster.

She wagged a finger at him. "I am not the only believer. And believers do not need proof."

"But he killed a woman. She might have been innocent. He might kill more. We cannot do that on his word alone."

She shrugged and went back to picking at lice in her bedding.

Stefan was alone in his doubts. Earlier everyone had filed out of Mass, eager to rush the day along, rush along with the business of living so they could return and see another witch burned. None of them would have let him confess his doubt to them. He had no refuge, save for his faith, and his words—words that had proved worthless to Catarina and Cronwall, words that had condemned Rose. Words in Latin, a language he did not even understand.

"Wait," he said. "Did Bastion give any proof that you are a witch?"

She scooted around to look at him. "Yes. I had lost a babe not long after it was born. He died in his sleep. I told everyone that I didn't know how it happened, but I knew it was my fault. A good mother would have known something was wrong. She would have saved him."

"And then Bastion accused you of being a witch?"

"No. He showed me the evidence. One day I worked in the fields, and I said, 'I believe it is going to rain today,' and it did. We were in a drought, Father Stefan."

"'Tis not witchcraft to feel a rain coming."

"Only witches know the future, Bastion said. He showed me who I truly am. I must be punished. If I am punished, my son will see the face of God. If I am punished, enough of my sin will be burned away that one day I can see my son again. I want to burn,

Father Stefan. It is all I want. Bastion will deliver me from this body of death, but I must serve him well first."

"No, no. 'Tis not right. 'Tis not right at all."

"I don't want you to speak to me anymore. I want to burn. Why can you not understand? I want to see my son."

"What if Bastion's words are wrong? What if you're not a witch? What would your son think of your punishment then?"

"He'd know I deserved it. Please, let me die. You have words. Bastion has words. I have already chosen whom I believe."

"Stop! Stop right there!" Dame Alice's scream interrupted Stefan's reply. Turning, he saw a line of women tied together by a rough rope, being led to the church by Bastion. Dame Alice screamed at Bastion, trying to grab the rope away from him. He pushed her back and kept walking. Dame Alice saw Stefan and screamed at him next.

"This is not right!" she shouted.

Stefan backed away from Ava's cage, saying nothing, then turned and ran back into the church, locking himself in, tears stinging in his throat.

Erick ran down the aisle to him. "Father? What's happened?"

"Don't go outside."

"Why? What's happening?"

"Bastion has authorized Bjorn to arrest more women. He's bringing them into the jail for interrogation."

"Women from our village?"

"Yes. I think so."

"Are you going to stop him?"

"I don't know how. Everything he says sounds right to my ears. But not to my spirit."

Erick lowered himself to sit next to Stefan on the floor. "You think he's wrong?"

"Yes."

"Praise God. I thought I was the only one." Erick rubbed his palm across his forehead, then through his hair. "What are you going to do?"

Stefan's chest hurt as if crushed from all sides by a heavy weight, a malicious embrace he could not escape. He was confused beyond all hope of reason. For every action he thought seemed right, his mind shouted five reasons it was wrong.

The door behind their backs thundered and shook as Dame Alice first tried to swing the doors open, then began beating against them with her fists.

"Father Stefan! I know you're in there! Come out and help those women!"

"I don't know what to do!" he shouted through the door, then looked at Erick and spoke quietly. "I was never taught about witches, or women, or how to tell lies from truths. I don't know any prayers for this. What should I pray? Deliver these people from my stupidity?"

"It's a start." Erick's face offered no compassion.

"Erick!"

A shadow at the window caught Stefan's eye. Dame Alice was trying to peer in through the cheap, muddy glass, looking for him.

Erick grabbed him by the shoulder to get his attention. "I know two things about God, two things you have taught me. He is a Father. And He is a Savior. I have never had a real father, but I imagine that a real father, a real savior, doesn't wait for his children to say the right words when they are hurting. He would throw his arms around them, wanting to save them. Why is it not enough for you just to cry out to Him? Why do you depend so much on what you say, place all your trust in words instead of His heart?"

"Words are all I have as a priest. Those words are who I am."

Dame Alice knocked on the glass. "You can't hide! You must act!"

Stefan stood. "Please get rid of her. I need time to think."

$$\sim\!\hat{\mathcal{L}}\!\sim$$

With Bjorn asleep for hours, his heavy breathing unbroken, Mia set out. Margarite and Alma had dozed off in the early afternoon, just after the noon meal, and Mia could wait no longer.

Though the sun burned bright, she took care on the winding uneven path through the forest. Low-lying birds' nest pines were always a cause for stumbling, and the moss could hold the night rain and be slippery at any hour. Still, she moved with good speed, feeling her spirits lift again when she walked through a portion of the path lit by the sun. Mia had had enough of darkness. She did not relish those portions of the path that made the journey difficult.

At last the town square and church were within view. Mercifully, Dame Alice was not on her steps. Mia surveyed the house freely now. Mia had tried to walk where the old crow couldn't see her. She did not want to be invited inside to eat. When Mia came to this village she wanted to forget who she had been, why she was broken. Dame Alice pried too hard too often. Mia did not trust herself to stay strong if Dame Alice fed her and spoke kindly to her. An unearned kindness might destroy the hard shell she had built around her heart. Mia knew that such kindnesses, and Alma, were her only weaknesses.

Mia saw the caged witch sleeping on her straw. A group of people stood across the street from the church, each peering at something in the jail through its windows. Mia paid them no mind. She had no time for curiosity. She wished they had slipped the cover back over the witch.

Heaving open the wooden church doors, she removed her head scarf and inhaled the perfumed air, the scent of burning wicks and incense, of the oiled wood altar and fresh straw on the floor. Stefan was removing his outer robes. He must have finished Mass. Mia had missed it, one more sin she would have to atone for.

He froze when he saw her. He did not look pleased.

"Father Stefan?" she asked. "May I speak to you?"

"I am busy," he said, folding his robe and smoothing out the wrinkles. "You can stay and pray, but I must attend to my work."

"I will not take but a moment. Please?"

"Is it confession?"

"No. It is not confession. I need help."

"What help can I give you, Mia?" Stefan raised his voice. "Why can you not solve your own problems? I can offer confession, I can offer Mass, I can offer sacraments. But these are never enough for you, are they? What could I possibly help you with?"

Mia burst into tears. She didn't mean to, and she wanted nothing more than to stop, but she felt like a small, stung child with no mother to run to. No one wanted to help her except the one man whose help she should refuse.

"Sit," he said, groaning, flinging his hand at a bench. Mia sat.

He sat down an arm's length away.

"What is it, my child?" he asked in a brittle voice.

"I think I am bewitched."

Stefan stood. "Get out."

"No, Father Stefan. Hear me."

"I want no talk of witches, not in my church, Mia. If you fall prey to this madness, then you will suffer it alone."

Mia's shoulders fell. She cleared her throat, trying to soothe the burning lump starting inside. "I have nowhere else to go, Father. Something is terribly wrong."

"You can go home, Mia. You can tend to your child and to Bjorn. Go earn your good name."

"What good name do I have?" Mia said. "My husband cares nothing for me. I have no more friends. The one friend I trusted abandoned me, and now you, my own priest—you want nothing to do with me either."

Stefan sighed, putting his head in his hands for a moment.

"I just want to ask one question and then I'll leave. How can I go back, Father? How can I undo my mistakes?"

"What do you know of mistakes? Forgetting to make bread? Using too much salt? I know about real mistakes."

"Bjorn is bewitched because I failed him as a wife. I left him vulnerable. He has lain with other women. And Bastion has said these same women bewitched Alma. It was why she was so often sick, despite my prayers."

"No woman in this village would curse a child."

"They have to. Bastion says they do. They have to murder children, 'tis how they get blood to make their magic potions."

"This madness offends God."

"Then why did God heal Alma?" Mia asked. Her heart quickened. She hadn't said that out loud before.

"Alma has been healed?"

"Yes. Alma was healed that night after Bastion's first service. Doesn't this mean God is blessing Bastion's work?"

"We should not mistake success with men as a sign of God's blessing."

"I do not want to believe this is God's way either, but God is a mystery to me. Why would He heal Alma when I have made so many mistakes?"

"Because you asked Him to. He is a Father and a Savior."

"I've asked Him for lots of things."

"So have I."

They sat in silence. Mia knotted the fabric in her lap, then released it.

"Bastion troubles me a great deal, Father. I don't know who else to turn to."

Stefan stood and approached the altar, staring up at the crucifix, his hands behind his back. "God did not answer me or grant my prayers for Alma either. Why do you come to me, then?" Stefan asked, then turned to face her. "Why come to me at all, Mia?"

Mia wrapped her arms around her stomach and looked away. "I thought you would have answers."

"You have to choose. Bastion's words or mine. Choose whom to believe, or neither of us can help you."

"I want to believe you. But Bastion has done great things, things worth believing in."

"So why come to me now? My words seem to produce no effect. You said it yourself."

"Because you are my priest, and I have sinned. I am confused. I do not know how to repent, whether it is my nature to sin or some devil at work." She paused, taking a deep breath before releasing what burned in her heart. "I tempted a man, Stefan. I did not mean to. I am afraid God will take away Alma's healing, afraid I'll do something worse."

She lied just a little. True that she had not wished for this or invited Bastion's kiss, but now she knew desire. Her pains melted away when she thought of the kiss. She would not confess that.

"Bastion would say there is nothing you can do," Father Stefan said. "Women stir up lust in a man."

"I didn't mean to."

"It is in your nature. It is the way God made you. That is what Bastion teaches, is it not?"

"Name any penance. I do not want to be this way."

"Go home, Mia, and stay there. If you live by Bastion's teaching, then you will suffer by it too."

"But …"

"Go away!"

Mia stumbled out of the doors, shielding her eyes from the bright sunlight as tears streamed down her face, shaming her.

Strong arms caught her before she tumbled down the steps.

"Mia? What is wrong?"

Bastion had hold of her. Mia was so grateful for his touch, his arms taking hold of her, but she thought of running. Running would be right.

"Tell me what has happened," he said.

"Is something wrong with me?"

He led her a few steps away where she could lower her voice—a kind thing for him to do. Her comfort mattered to him.

"Bastion, why do people treat me this way? Even Father Stefan is sick of me."

Bastion made a little scolding sound, shaking his head.

"Don't mock me," Mia said, unable to raise her eyes to look at him. "Why is Bjorn so cold to me? Even you—you would not flatter me if I was not desperate, would you? That's what makes me attractive to you. I was desperate when Bjorn married me. I don't provoke desire in any man. I provoke pity. Pity and scorn."

"Are you done?" Bastion asked.

She made everything worse every time she tried to speak. He probably thought her a fool.

"I owe you my deepest apologies, Mia. This is my fault."

Mia got up the courage to look him in the eye. He did not mock her.

"I forget that all this is so new to you. You misunderstand the signs around you. Shall I help you understand? You might feel better."

She nodded, taking a shuddering little breath.

"I have not yet rescued Bjorn, and for good reason. But you must first understand how their magic works. A witch casts a spell on a man, and the spell cannot be removed by anyone other than a witch. A witch's death does not break the spell. Only another witch can do it. Do you understand? There will be time to rescue Bjorn. But you must be patient while I work, and if you know of any witches, you must turn them in. I want to see you happy."

Bastion ran his fingers through her hair, pushing it away from her face. In her rush, she had forgotten to put her scarf on. Her hair fell loose around her shoulders. No man should have seen this; it was as if she was naked before him, before them all standing on those church steps.

"You don't know any witches, do you, Mia? Anyone you would wish to turn in? You don't have to have proof. I know you to be a good woman. I will accept your word."

She ran her hand through her hair, pushing his out.

"Of course not," she lied. If she said anything about the old healer in the forest, Bastion would have the woman burned. Mia could not live with that guilt too.

"There is no one you suspect?"

Mia saw the village spread out behind him, the women busy at market, returning to their homes. She had chosen work, and silence, over friendship, even more in the years since Rose turned away from her. The women had taken Rose's side, eyeing Mia with distrust. Or disdain, as if there was a difference. Mia understood what Bastion offered her. He offered her the chance to judge them all. With one pointed finger, she could have revenge.

"No. No one."

"I know you want to be loved," he said, leaning in. "But I do have a problem."

He inhaled, trying to smell her hair. Mia stood very still as he spoke.

"If the spell on Bjorn is broken, how will we know? Has he ever truly loved you?"

Mia's cheeks burned, and she did not answer.

"If you will never be loved by Bjorn, come with me. When my work is finished here, come with me."

Mia shook her head.

"I want to save you, Mia. You are a woman worth saving."

Mia's nose stung, the first sign of returning tears. She swallowed hard.

Bastion stroked her cheek, his smooth hand finding the contours of her cheek, then stepped back.

"Consider my offer. But if you want to stay, if you are so determined to save this husband that may never love you, think of this: I can command a witch to remove the spell over Bjorn. But why should I, Mia? Should I set Bjorn free only for you to discover that he never loved you? Should I see your heart broken and know I broke it?"

He grabbed her by the waist and pulled her to his chest, leaning down and kissing her before he released her. She recognized alcohol on his breath.

"If you want him back, I will make sure you know what it means to be loved first."

He turned and strode down the steps, leaving Mia there with her heart thundering in her ears, her legs unsteady. She saw villagers staring at her, the women with their mouths open. A stray cat dashed out of the church, past Mia's feet, startling her. When she looked back at the people, no one raised their faces again to look at her.

Mia understood.

Who would dare speak against me now? she thought. *If I hold Bastion's heart, then I hold their lives.*

Mia put her hand over her mouth.

"Who am I becoming?"

Chapter Nineteen

Stefan sat on the pew, his face in his hands. Erick hadn't returned from dealing with Dame Alice. Mia had fled after his outburst. The church was dead in its silence. He stood and faced the wooden cross hanging above him.

"I'm no use to anyone if I stay in here." He tapped his toes inside his shoes, then turned and rushed for the doors, trying to move fast before his fears caught him. He stumbled down the steps, shoving people to his right and left, causing them to cry out. Stefan pushed them away until he stood facing Bastion.

Bastion sat in a chair, one leg crossed over the other, gesturing with ease as men from the village crowded around him, listening to his counsel. At his feet seven women from the village crouched on their knees, heads bent to the dust, weeping. Dame Alice faced Bastion, shaking her finger at him.

"These girls are like daughters to me, all of them! You can't just tie them up and take them away! If you have questions about their character, you come to me!"

Bastion indulged Dame Alice with a smile. "Mother," he said, "have no fear. Any woman I find to be virtuous will be released."

As Stefan approached, he saw what had kept Dame Alice safe so far: She was not young or beautiful. Bastion had only the dullest interest in her.

Erick pulled on her arm, trying to move her to safety—somewhere her tongue would not lead to her arrest. When he saw Stefan, he rolled his eyes and let go of Alice. "She's going to get herself arrested. And me, too. I can't even repeat what she called me when I tried to stop her."

Stefan took Alice by the arm, and she glared at him.

"Dame Alice, please. I will resolve this. But you need to be quiet. No sense in getting yourself arrested."

Bastion said something to the men behind him that made them smirk, and he stood. "Stefan, it is good of you to come. This is your work too, after all." Bastion gestured over the women kneeling at his feet.

"Humiliation is not my work."

Bastion opened his arms, welcoming all to listen. "Father Stefan expresses what many of you think, yes? Let us remember why I have been called here, with some urgency, by your Father. Did you not have two murders here?"

Stefan saw them nod.

"Did they show signs of witchcraft?"

Bastion waited less time for the nods.

"Did not King Saul consult a witch in his hour of great distress?" Bastion asked, another Scripture story he seemed to know well. "And King Saul brought wrath upon himself for his wicked ways, upon his whole family, upon his whole kingdom. His sons died. His warriors died. What does the Bible command good men of God to do with a witch?"

The answer burned in Stefan's mind. He had heard this one verse quoted for years. He never imagined it would matter to him.

"'Thou shalt not suffer a witch to live,'" Bastion called. "God commands it. God does not say it is pleasant work. Who among you is a Christian? Jesus says only true disciples obey His commands. This is a test from God, I tell you. The true disciples of Jesus are being revealed. Woe unto him who fails the test. Woe unto him who betrays His Lord. May Judas be cut off from his people forever."

"No." Stefan stepped forward. "It is I who will put you to the test. You must prove your claims or release these women at once. Prove to us that you do God's will."

The women had turned their faces up to Stefan to see their savior. He scowled. They must have done something to be arrested. Women's foolishness had made his own mistakes that much worse.

"I have always allowed these tests, my friends," Bastion said. "There are lawfully prescribed tests to know if a woman is a witch. Woe unto me if I am not careful in my work, for the very souls of these women are in my hands."

"Prove to us they are witches, or leave this village today," Stefan said.

"If you had labored with me, Father, you would have seen proof already, but you have chosen to spend your time cowering in your church, too afraid to confront the Devil. Did I not see even Dame Alice here trying to drag you out? But to appease you, let us test the women."

Bastion grabbed Nelsa by the elbow, pulling her to her feet. Nelsa stood much shorter than Bastion, her head coming to his shoulder. Her face grieved him. He had never seen it so red from tears.

"Tie her with her wrists around her back," he ordered. A man stepped forward, taking a rope from Bastion's chair.

"What is the test?" Stefan asked.

Bastion waited for the knot to be tied, then took hold of her arm and walked through the crowd, dragging Nelsa behind him. She began to cry again. Dame Alice lunged after her, trying to grab her away, but Erick restrained her, pressing her face into his cloak, whispering in her ear, trying to calm her. He looked at Stefan with an awful expression. Stefan shook his head. He had no answers. He had done everything he knew to do.

"Mercy," Nelsa cried out, searching for a face that had kindness upon it. "Mercy. I am no witch."

"Then why did my son die in your arms?" a blacksmith called from the crowd.

"Sir, I do not know! That is the work of God, not me!"

"God would never allow that! You should burn for your crimes!"

"What is this test?" Stefan yelled, trying to catch up and cut through the crowd following Bastion. Bastion led them to the river, which stood at the south from the village. Stefan heard it before he saw it, the sound of the moving water and the life in the trees that went right to the edge. Bastion led them through the trees, into the water, walking out several paces with Nelsa, turning her to face the crowd.

"It is a well-known fact that a witch cannot drown. A witch has given the Devil everything that has made her human. In the water, without heart or spirit in her body, she is weightless." Bastion walked Nelsa further out into the fast-moving water. Stefan saw the whitecaps moving in the same direction as the dark clouds touching the horizon.

A storm descended. Bastion walked her out until the water came to his chest and nearly to her chin. He shoved her deeper in and let go.

Nelsa screamed, just once. Stefan saw her head bob up, her mouth gasping for air. But the whitecaps slammed water in her face, and she took in more water than air.

"Save her, Father," a woman beside him on the banks whispered to him.

Stefan turned, sick from the vision of Nelsa. "What can I do?"

Nelsa did not surface again. Bastion walked back to the shore, shivering. The villagers stood, dazed, watching the water for signs of life. The whitecaps rolled on.

Stefan grabbed him by the arm. "She did not float. She drowned. She was innocent."

"The water ran cold today." Bastion rubbed his arms, shivering.

"She was innocent," Stefan repeated.

The villagers looked back and forth between the two men.

Bastion turned to them. "Did you see the way she fought? Did you hear her scream? She did float—I saw it—but Satan took her under. She wanted to confess everything." He clucked his teeth. "You are in greater danger than I imagined."

Someone took off their wrap and offered it to Bastion, who accepted it with thanks and set back toward the village.

One by one the crowd turned and followed Bastion. None of them looked at Stefan again. Stefan waded out into the water, his hands skimming the surface. As if she might surface, as if it were not already too late for her. And for him.

Stefan stood in the green water, motionless. He watched it flow past, the current urging him to follow Nelsa in death. He closed his eyes, imaging the sweet, cold water flowing over his face, pushing him down, underneath the world, to a better place, a quiet place where God alone took responsibility for suffering. A place where God answered every question from a crystal throne. A place where His rule gave perfect clarity. Stefan would be just another soul in His care. His troubles would be over. There would be no more riddles, no more confusion as he stood helpless beneath the cross.

Stefan took another step deeper out in the water.

A hand grabbed him around the ankle, and he heard a cry again, but as if from another room.

He screamed, pushing back through the water for the trees, finding his footing and running until his side burned so badly he had to stop and breathe. He had imagined that. He was distraught. A branch had caught him by the hem. He glanced back in the direction of the river. Nelsa's body was already far from here. She was dead.

"You must choose," someone whispered.

Stefan covered his ears with his hands.

"What do you want from me?" Stefan screamed. "Am I in the place of God?"

"You must choose. Are you a shepherd or a hired man?"

Stefan saw no one near, no animals fleeing in fear. Alone he cowered under a tree.

"Choose," came the voice, much further away, an echo from the mountains that surrounded the river.

"Choose."

Stefan watched the full moon outside his window in the dormitory. He could not sleep, not with the outrageous light pouring in his room at this hour. Prayers would begin soon anyway. *There is no point to sleeping,* he thought. *I cannot find rest. I do not know what I heard or what it meant.*

Bastion slept at the other end of the room and did not stir. His sleep was always deep and calm.

Bastion finds rest. What is wrong with me, that I try to do what is right and cannot sleep? he thought. *He brings terror, and God blesses him with sleep. Have I been so wrong about You, Jesus? Do I even know Your voice?*

Stefan sneaked out still in his bare feet, the wood floor blessedly quiet. He stood blinking in the moonlight, listening to the sounds of the sleeping village. He heard rats rustling through the gutters and empty market stalls across the lane. Rats here grew to be the size of cats, and the cats had given up trying to catch and eat them. The air, so crisp and clean it almost sparkled, told him that no one had begun throwing wood and manure into their fire to cook breakfast.

She's not sleeping, he thought. *She can't be, not in this moonlight.*

Stefan approached the cage. The cover lay on the ground. The witch Ava looked up at the moon and turned when he came near.

"Would you cover me?" she asked. "I do not want to see the moon anymore."

"It is beautiful tonight."

"I like being covered," she said.

Stefan lifted the cover and began throwing it over the edge of the cage, moving around to each corner, pulling and tugging it into place. He stopped when he reached the last end. He couldn't see her very well now, just her silhouette. She sat, her legs crossed, facing him.

"You should speak it out loud," she said. "It's why you cannot sleep."

Stefan looked up at the sky. He couldn't see any stars. Just that brilliant white eye, staring blindly at the world below.

"You are not a true believer," she whispered.

"In Bastion? No."

"In God. Why else would you be here, talking to a condemned witch before dawn? You cannot sleep because you do not believe."

"I do not believe in myself. Nothing I say seems true."

"You believe in the power of your words. That is the poison you drink."

Stefan yanked his head back as if she'd scratched him.

"Bastion teaches with words, yes," she said, "but he is a man of action. He has worked since he arrived. That is why he sleeps so well."

"Bastion is wrong," Stefan said, glancing behind him.

"Are you jealous? He has many followers, even here in your own village. Your own people love him over you."

"It's not love. It's fear. What he does makes them fear."

"Then make them fear you. Or love you. It looks the same to me."

Stefan groaned and flicked the cover over the last portion of cage. *I should sleep,* he thought. *This will profit me nothing.*

"Father, look upon me. Bastion offers me freedom. He has given me a way to atone for my sins, to satisfy this guilt that is eating me alive every minute. I gave him a witch, a woman to terrify the crowds. But you and I? I can offer you nothing. And what have you offered me?"

"I offered you the truth." He pulled the cover back up. He wanted to see her face.

"But what good is your so-called truth to me?" She scrambled to him, her face inches from his, her filthy fingers wrapping around the bars. He flinched, but she could no longer hide the humanity in her eyes. "Will your truth mend my heart?" she continued. "Will it make me forget my son? Will it set me free of the guilt and pain that pierces me through every time I take a breath? I don't want your truth. I want peace. I want my son. Can you give me that?"

"No. But I can bring you beer," he said. *Saints help me,* he prayed. *I am losing my mind. I am reduced to offering drink instead of wise counsel.*

She wiped her face, streaking black from her palms across her cheeks. She blinked rapidly before answering. "Yes."

Stefan returned with a tall mug of his best beer. Water would kill a woman in such a weak state, but he used the best grains, the most careful attention, for his beer. Many ailing people felt renewed after a mug. Probably the only miracle he had ever offered or witnessed.

He couldn't fit it through the bars, so she pressed her face against the bars, opening her mouth, and he poured it in. He tried to be careful and not spill it, pushing the mug against the bars, watching how he tilted it, willing the stream to go slow and not spill over.

She drank it all, using her long skirt under her shift to wipe at her mouth, leaving a wet stain across it.

He looked at her, this mess he had created. She looked down at herself, then at him and burst into laughter.

"Shhh," he urged, glancing behind. "I would be stoned for this."

"I have not tasted beer since my arrest. Just spoiled wine reeking like vinegar, whatever dross Bastion did not trust to give the village pigs. And never clean water, though I am tortured by the sound of the rivers as we travel. You cannot imagine my thirst."

She looked up at the moon, squinting.

"One time," Stefan said, "I ruined a batch of my father's beer, spoiled the hops, letting them ferment, so I fed them to my mother's pigs. I didn't know pigs could get drunk. My father came home from the fields and found all his pigs staggering about, foaming at the mouth. He thought them possessed, so he ran them all off into the forest out of fear for his life. We had no bacon that winter."

She laughed, and Stefan did too, shaking his head.

She reached her hand through the bars at him.

Stefan remembered the beating she had given him, but he did not step away. Her hand touched his face. He reached up and caught her face too, and they stood in the strong moonlight, not looking away from each other.

A light shifted in the dormitory windows as someone inside walked past a candle.

Stefan dropped his hand and replaced the covering. He ran inside the church before his crime could be discovered.

ﮩ

The next morning Mia set out to find a bit more firewood. She had used up her winter supply. She hated the forest and worked quickly, bringing home just enough fallen, dead branches for today.

As she opened the door to her home, a sword winked at Mia as Bjorn turned it over, wiping down the blade with a polishing cloth.

Bjorn did not look up as Mia came through the door. She held her breath and entered as Alma grinned and rushed for her legs. Mia bent down and scooped her up, kissing her on the cheek, exhaling with relief. Alma made everything better. Even when Alma was frightened by a noise outside the window or a flash of lightning in the sky, it was Mia who felt comforted as she cradled Alma. Alma could never know the deep relief Mia had on those nights just touching her, holding this soft, trembling little flower. Alma gave Mia a reason to be brave. God let women bear children so women would never give up hope. Even if here on earth women were denied everything else, God would always let them bear children. Alma hinted at His goodness. Children were a promise brighter than the rainbow.

Mia sat Alma back down, swatting her on the rump to nudge her in the direction of her doll. Alma grinned and went back to it.

Bjorn had still not said a word nor even looked at Mia. She kept watch on him out of the corner of her eye, her body stiff with dread. Stefan had given no comfort or help yesterday. Mia had gone to Mass early today anyway, careful not to look at Stefan in the eye. She had focused on the statue of the Virgin Mary, who remained blind to her too. No one in town said a word to her as she left.

"I am sorry," she said. She was sorry for it all: the missing dinner, the leaving with no word yesterday, the anger.

Bjorn looked up, his eyebrows arching. "For what?"

"I am surprised you need ask."

He stood, lifting the sword, turning it to catch the light from the fire under the cooking pot. "I'm going to ask you a question, Mia."

She waited.

Stepping closer to her, he offered her the sword, hilt first.

"Would you kill me? If you knew you could not be caught?" he asked.

Mia pushed the hilt back with her palm, slowly, careful not to push the blade into his stomach. She turned and bent over the cooking pot, pretending to stir. It had gone bone dry while she had been out. Any good wife would know this meant disaster. Anything she put in it now would scorch or curdle. Bjorn would taste her neglect for weeks.

"Does it look good?" he asked. "I would like a good meal tonight."

"I can't say. I need to fetch some water for it."

He caught her by the arm, pulling her face to his.

"Where were you?" he asked.

Mia looked at the floor. Always best not to look someone in the eyes when they grew angry. Thomas had taught her that, though not because he beat her, as others would, but because he relied on her hard work to buy his beer.

"I went to Mass. Then I got some more wood, for later today. I ran out of wood."

"You went to church? Father Stefan was there?"

"Of course."

Bjorn moved around her, to her back. His arms went round her waist, one of his hands still holding the sword.

"But you went yesterday, too. There could be only one reason to go back again today."

"Mass makes me feel better. That's the only reason."

He brought the sword up along her body, resting it under her chin, the sharp blade cold against her throat. Alma dropped her doll, her eyes wide.

"And what did you say to the good Father today?" Bjorn asked. "Did you complain about me? Did you whisper my secrets to him? Are you the reason he resists Bastion and me?"

"I don't know any of your secrets. I didn't know you had secrets."
She tried not to think of what Bastion had told her about his adulteries. Bjorn would hear those thoughts in her tone.

"Then you've told the other women. Everyone knows the women of this village love a bit of gossip. How they must enjoy yours."

"They don't talk to me." Mia would not add that they did not like her, that they treated her with indifference. She would not humiliate herself to escape his wrath. She had grown tired of that escape.

"I may be bewitched by another woman, but I will not be cuckolded by my own wife. Keep your petty complaints, your stupid, baseless suspicions about me to yourself from now on."

He lowered the sword but did not step back. His body pressed into the curves of hers.

Alma's expression changed to one of anger. She marched to Bjorn, holding open her palm and pressing her other hand into her stomach. Bjorn stepped back with a short laugh. "Give your child something to eat."

Mia tore a piece of bread from the morning's baking and gave it to her. Alma flopped to the floor, tearing at the crusts, nibbling at it like a mouse, her eyes watching Bjorn with a fierce interest.

"Why did you marry me?" she asked.

Bjorn replaced the sword over the doorway.

"I asked a question," Mia said. She kept her voice soft, more interested in an answer than in an argument. She moved away from Alma so she would not hear.

"I never wanted to marry," he said. "It's too much effort to please a woman you have to see every day."

"So you married me because I did not need to be pleased?"

"I needed a wife. You did not ask questions back then. I thought you would give me peace. I thought you would be a good wife."

"Am I not?"

Bjorn laughed.

"What will become of us?" she asked. "When Bastion is gone and the village is quiet?"

Bjorn ran his hand over his chin, walking to settle himself at the table for his meal. Mia ignored the rising panic, knowing she had no meal to feed him.

"Nothing," he said, his eyes cold and hard. "Nothing at all."

The word sank like a stone in her stomach. Mia looked around the little home, her pathetic attempts to copy the other women of the village by setting things in order, behaving as the marriage book had said she should, trying to please Bjorn no matter how it crushed her spirit. She had failed. Everything looked a mess. She had no meal to feed him, never mind her own empty belly.

Bjorn reached for the plate on the table with a glare toward Mia. He knew the pot held nothing for him. She saw it in his eyes, everything it told him about her and these years together. She had nothing to offer him.

Mia rubbed her hands together, nodding.

She bent down by Alma, whispering in her ear. Alma stood, raising her arms over her head. Mia scooped her up and walked out.

Mia could not pretend any longer. She had no energy left to try. If she stayed, if she tried again, desperation would cling to her, seeping into her voice and expression. Bastion would smell it out when he came calling again. She would have no argument, no defense. She would have no reason not to give up, no reason not to fall into his arms and let him take her far from this life.

Except for Alma. Mia would not give in, and never give up, because God had given her Alma. He healed Alma for no cause Mia could think of. He dwelled in shadow and mystery, to be sure, but Mia knew one thing about Him now, one thing forever: This God of mystery and shadow gave good gifts, even to those who failed Him. Even if she failed Him again and again, she believed He would still be near, walking with her in her darkness.

And Mia knew something else, too: She would choose to die in the forest before she broke her promise to God to honor Bjorn. Bjorn wasn't worthy of it. God was. She would be true to this mysterious God, and by setting foot into the forest, without sword or knife, she knew she chose to die.

"I will take care of Alma," she whispered to God. "I will take her as far from here as I can."

Mia stepped into the shadows of the trees, cradling Alma in her arms. The forest rested quiet in the day. Those with hungers slept, waiting for night. Mia saw paw prints in the earth, one set, each print about the size of her palm with four toes, each with a claw curving in toward the center—the mark of a large wolf. A wolf had found her house last night. Bjorn had killed one wolf, and another had sprung out of the darkness to take its place, pacing back and forth, watching. Mia picked up her pace, hoping the wolf would not wake.

The foolish virgins, Mia thought. *I am no better than they.* Mia had heard the parable of the foolish virgins from Father Stefan. Ten beautiful young virgins waited at night for their groom. But the wait proved too long, and the night was so dark that all ten virgins fell asleep. At last the cry rang out, "The groom is here! The time for the feast, the wedding, it is upon us!"

But five of the virgins had no oil left for their lamps, so they couldn't make their way to the feast. They went out into the dark streets, searching for oil, searching for help. And the five wise virgins, the ones who had stored up oil, the ones who were ready for a long, dark night, these women won everything—even love.

The five foolish virgins mocked Mia as she picked her way through the last of the afternoon light, through this thick forest, with Alma clinging to her, every step difficult and painful. Green boughs scratched Mia's face and caught her by the hair. She continued forward, letting the bough take a piece of her hair with it. She only wanted to save Alma.

Mia had let herself get too thin, too weak, and knew she did not even have strength to last the remaining minutes of light. Night was settling around them fast. Mia realized now that they would both die when wolves and bears and boars woke and went hunting for the foolish and the weak. The five foolish virgins were never heard from after that, apparently, because they were never mentioned again in the Bible. *Probably eaten,* Mia thought.

Her arms burned with the effort of carrying Alma, but when she tried to set Alma down, the child moaned in fear, scrambling, scratching, and grasping for Mia's embrace.

Alma had never experienced the fear of being unwanted. Mia nuzzled her cheek against Alma's as reassurance. Mia had known the life of a fugitive long ago. She knew how to bury her sorrows and fears, how to drive them down deep into the mud and run.

Mia was a woman now, and everything on her stove had gone to giving Alma more strength, and to Bjorn's big appetite. Nothing remained for Mia.

The last light faded as Mia pushed on. An hour later, exhausted, she collapsed beneath a tree. She could hear the animals scurrying overhead and the insects scurrying underfoot. Heavy footsteps frightened Alma, but Mia suspected it was a deer. Tired of chewing on the birch trees through the winter, deer would be grazing on spring's new growth with no thought of danger. Around her, toadstools glowed blue-green in the darkness, moonlight breaking through the canopy above in rare, distant spaces.

Alma curled into her lap, sucking her thumb, falling asleep. Mia blinked in the darkness. The forest writhed to life. Predator hunted prey, insects sang and chewed through the leaf litter, owls flew past not more than an arm's reach away. She heard tiny screams of a mouse or rat as an owl caught it.

Mia had always cooked her meals in a pot and acquired food by digging through dirt or paying a butcher for cuts of meat. She had never hunted or heard claws tearing flesh. Suffering came to everyone in the night.

Bastion and Bjorn would be searching in the village tonight for signs of more witches. The women arrested would sit in the jail and think tonight of what must soon happen to them. Sleep was mercy. Everyone and everything still under the curse stayed awake to suffer.

Mia knew those screaming, scurrying animals had a better lot, dying before dawn. Mia would die slowly, over the course of days. If God had mercy, she would find a place for Alma to live before that happened. Perhaps there would be a woman who could not have children of her own. Perhaps she could take Alma in.

If Mia could muster the strength to carry Alma just a bit further, she would find a town. Surely she would find a town.

A scream startled Mia awake, her heart pounding against her ribs. An owl repeated the call. Mia blinked, wondering how long they had slept like this, Alma in her lap and Mia slumped against the tree.

Steps in slow cadence broke branches in the distance. Something heavy approached, something not hunting, but searching. Mia froze, tightening her grip around Alma.

Bjorn would not have followed. He did not care enough.

Mia's stomach burned from the rush of spiked fear, a cold iron mace being swung through her body as she saw the ghost. A woman's image glided in between two huge beeches ahead. She had long silver hair, unbound, spreading across her shoulders, flowing down to her elbows. Nothing more than a skeleton's body hung underneath her plain shift. The ghost stepped, cracking a twig underfoot.

Ghosts do not break twigs, she thought. *This must be a woman of flesh and blood, living.*

The woman turned and came right to her, not blinded by the darkness, not dependent on the patches of light. It was the healer Mia had spied in the village. She carried a thick rope at her side.

Mia closed her eyes as the woman got closer, leaning down and burying her face into Alma's back. *Better to be taken by an owl. Victims saw the stars before they died.*

"Get up," the woman said.

Mia could not move. Her limbs were numb.

"Do not fear me. Stand up."

Mia tried to bend her legs but only whimpered, the sound drowned out by the piercing of crickets.

The woman's hands took her by the arms, cold bones like frozen straw under such thin skin. The grip tightened. The woman had surprising strength. The pain of these old fingers digging into her arm comforted Mia. The pain broke the spell of numbness, the blankness of exhaustion.

"Get up, or I will leave you here." She released Mia and stepped back. A wolf appeared behind a tree just feet from the woman. Its black lips curled up as it growled. Mia froze. The woman turned to the wolf and clicked her teeth at it. It stepped back, watching something near Mia.

A snake slithered away from Mia under the leaf litter. Leaves bobbed up and crunched as it moved. The wolf whined as the snake fled.

With a grunting series of shuffles, Mia managed to stand, lifting Alma into her arms. She could not set Alma down again here. Alma did not wake but recognized her mother's movement and wrestled into a comfortable position against Mia's chest.

The woman dropped the rope to the forest floor, holding one end as it fell. She stepped closer until Mia could smell meat on her breath, and fresh sage. The woman ate well. She was strong. She tied the rope around Mia's waist and stepped back, giving it a tug. Mia stumbled forward but the knot held. The woman clucked her teeth at her and began walking. The rope dug into Mia's back, forcing her to follow or fall.

Mia walked in the darkness, not able to see the woman, only seeing the rope extending a few feet in front of her. With the rope taut, Mia knew which way to face, where to set her feet. She walked until her arms returned to life, burning. She tried rearranging Alma, setting her up more to her shoulder, then more on her hip, but it did not give much relief. Mia had never known such pain. Still, she focused only on the rope, only on the next step. She tried not to hear the softly padding steps of the wolf behind her. She tried not to hear the wolf calling to its pack, and other wolves appearing from between trees along the path.

The woman led her to a clearing. Under the generous new supply of moonlight, Mia saw a thatched home, much smaller than her own but more inviting. The windows held a golden welcome, a sign of a fire inside at the hearth. Mia fell to her knees, unable to take another step, letting Alma tumble down onto the grass. Mia's arms were of no use. She knew she should cry out for help, but who would hear except wolves and this strange woman, this witch?

As if she heard Mia's thoughts, the woman turned back just once more. "My name is Hilda." At that, Hilda dropped the rope, opening the door and disappearing inside. She left the door open.

The black hungry forest stood at Mia's back. Predators crawled and called, scratching against trees and uprooting rocks. The wolves circled and waited, pawing at the ground, sniffing the air.

Alma had opened her eyes and was smiling at Mia, looking with curiosity at the clearing and the small house with the golden windows. Mia nudged her, turning her face so she would not see the ring of wolves so near.

Mia stood, praying for strength, groaning at the heaviness in her joints. She took Alma by the hand, stumbling toward the open door, the rope trailing more behind her with every step.

Mia took painful, heavy steps. The door seemed to move further away with each one. Mia did not have the strength. She stumbled, forcing herself back up. A wolf stepped into the clearing, too near. Mia's heart beat faster, her breath burning in her chest.

Alma moved in front of her, still grasping her hand, and pulled. Mia followed, letting Alma's strength overpower her dead muscles. Alma pulled Mia to the door. Mia pushed a fist into her chest, trying to breathe. Pain squeezed at her ribs.

Mia fell to the floor as Hilda closed the door, scolding the wolves for coming too near. The last thing Mia saw was Hilda leaning over her with hollow eyes and sunken cheeks. Mia remembered raising her hand, pointing to Alma.

"Her name is Alma," Mia said, slipping away. "Please do not let her die."

Chapter Twenty

Stefan poured fresh water into a bowl and scrubbed until his face and neck glowed red. He had looked into Ava's eyes in the glowing white moonlight and had seen himself. He believed everything he had been told and too late realized not everything had been true. Not about God. Not about salvation and sin.

Bastion sighed, running his hands down his robe, down his vest, smoothing out wrinkles. Stefan took a moment to smooth out wrinkles too, with extra care to pick at stray hairs. He pressed hard, trying to stop his hands from shaking. The last secret he had kept was his decision to call for an Inquisitor. Stefan did not trust his own judgment now.

"You look good, Stefan."

"Do not speak to me."

"You are afraid. Do not mistake fear for wisdom. You'll do something stupid."

"I am not afraid," Stefan said, digging his nails into his palms. He shook them out. "I trust God will avenge His name."

"Perhaps He will. But how do you know He is not angry with you? How long have you shepherded these fine people? When was the last time you saw true salvation in any of them? You've strung them along—that's what I think. You promised life and salvation and couldn't deliver. That's why you called me in. You're no better than a man who cannot satisfy his own wife and sends her off to find a lover."

Stefan lunged at him, grabbing him by the neck, slamming him into a wall. Bastion relaxed, going limp, a gentle expression on his face. Stefan dropped his hands and stepped back. Bastion reached out and tried to pat him, but Stefan pushed his hands away.

"We both knew you couldn't do it," Bastion said.

Stefan shook his head, staring at the floor.

"Look at me, Stefan."

Stefan refused. Bastion stood closer, bending down to see Stefan's face.

"Your war is not with me, brother. Your war is with yourself. I will finish the job you brought me here to do. I will gain confessions from these women, and I will burn them. Then I will leave. But you will still be here. You will still be their priest. I do not want that job. I am not fighting you for it."

Bastion stepped back and straightened up, then breathed into his palm. He poured fresh water into his hand and slurped it, swishing it in his mouth before spitting it out into his bowl. "These people will need a good priest when I am finished. I hope you are that man." Bastion walked out toward the crowd waiting for him to conduct his interviews.

Stefan had a Mass to do. No one would attend, of course. They would be with Bastion. He tugged at his tight collar. The air in the room was stifling.

He walked out of the dormitory but decided not to follow the path into the church. If Stefan could do nothing else, he could stand with his flock.

He turned at the gate and walked toward the hungry crowd. Bastion saw him coming and raised his voice to keep the crowd's attention.

Bjorn caught up to him, pulling at Stefan's arm.

"Let me go, Bjorn."

"I know Mia came to see you. I want to talk to you."

"No, not now."

"Mia's life depends on it."

"Have you harmed her?" Stefan stopped, turning to face Bjorn.

"Do what Bastion wants. Help us destroy the witches in the village. For Mia's sake."

"If you love her, get her far away from here. Save her from this."

"Save her? You do not understand. I am the one that needs to be saved."

Stefan pushed him aside, taking each step up to Bastion.

Bjorn climbed the steps and took hold of Stefan's arm. "Let Bastion finish this work. We can be free of all this." Bjorn gestured to a clump of women huddled together behind Bastion. Some bled from the nose, others had hot red marks slashed across their arms. None looked up. They pushed together with moans like frightened sheep.

Stefan shook off Bjorn and went to the women, kneeling. He removed his outer vest and spit on it, using it to wipe at the blood, pushing hair out of faces, trying to help, touching his women for the first time. Tears ran down his cheeks, blinding him until he could do nothing more for them. Then he stood.

"Witchcraft has not been proved! These are your sisters, your neighbors, your wives! You cannot let Bastion have them!"

Bjorn grabbed Stefan with more force. "Come down, Stefan. This is the only way. You do not understand."

"He can't set any of you free of your sins! He does not offer salvation!"

"If he doesn't, they will all die anyway."

Stefan pulled his arm free, and Bjorn grabbed him again, pushing him to the ground. Stefan went limp just as he had seen Bastion do. Bjorn released him. Stefan got to his feet, slugging Bjorn in the cheek, sending him spinning down the stairs. Stefan turned to go after Bastion, but men from the crowd jumped on him, wrestling him back, kicking him until he could move no more.

"Stop." Bastion's voice shot through their grunts and curses.

Stefan looked up and saw their faces receding and Bastion peering down at him. Bastion clucked his teeth as Bjorn jerked Stefan to his feet, shoving him in the direction of the jail. Stefan couldn't feel his legs. *God's mercy,* he thought. They were bruised beyond anything he had ever felt.

Bjorn dragged him through the wooden jail door, the rough frame catching Stefan on the shoulder, ripping threads from his robe. The jail resembled a row of horse stalls, all wood with a filthy main aisle and sunlight peeking in through gaps in the roof where the wood had rotted. The jail stank. Stefan held his breath.

Bjorn pushed Stefan into a tiny stall. Stefan saw that he had no way to lay down, nowhere to relieve himself, no window to see out into the village. He could see Bjorn's profile in the small cutout window in the doorway to his cell.

"Save Mia and Alma, please. For me. Send them to another village. She came to me for help, confused, and I screamed at her. God willing, it will be the last mistake I make in this village."

"She ran away last night with Alma. She has not returned."

"That does not mean she is safe. You know as well as I about what lives in the forest. You must keep her safe, or nothing you ever do will be enough to purge your guilt. And mine."

"Am I guilty, Stefan? Or am I bewitched? I sat in your church every day, years upon years, and it did nothing to stop the vile desires of my heart. I've sat though your Mass and partaken of the Host, then left to ravage a woman. I did that, Stefan, after receiving your blessing, your pardon in God's own name."

"Bjorn." Stefan covered his eyes with his hand in sorrow.

"So tell me, Father, why could I not stop? I wanted to."

Stefan could say nothing. Bjorn slammed his fist against the door.

"Who compelled me to sin: your merciful God or a witch?"

"Neither."

"No. If a man wants to stop but he can't, that is a sign. He has been bewitched."

"It is not a sign. It is sin. And Bastion can't set you free from that. Punishing others can't set you free from yourself. Bastion has arrested almost a dozen women by now, hasn't he? He's even burned Rose. And are you free? If so, where is your peace, Bjorn?"

Bjorn did not answer, but he did not turn away. He had to listen. Truth riveted anyone. Stefan knew with more confidence than he'd ever felt before that he was speaking the truth.

Stefan saw the shameful expression on Bjorn's face and inhaled a long, sharp breath, when he suddenly realized yet another truth. "Rose carried your child, didn't she? You're the reason she turned cold to Mia, refused to speak to her again. And Catarina? Cronwall?"

"Ah, Catarina. She was not a compliant woman. I had such sympathy for Cronwall after a while. I had to do it, or she would have destroyed my good name. I could have been arrested, and now I see I did not even commit a crime. It was not me at work at all; even Saint Paul says the Devil is at work in our flesh. You should hear Bastion preach on that."

"But why Cronwall, too?"

"Cronwall was first, of course. I killed him instead of the wolf one night. He was half drunk, though. He was going to kill me if I didn't stop him. I don't understand, actually, how he could treat her like that and become so enraged when I touched her. That man was an utter mystery."

"But why did you dump them on the church steps? Why did you not try to hide your crime? Were you proud of what you had done?"

"Don't you understand? It wasn't me. If you want to talk, you have to stop these lies, or I will walk away."

Stefan bit his lip to keep himself from shouting. "All right, then. Why did the Devil prompt you to dump the bodies there?"

"The Devil's most famous sin is pride, Father. Even you teach that. So I suppose that was one reason. But I think it was an accusation against you, against God. Think now: I hardly ever missed church. I asked God to stop me from coveting what was not mine, every day. But the urges were always there. Nothing could stop me. I began to doubt God even existed. A good God would not let me suffer like that. And then Bastion came. He showed me that belief in

God wasn't the problem. I had no belief in the Devil. That's why the Devil found it so easy to control me. That's why I had to hurt others. He had control, and I did not know it."

"Let me out, Bjorn. We will go and seek help from the bishop, from the church fathers."

"It's too late. You brought Bastion. You did save me, in your way. I will not forget that." Bjorn began backing up. Stefan was losing sight of his face.

"Bjorn, wait. The blood of these women is on my hands too. We are both guilty in the eyes of God."

"No. I am not guilty. I am bewitched. You failed those women. You failed me."

"Then do not let me fail Mia, too. Or little Alma. Bjorn, she tried to come to me so many times for help. I thought she was the problem. I blamed her. I did not help her."

"I can't stop to help Mia now. I should continue my work with Bastion. I have not harmed a woman since Rose burned. It's working, Stefan. The curse is lifting."

"Just find Mia and Alma. Guarantee their safety. Do this for me, so that my guilt will not be so great in the eyes of God."

"Why would I do this for you?"

"Because soon everyone will know what you did. But one act of kindness, of loyalty to your wife, will prove all that you say—that you were bewitched. That you are a good man in your heart, and that the Devil worked through you. And not just prove this to me, but to everyone in the village, everyone who hears of our great struggle here. You will become famous, the man who escaped from the clutches of the Devil."

Mia watched Hilda swaying back and forth, her back to Mia. Mia blinked, hoping to steady the image.

Hilda turned around and shuffled to her. Mia stared at the old face, swollen and doughy, with a fish's mouth, lines drawn up tight around it. The woman had silver-colored hair hanging listlessly between stalks of white that clumped together in places. Mia closed her eyes.

It had been foolish to run, with no plan, with no hope, with only a determination not to give in to temptation.

Breath tickled her cheeks, and Mia opened her eyes. Hilda's mouth hovered inches above her face. The old woman snapped her teeth.

Mia flinched, banging her head on the wooden beam supporting her pallet.

"You're fine. Sit up," Hilda said.

Mia pushed her feet over the edge of the pallet, touching the dirt floor. Alma slept on another pallet, her thumb stuck in her mouth, her hair done in beautiful braids.

"I kept her happy as you slept. She is a fine child. Healthy and strong."

Hilda shuffled over to a black pot covered in burned drippings down all sides and filled a bowl with broth. She brought it to Mia.

"Drink this."

Mia lifted the bowl to her nose and inhaled. It smelled better than most of what she cooked. She took a sip and pleasure shot through her veins. Mia lifted the bowl and gulped, letting food dribble down her chin.

Hilda sat on her haunches, watching Mia.

Mia lowered the bowl, gasping for air. The old woman looked shocked at her manners. "I am sorry to cause such trouble for you," Mia said. "I was foolish to run into the forest."

"Are you done, then?" Hilda asked, reaching for the bowl. Mia moved it away from her. If the woman would only turn her back, Mia would run her fingers through it and lick what she scraped up.

"I don't want you here. Because you are a woman, because you are lost, I feed you. But I do not want you here. Eat and leave. First light has come."

"Where should I go?"

"You do not know where you want to go?" She squinted, leaning toward Mia. "Did you plan to die in the forest?"

"I was already dead. I just wanted to save my daughter. And my conscience."

Hilda sat back, chewing her lip, studying her. Mia stretched, her chest still sore. Her arms were heavy and numb.

"Tell me your name."

"Mia, wife of Bjorn, sheriff of Dinfoil."

The woman covered her mouth with her hands. She hobbled to the door, leaning out and peering in all directions before shutting it.

"No one followed you?"

"No. Bjorn wanted me gone."

"I'm sure he did."

The woman paced the short length of her home over and over, then turned back to Mia. "You've got to leave right now. I fed you. You're strong. Go."

"Where?"

"Leave here and walk toward the sun. Find the path and follow it. Do not return to your home. I will give you money, but you must never return to this house, either."

"But why must I go right now? No one followed me, certainly not Bjorn. Why would you be afraid of him?"

"So it is true?"

"What?"

"And you did not run to me? You did not run thinking I would save you, just like the others?"

Mia shook her head. *Others?*

"You know nothing?" She kicked with one foot at Mia, spraying dirt over Mia's feet. Mia just shook her head again, lost. "I don't believe you."

Mia reached down and brushed the dirt away. What did the woman want her to say? Some sort of confession or accusation? Mia would not accuse anyone, not for Bastion, and not for this strange woman.

"Thank you for the night's shelter," Mia said, standing. Mia walked to Alma and whispered in her ear, wiggling her hands underneath the sleeping child to lift her. Mia did not acknowledge the surprised expression Hilda wore.

"You really know nothing? And you would walk through the forest, without any protection, for what, you said? Your daughter? She'll get eaten."

Mia removed her hands from underneath Alma, who stirred and woke with the interruption.

"You do not want to give me help," Mia said. "You are no different than any other woman I know."

"It's remarkable," the woman said, moving to sit on the pallet Mia had slept on.

Mia closed her eyes and shook her head before answering. "What is remarkable?"

"That you ran straight to me, that I was out collecting toadstools at that very moment, that I saved you. We must think of what it means."

Mia frowned. "Do I owe you money? Is that why you tell me to leave and then tease me into lingering and asking questions? Do you want to be paid?"

The woman gasped and kicked more dirt at Mia, as if punishing her, or pushing her to reveal something more.

"Stop doing that!" Mia said.

The woman sneered. "You are not what they say."

"Why are you teasing me? Do you want me to stay? Or do you want accusations? I won't give you names."

The woman's face grew dark and angry. "I do not want names. I know their names. And I know that many of them will die."

"If some women have become witches and consorted with the Devil, how is that my burden? Let each pay for her own sins."

"Do you believe that? Each one of us must pay for our own sins? Our own sins and not the sins of another?"

The door stood only a few paces away, if she could get past the woman. Hilda could not be trusted. She was not even a Christian woman. She would only lead Mia deeper into deception and danger.

"I know more about you than you know," Mia said. "You are a witch, a forbidden healer. All the women know about you. We see you in town, buying herbs, scowling at Father Stefan. If Bastion knew of you, where you lived, he would burn you on the spot." Mia hoped the woman did not miss the threat in her words.

Hilda laughed and patted her knee. She had no reaction other than amusement. Mia must have made a poor enemy. "Come and sit with me."

"No, I will not. If you consort with the Devil, then you are no good Christian woman."

"You are the one who consorts with the Devil."

Mia gasped.

Hilda grinned as her eyes narrowed. "I have heard stories of you, Mia, an innocent who married Bjorn without thinking, without caution. Rose tried to befriend you, to help you see who he was, but that ended so soon, didn't it? Yes, I have heard the stories."

Mia could not let Hilda sense the dread building in her heart. What Hilda said might be true. And Mia had made it all possible for Bjorn.

"You speak nonsense."

Hilda crossed the floor in three fast steps. "Do you wonder where Bjorn goes at night? Do you wonder why women are cold to you? Can you not see fear on their faces?"

"Can you not speak plainly?"

"I want you to say the words to yourself first. They should not come from me."

Mia laid her hands on Hilda's shoulders. "Whatever it is, say it."

"No."

"Then I will leave."

"There is a monster in your village—a man who creeps round at night, finding women alone. He does terrible things. He holds all power. They do not resist. But they hate."

"If you accuse Bjorn …"

"He has never been able to find me. He would like to, for he knows that I am a refuge for the women. When they come to me, I give them medicines for pain, for sorrows, and to make sure he does not give them a child. I cannot give them justice. I give them a chance for survival."

"Nothing you say is true." Mia grabbed Alma and rushed her out the door. Rain spattered the ground. Thunder roared overhead. Mia did not know where to find the path.

Hilda came up behind her.

"Tell me, did you get your pearls back? They were given away to shut a woman's mouth. Bastion returned them, yes? And you rewarded him well?"

Mia stopped and turned to face her. Raindrops pelted her cheeks.

"Who told you of my pearls? What do you know of Bastion and me?"

"Women are talking about you, Mia. You are not imagining that. They wonder how much you know. They wonder why Bastion prefers you. What shall I tell them?"

"Tell them I was ashamed to be rescued by a witch who spews lies."

"I have not rescued you. It is far too late for that."

Hilda turned and went back inside. Mia tried to find a path and be free of this place, but the rain came faster. Not much light fell to the bottom of the forest on good days; now none made it down. Mia felt along the trees, with Alma clinging to her skirts, trying to push through the narrow openings between the slender firs, trying to make sense of the forest. She looked in every direction and saw no hope. Worse, Alma was getting soaked. Mia tried to pick her up, but her arms ached so badly she couldn't. Alma shivered, cold and wet.

Mia beat her fists against a tree. "Where is the path?"

Hilda opened the door to her home. Mia could see the light and Hilda's thin, bent body standing in the doorway. Hilda could keep Alma dry. Mia did not have to listen.

Mia led Alma through the trees, trying to keep a hand over the child's head to shield her from more rain. Through the door they came, and Hilda shut the door behind them.

"Can you shelter us until it stops raining?"

"You are a good woman, Mia, but you cannot be trusted. This is what I will tell the women. It is what they suspected."

"What would you have me do? Ask my husband? What would he tell me?"

"You believe he is innocent?"

"He might be bewitched."

"Well, now, with that, I can help you. But only if you are willing to know the truth. Not everyone thinks you are. Only Dame Alice thinks you are an innocent. She tried so hard to help you. But you do not want help, or friendship, or even the truth."

"They're wrong."

"Then I will give you a serum that breaks all spells and charms. Once a man has drunk it, he will be set free, never to be bewitched again. All the evil he has done will be finished. If you want the truth about Bjorn, if you truly believe he has been bewitched, then give him the serum."

"I should not test him. It is not God's will that we test our husbands."

"Leave God out of this. With this potion, you can set Bjorn free of all lusts and ungodly desires. If he has been bewitched, as you say, it is the right thing to do. Prove to us you are a good wife."

"What if he has not been bewitched? What will drinking the potion do?"

"Do? It can do nothing. It's only a counterspell, powerless if there is no spell to break."

Hilda fetched a small vial of opaque green glass, holding it between two fingers, dangling it at Mia. "What shall I tell the women? Do you want the truth?"

Mia listened to the rain hitting the thatched roof. A few drops burrowed their way inside and left dark streaks on the floor. A chill crept around her.

"If I take this potion from you, will I be guilty of witchcraft?"

"No. You are not making spells. You are only breaking a spell. And you have greater worries than accusations that cannot be proven."

The cottage darkened as Hilda spoke, the storm coming closer. Alma shivered and Hilda retrieved a shawl, handing it to Mia.

"Have you something else to say to me?" Hilda asked. "You do not take this vial? What else are you hiding? What is the real reason you ran?"

"I just want to think."

Hilda opened the door and peered out. Rain struck hard, rattling the green spring leaves above. "Women travel many miles to find me. When they arrive, they need time to find their voices. But you do not have time, Mia. You must tell me, whatever your burden is, right now."

"I am confused. I want to pray, and I cannot ask a witch for counsel about God. And it is God that I most need right now."

"Oh, I may know God better than you imagine. I find Him here, in the forest, quite often."

"Blasphemer."

Hilda cocked her head and waited.

Mia chewed on her lip, looking away from the vial. If Bjorn was bewitched, it was logical to believe that only another witch's work could set him free. This vial could give him hope. It could deliver him. Hadn't he provided for Alma? Hadn't he kept them both alive and clothed, no matter how lean the years were? Bastion could not be trusted to do it, not if he desired Mia for himself. She had no way to break that spell. It was not witchcraft, she knew, but just a common evil.

"I ran away because I was afraid. I had wanted to die in the forest. But you found me."

"What were you so afraid of, my child?"

"Myself."

Hilda threw back her head, laughing.

Mia put her hands to her face. She would not cry in front of this woman.

Hilda shuffled forward, putting her hand on Mia's arm.

"Mia, when I was a girl, I wanted to be a wife and a mother. My mother and my sisters died, three of them in all, and my father left me forever, alone in this little home. I was twelve. One day I found a

woman wandering in the woods, delirious with fever. She had tried
to abort her unborn child by drinking a potion she had bought from
a wretched peddler. The pregnancy had ended but not expelled, and
she was dying. I pulled her into this home, and I cared for her until
she died. She is buried behind the home, and she is not alone. Many
women since then have come to me. I have learned many recipes
and charms, but not everyone lives, no matter what I do. Imagine it:
an old woman with a garden of dead women. Think of how it must
look to a stranger. But I know the truth about myself. I am not an
evil woman."

"But the whisperers in town say you are not a good Christian,
either."

"My methods are outside the church, yes. But they work. Can
you always say that about your prayers, your penance, your devotion?
You go to church but don't get answers. I make my little recipes, and
I always get results. I have answers for my women. I cannot believe
that a good God could be angry if I only try to fix what is broken."

Mia reached for Hilda's hand and took the potion, holding it to
the light. The dark glass vial revealed nothing.

"You say this will release Bjorn from witchcraft? He will no longer suffer bewitchment?"

"Never."

"Is there no other way to set him free?"

"None. I give you a pledge that is certain."

Mia inhaled, not looking at Hilda. "Will it make him love me?"

Hilda's face spread into a slow smile. "Ah. Now I know why you
ran."

"Don't embarrass me. Just answer."

"No, it will not. But a good wife would see that he drank it, just the same. I can make another potion, if you like, one that will bring you happiness. One that will make your heart lighter."

"No, thank you. If I do this, will you keep Alma here? I will return when I can."

Hilda shuffled to her and rested a hand on Mia's arm. "I will watch over her with all love and care."

Mia tucked the vial inside the tiny bag on her belt. She went to Alma, sitting in her pallet. She took Alma's hand and kissed it, rubbing the pudgy little knuckles with her own finger. Alma was perfection. Mia kissed the top of her head. "I will be back for you when it is safe. Try not to be afraid."

Alma teared up and buried her face in Mia's skirts.

The door flew open. A flash of lightning illuminated a man standing in the doorway.

"Bjorn." Mia gasped.

Chapter Twenty-one

"Mia?" Bjorn did not move. He squinted, the hard rain showing him no mercy, pelting him from above, causing rivers to flow from his brow to his mouth. He wiped at his face and stepped in.

"This is your husband?" Hilda asked, shaking her head, moving to the back wall.

Alma ran to him, shoving her arms against his shins, pushing him back through the doorway. Bjorn picked her up, pinning her arms against his chest, leaning his head away from hers as she thrashed.

"Alma," Mia yelled. "Stop."

"What are you doing here?" Bjorn asked. "I thought you ran away. I thought you were in danger."

Hilda's hand had closed around a knife, and she pointed it at him. "Get out. Get out, or I'll do worse than curse you."

"You are the witch the women speak of, aren't you?" Bjorn said. "Mia, what have you done?"

"She found Alma and me in the forest and brought us here. I didn't come looking for her."

"Mia, are you a witch too? Did you start it all?"

"Get out!" Hilda screamed.

"My own wife has done all this to me." He looked mystified.

"No. I am not a witch. You must believe that."

A flash of lightning cut across the sky as wolves howled, shrill calls above the low growls of thunder. Bjorn stumbled through the door into the room, almost landing on his knees before regaining his balance.

"He doesn't believe anything good about you, Mia." Bastion pushed him out of the way, stepping into the room. More men stood behind him. Mia recognized them from the village. She felt a cold wind blast in through the door. The great storm that had been lingering on the edge of winter, on the edge of the village, had come.

"Thank you, Bjorn," Bastion said. "I had every faith you would lead us to Mia. But this," he said, pointing at Hilda, "this is a surprise. This must be the witch the women confessed to, the one who undermines the village."

Bastion picked up Alma, stroking her hair as the men poured into the home, dragging a screaming Hilda out into the rain. Alma went limp, her eyes wide with fear. Bastion smiled at Mia.

"I am surprised you ran away. You knew deliverance was at hand."

Mia took a deep breath and forced herself to look Bastion in the eyes. "Put her down. You came for me."

Bastion turned to Bjorn. "I know why I followed her. But why did you, Bjorn? Why are you here?"

"I did something stupid. I should have known better. But I listened to Father Stefan. He said if I found Mia, if I guaranteed her safety, it would prove I was a good man. It would prove my claim of witchcraft."

"As if you need proof. But you should admit the truth to cleanse your conscience. Why did you follow her? For her? Or for yourself?" Bastion watched Mia as he waited for Bjorn to reply. Mia looked at the floor. She did not want to be won this way. She did not want to be won at all.

Bjorn did not look at her again, but shrugged like a child caught in a lie. "I did it for you, Bastion. For your work to continue." Mia looked back up as Bastion smiled at her, his eyes half closed. He heard the lie in Bjorn's words just as well as she did. Bjorn had come here only for himself. Not for Mia. He had done nothing for Mia and never would.

Hilda's scream from outside the home broke through Mia's heart. She lunged for the door. Hilda was an old woman. No one should hurt her.

One of Bastion's men grabbed Mia by the arm. Bastion and Bjorn lunged for him at the same time. Bastion moved faster, throwing the man to the ground in front of Mia.

"Do not touch her!" Bastion said.

Bjorn stepped over her. "Leave her to me. A man has a right to punish his own wife."

Hilda screamed again, a clotted sound. Bastion glanced in the direction of the door.

"Bjorn, you must see that the men use some restraint with Hilda. Try not to let her die until I can question her."

Bjorn glanced between Mia and Bastion, then went out the door.

Bastion set Alma down. "Go and sit on the bed, little one."

Alma stared at him and did not move. Mia reached out and nudged her arm, not taking her eyes off Bastion. "Go on, Alma. Go sit." Alma obeyed, sitting on the bed, then curling into a ball, suck-ing her thumb, her eyes like deep white moons.

Bastion slapped Mia. "What have you done? Why did you not trust me?"

Mia covered the burning spot on her cheek with the palm of her hand, too stunned to cry. "I do not trust you. But neither do I trust myself with you. That is why I ran."

Bastion pulled her in, and she did not resist, her limbs cold with fear. He moved her hand and kissed her red, stinging cheek.

"Was there ever a woman like you?" He pressed his mouth and nose into her neck, inhaling deeply. She felt his chest expand against hers, his warm hands on her cold arms. She tried not to close her eyes.

He nuzzled her as he spoke. "You must stop listening to your little fears. Do you want to die? Do you want Alma to die? In the village I came from last, they burned no fewer than five girls."

Mia let out a breath.

"I can still save you," Bastion promised.

Her mind presented answer after answer, dozens of them in the space between two blinks of an eye. She should reject him and call on the name of the Lord. She should ignore her conscience and do whatever he asked to save Alma. She should scream for Alma to run. She did not realize her mouth moved as she sorted through all the choices, until he put a finger to her lips.

"This is what you will do. Admit nothing. Insist on your inno-cence. I will see to it that you are cleared."

"And Alma?"

"Alma, too." He sounded surprised, as if he had forgotten about her.

He went out the door and yelled at the men as a chilling breeze swept in. Bjorn appeared in the doorway, removing his belt, his hard and determined gaze making her shiver. The men talked quietly, but the cold wind brought the words to her ears. Hilda was dead. She had confessed nothing.

Bastion chastised the men, his back still turned. Bjorn took a step toward Mia. She flinched as she imagined the belt across her face. Still, she motioned for him to come nearer. She had to try to do the right thing, no matter who he was inside, no matter that he wouldn't do the right thing for her.

"I am no witch," she said as calmly as she could. "But I do know how to break the spell over you," she said, taking the bottle from her bag. "Bastion told me that only another witch can break a witch's spell. Hilda gave this to me when I begged for help for my husband. Drink this, and you will be completely free. It's the only way to be free."

Bjorn walked behind Mia, pulling her arms behind her back, using his belt to bind her wrists together. He ran one finger down the soft length of her forearm, then he took the vial from her hand.

Bastion returned. "Use my rope, Bjorn. It is easier to pull a woman along a path than to push."

Bastion walked to Mia, carrying a rope, and ran the rope once around her waist, moving in front of her as he tied it off.

The tears on her cheeks shamed her in front of Alma, who looked at her with fear and anger.

Bastion handed the rope to Bjorn.

"I shouldn't lead her. She is your wife."

ﻪﻠﻟ

Stefan could not get used to the smells inside the cell. Bjorn would not have washed them. Bjorn would want a criminal to suffer in every way, and once, Stefan would have agreed.

He hoped he would get used to it after the first hour, but two nights had passed. Every time he relieved himself it grew worse. He could hear very little weeping today. The women in the cells flanking him had worn themselves out. Without family to pay for food and drink, many now saw their third day of starvation. Stefan hoped the other women, those who had families unafraid to visit them, shared their drink and food. If they did not, women would begin dying before Bastion could burn them. Stefan wondered if they preferred that. He wondered where Bastion and Bjorn had been and when they would return. He did not want to speed that hour, but neither did he want to remain here.

"Pray for us, Father," a woman called to him.

Stefan could hear a guard fling the cell door open to another cell. He heard the crack of palm to face and the guard's voice. "Do not blaspheme. Not on my watch."

"My son," Stefan called. The guard appeared in the square window on the cell door.

"Perhaps you are thirsty?"

The guard frowned at the question.

"If I give you my keys, you will have complete access to my beer cellar."

"Getting me drunk so you can escape?"

"I am your priest. I answer to a higher authority than yours. Even if I could break down my cell door, I would go nowhere, for God has sent me to serve you and this village."

"You tried to hurt Bastion."

Stefan nodded with a forced grin. "Have you ever had too much beer and done something foolish? My son, take these keys and bring a good priest a drink, won't you? You know we are all well secured here. Nothing will happen."

Stefan handed the keys through the window to the guard. He heard the guard rattling each cell door as if to check for strong locks, then heard the main jail door open and close.

"Is everyone all right?" he called out.

No one answered.

"We are alone now. The guard is gone. Speak!"

"We cannot trust you," a girl called out. "Whatever we say will be twisted."

"No," Stefan called. "Am I not in jail like you? I can be trusted."

"You will not be burned," an older woman's voice said. "Nothing you say can save us."

"Why not let us die in peace?" another woman called. "It is too much work to convince you of our truths."

Stefan did not recognize their voices, though the women must have been from his flock. He wondered if he had ever really heard them.

"I have made many mistakes," Stefan said. "I will do everything I can to save you, but it may be too late. Just tell me, in what manner did Bastion accuse you? What is his proof?"

The first to speak was a woman Father Stefan knew well. Dame Alice. He closed his eyes in gratitude. Her voice was rough with no refinement. He had cringed often when she confessed to him, unaccustomed to a woman so devoid of interest in affectation.

"I was brought in for questioning just after I tried to save Nelsa. His proof? My back was sore."

"What's that?" he asked. "How did a sore back make you guilty of witchcraft?"

"Anything would have done. But Bastion is clever, I will admit to that."

"But how did he do it?"

"Mary, the dairyman's daughter, thought a witch had caused the milk to dry up on her prized cow. On advice of Bastion, she hung an empty kettle over the fire. When it was red hot, she began to beat it with a stick."

Mary's voice shot out from that same cell. "Bastion promised me that every blow would land on the witch's back." She sounded unrepentant.

"Bastion will see you dead too, Mary. You should realize that by now," Dame Alice replied. "Father Stefan, you know my back is often sore. My babies were the biggest in the village. That's no witchcraft."

"Mary," Father Stefan called, "why did you think a witch would have reason to curse your favorite cow?"

"Bastion spoke kindly to me, and I feared other girls might be jealous," she answered. "He would be a fine catch for me, seeing my father has no money."

"But why would Dame Alice care? She did not desire Bastion for herself."

"I don't trust her, Father Stefan, and neither should you. She's always sheltering strangers, trying to feed people who wander about. She has no discretion. She takes anyone in. It's not proper. She even admits to trying to save Nelsa, who proved herself a witch in front of everyone. I wasn't surprised when Dame Alice was revealed as a witch herself."

"But Bastion spoke kindly to me, too, and I am no witch." A soft voice carried across the jail. Stefan was unsure who it was. "Would you like to see what he did to me last night?"

Stefan heard gasps. "What is it?" he asked.

"Iris showed us her fingers."

"And?"

"They are burned. He laid a hot poker across them."

"Iris? Is it true?" he asked.

No answer came.

"What is happening?" he asked.

Dame Alice answered. "She fainted. Poor thing. Her father hoped to marry her off this year. He hoped Bastion might be agreeable. Perhaps Bastion didn't like his terms."

Stefan took a few moments before he could speak again. "Dame Alice? Finish your story. How did Bastion link you to Mary's cow?"

"One of their cows had wandered into the square again, and I brought it home to them. Bastion said it was proof that I was the witch. I had their cow, and my back was sore, as if the blows had landed on me."

"But how did Mary get arrested, then?" Stefan's head hurt. *How many lies did Bastion have to keep up with?* he wondered.

"Bastion said I tempted him. He blamed me for liberties he took."

"He wouldn't be the first."

Stefan didn't know who said that, but heard stifled giggles.

"What does he say will happen now?" Stefan asked.

Mary replied. "We are to be tried. If we are found guilty, we will be burned. Pray for us, Father."

"It doesn't seem enough," he said.

Dame Alice answered. "Do it anyway."

"But I am the one who brought him here. I brought this upon you."

Mary answered. "Did you not know, Father? Have you not heard the stories of the witch hunters, that in some towns there is not a woman left?"

"I thought you were not like those women. You would not be accused."

"Have you not heard, Father?" Dame Alice's voice mocked them both. "Women are stupid, lusty, insatiable, gullible, given to imaginations. We must be driven from the garden."

"I have taught this?"

"You have taught nothing in its place. That's what will kill us."

"What can I do now?"

His cell went white with light, a crack of thunder chasing it. Stefan jumped, his heart pinching in fear. Lightning killed shepherds and servants, anyone who worked lonely days in the orchards and fields. Stefan always told children not to fear it, feeling stupid even as he said it. Lightning was God's creation, but so was hell, so what comfort was that? Impotent words, always. The lightning showed him his cell, his squalor.

"You have made your choice." The voice came from inside his mind. *"Well done."*

Stefan clapped his hands over his ears, and lightning lit his cell, thunder making the walls shake. He gritted his teeth and pulled his hands down, forcing them to his side.

"Father," a woman's voice moaned close by.

"Who called me?" He could not tell if the voice was weak, or he could not hear it well.

"I am here."

A hand reached through the dirty straw on the cell floor at his feet. Lightning lit his cell, and he saw the woman struggle to rise. She was nothing but grime, her hair hanging in thick cords, looking like wax candles hung upside down to dry in the merchant square. Her face, stained with dirt, with stray pieces of straw clinging to it, had channels down her cheeks where tears had flowed. Dried blood crusted around her ears.

"How long have you been in this cell with me?"

"You were asleep last night when I was brought in."

"Have mercy," Stefan gasped. The words loosened his legs, and he went to her, helping her sit up. She flopped over, and he leaned her body into his, lowering himself to sit behind her, pulling her against him. "Do I know you?"

"I sold you hops," she whispered.

"Elizabeth?"

"Yes."

"Elizabeth, did Bastion hurt you? Did he put you in here?"

"No."

She was sixteen, a lovely girl who worked for a farmer's wife. She had no parents to provide for her, but she had done well for herself, finding a childless couple who needed the help and a young companion.

"Who put you in here, child?"

"He said you knew everything, that you would say this was my fault, that he was bewitched and could not be blamed."

"Bjorn did this to you?"

He tried to turn her around.

"No. No. I do not want you to look on me."

The jail door swung open, and he heard happy whistling.

"Excellent beer, Father. I will be enjoying some more tonight."

Stefan helped Elizabeth sit up against the wall.

"Did you bring any back?" he called out to the jailer.

"Not a drop."

"There are women in great need here. Bring them some of my beer, I beg you."

The jailer's face appeared in the small square window in the door.

"You know the law."

"Yes, but it's my beer. Surely I can offer it to these women."

"If they want something to eat or drink, their families must provide it. I'm not your errand boy, and I don't break the law."

"But there is a girl in this very cell who needs a drink, and one more in the next."

The jailer peered around Stefan.

"She doesn't need a drink now."

Stefan turned and saw Elizabeth face-first in the straw, her body slumped over, her arms behind her. She was unconscious. Stefan lifted his eyes to the wooden crossbeams of the ceiling as if to pray here in his squalor.

Outside, wind shook the building, and the night began to build in violence.

Chapter Twenty-two

Bjorn led Mia through the streets to the jail, through steam rising from the ground. The storm had passed by in the night here, too, punishing the town. Green buds littered the streets, torn from trees before they had the chance to bloom. She did not look up at the wounded, bare trees, or to the side to see what faces were in the windows, watching. She had never entered his jail before. She had always stayed clear from it, from Bjorn's work, wanting to be home with Alma, not wanting to know who was imprisoned or for what crimes.

She watched Bjorn's boots, still thick with mud and forest leaves. Bjorn had carried Alma for the last mile; it had driven his boots deeper into the sludge. He would be so angry. He hated muddy boots. Mia wondered what to do.

The door opened, and she felt the screech of its twisting hinges in her belly, the heavy wood swinging at her as if to strike her dead for her shame. He pulled on the rope, and she marched forward, struck by the smells inside. She could smell beer on the guard, standing close to Bjorn as he passed by, and she could also smell the salted metal of blood and urine. The jail was nothing more than a long, dirty hallway with horrid, dark cells on each side. Mia avoided

looking through the square opening cut into each wood door, afraid
to see what or who cried out from the darkness.

"I didn't know...." Mia said. She had thought Bjorn's work, the
work of justice, was a good and orderly affair.

Bjorn grunted. "You didn't want to know. Did you?" He untied
her hands and put his hand on her back.

Mia started to close her eyes before being pushed into the dark
hole before her. Then a new fear struck her. "Your mother! Who is
caring for her?" Mia asked.

"I sent her to another village with a sheriff I know. She is safe there."

He pushed her through the door into a dark cell. He pushed
Alma in after her and stepped back to lock the door.

"Bjorn. Look at me, please."

Mia clutched Alma to her chest, shrouded in darkness. Bjorn
stood in the door, light illuminating him, a frightening angel with
a black shadow across his face. He did not seem to be looking at
her, though she had called him. His head was bent low, as in prayer.
Perhaps his heart had softened at last.

"My boots are filthy." Bjorn used one foot to pull the other out
of one boot, kicking it across the floor, striking Mia in the shin. He
pulled off the other and flung it into the darkness. It landed near her.

"I've nothing to clean them with." She meant it as a request.

"The shame you've brought me? Visiting a witch? Gossiping about
me? Whispering about me to strangers? You should lick them clean."

"No. You're wrong. Drink the vial I gave you. Then you will
know I am a good wife."

Bjorn shut the door, leaving her in total darkness. She heard his
steps fading away.

Mia heard voices from other cells. They spoke as if she couldn't hear them, treating her like an enemy. No one was indifferent now, not after Bastion's kiss on the church steps. Mia was an enemy, even if she was jailed too.

"Mia is here. Bastion must have changed his mind again."

"What vial did she give him?"

"Where did she get it?"

"Who is there?" Mia called into the darkness. The voices softened into whispers so Mia would not hear.

"Mia? Is that you? Are you safe? Is Alma with you?" Father Stefan's voice rose above the whispers.

"Yes, Father Stefan. We are together. And we are safe."

Mia stroked Alma's hair as she spoke. Alma did not seem afraid, because Mia was always there in the darkness with her.

Her closed, scarred heart broke open as she understood the truth of what she had said. Mia gasped and hugged Alma tighter, mercy and grace exploding in her heart so hardened from fear. Mia saw her past, illuminated at last, the brittle wall around her heart shattering and falling away.

Sitting in the dirty cell, she had never been so free.

و

As the hours wore on, Mia had nothing to feed Alma and no relatives to supply their meals. Surely, though, Bastion would think of this, even if Bjorn did not. Surely Bastion wouldn't let Alma starve. He had made promises.

Mia could not be afraid, not for herself, not anymore. But Alma might still be frail. She needed food. Mia would wait. Someone would come, someone to help.

Hilda had not been brought here. Perhaps it had been better for Hilda that way. Perhaps her heart had given out, and no one had touched her. Mia hoped the men buried her. Most criminals were not buried. Their corpses were left out to be despised and abused.

She remembered that. She remembered how her father had hung from a beech tree until the birds came and picked him clean. She had stayed hidden in the streets, only coming out at night to steal, looking on his bones that fell, one by one, beneath the tree, watching as dogs carried them off, tails high and wagging.

It had all started, or ended, on a beautiful morning, cool air and burning sun. The miller's grindstone had just begun its low growl as it started to turn for the day. Chickens pecked at bugs in the dirt outside her father's shop. She had gone to fetch a remedy from the herbalist. Her father had been out drinking the night before, celebrating the completion of Tyndale's forbidden Bible. Her father did not often have time to get drunk, so when he did, he did not do it well. He had no experience in it. He had been lying in bed that morning, groaning when the light hit his eyes, ignoring the other jobs begging to be done at the press. The last chapter of *How to Be A Good Wife* was yet to be printed. Mia danced around the press, yelling for her father to wake up and get on with it.

Mia knew the shopkeeper—a friend of her father's—would have something to make him right again, so she took a few coins from their hiding spot and ran out the door. The shopkeeper began acting so odd when she came into his shop. His wife pursed her lips and poked him, prodding him to do something. Mia could not guess

what. Without a mother of her own, older women were a mystery
to her.

"Wouldn't you like to look around?" he asked. "Surely that is not
all you're buying. We have excellent remedies for gout."

"What gout? My father's quite well. He's just hungover—that
is all."

"Yes, I know."

His wife butted in. "We all know, Mia. Your father was not himself last night. He told many tales, to many people."

"What do you mean?"

The wife sighed a loud, laboring noise. Her husband tried again.

"Wouldn't you like something for yourself, too? Maybe a treat
for a good girl who serves her father so well? Have you tried these
almonds my wife makes? They're spiced and so filling. You wouldn't
even need to make a meal today. Come, I will fill a bag for you."

Mia's stomach had tingled as if she should be afraid.

The shopkeeper came round the counter, reaching for her with
an odd smile. Mia didn't think it was a good smile. It was a smile that
hid something.

She backed up as he edged closer to her. She moved nearer the
bottles of remedies left by the door. She knew the one her father
needed to cure his hangover.

In a blur, he lunged. Before he could catch her, she threw her
money on the floor, grabbing the violet-colored bottle she had spied,
running out the door. Her heart pounded as he chased her out into
the street.

"Do not go home, Mia!" he screamed after her. "I am trying to
help you!"

People everywhere stared, something new in their eyes. They looked at her with something awful, something like pity.

She ran without stopping, losing the man easily. He threw his hands in the air and shouted after her, but she kept running. She did not slow until she turned the corner on the dirt path that led past the ivy-covered walls to her father's shop and saw horse droppings on the path.

No one Mia knew rode a horse. Not to see her father anyway. His business involved too many rebels and revolutionaries, men who did not sit proud and obvious on a horse's perch, men who had to sneak and hide and look over their shoulder.

Her father screamed. She ducked behind the wall, watching as men dragged him out of the shop, beating him until he fell and did not move. Smoke billowed out from the door of the shop, black and greasy.

"Where's Tyndale?"

"He'd not be fool enough to hang round the place."

"Is it all burned?" a man called to someone, someone still inside her father's shop. The man emerged, his face covered in soot, marred by hatred.

"Not all of it," the man said, kicking her father. She screamed, making the men look in her direction. Mia dropped the bottle, the glass shattering around her feet, the dark fluid wasted on the cold stone. God in His great mercy made her legs fly into a run, even before she knew what to do. Mia tore down the street, threading her tiny body through narrow passages and jumping out to run down other lanes. She ran until she found another village, where she stayed for days, coming out only at night to look for garbage to eat, to listen at windows for bits of news about her father and Tyndale.

Those men had raided his print shop on orders from someone important back in England. They had burned the press and everything in the shop. They had hung Mia's doll in effigy as a joke, a warning to anyone who tried to scavenge through the wreckage. A black greasy hole stared at her where his shop had been.

Tyndale himself was never heard from again. Mia walked miles some nights to return to the shop's empty space, thinking he would return for her.

He didn't.

Tyndale became the most hunted man in the empire, in all of Europe. If caught, his fate would be unspeakable. People speculated on what tortures would be applied, which limbs would be torn, how slowly he would die. Mia understood why Tyndale didn't want her. He would never allow her to be in his company again, not in these burning days.

Mia determined she would keep her promise. She would wait, if not for him, then for the burning days to end. And when they ended, she would read the book that stole her father and her beloved friend away. She would enter the new world their lives had bought her passage into.

But today, sitting in this dark cell alone with Alma, Mia had found her way to freedom. The burning days would never end; she saw that now. As long as the book was read, people would die for it. She had been wrong to wait, wrong to think a safer time and place to stand for the truth would find her. Truth made the world unsafe. Truth spurred evil into action. There would be no end to evil, not in this world, not while the book was still open.

And yet Mia found this one thing more to be true: She had been wrong to be so afraid, afraid of the darkness in the world, and afraid of the truth as well. She had survived the darkness, and she had survived the truth. She had survived the worst moments when she wished to die and the worst moments when she feared Alma would die. She had survived because God was not just in the church; He was in the world and in His Word. She had lost sight of that, frightened by the way people had responded to His Word, unwilling to lose another family for its sake. But He had never punished her for her weakness. He had healed and saved at wild, unpredictable moments, but He was here, and He was at work. They were together with God, right there, Alma and Mia, and they were safe.

Mia sat upon the bench, shifting her weight to ease the pain in her bones. Alma curled up like a kitten in her lap, and Mia bent over to kiss her head. Whatever happened now, Mia knew that this unpredictable, patient God was at work. She would choose to focus on this one thought and trust Him once more.

Worn by the streets, she had met and married Bjorn not many years after that awful year her father died, grateful for a constant roof and bed. She had stumbled into this good fortune and taken up his offer of marriage without question. And when her stomach swelled and the timely pains came upon her, she knew she had done the right thing. Her father and Tyndale, they would want her life to go on. They would want her to be a good wife and have many children and someday to teach them from the Book. If Mia survived this cell, she would do that.

She remembered Alma's birth. She remembered lying in her bed, too weak to help, too filled with joy to even speak, watching a midwife rub Alma with salt and wine. Bjorn had come home drunk, elated.

Mia reached for his hand. "You do not mind it is a girl, then?"

"What? A girl? Well, have another." He slapped his leg. "I heard news today, Mia, great news. A man causing much trouble for sheriffs, stirring up people—he got burned in Brussels last week. That's the end of his work."

Prickly black stars appeared in the corners of her vision. She could not focus on his face. The room shrank. Bjorn celebrated, but not for her. Not for them.

"Forgive me, Mia. I forget you are a good wife who stays home and doesn't go wandering about the streets picking up gossip. That's why I wanted you, you know. I knew you would serve me well. The man's name was Tyndale, though he had tried to escape us by changing his name, always running from one city to another. Some say he came here—can you imagine? I'd have gutted him in the street. He came here, they say, looking for someone, though he would not say who."

Mia was devastated.

Bjorn never spoke again of Tyndale or of her days spent near death after Alma's birth. He had turned cold and watched her indifferently, the way one watches an old cow that's gone dry, wondering if the meat is wasted too. He would have sold her in the market if he could—she knew that much.

Mia never told him anything of her past. She kept her eyes straight ahead, focused on days to come. She would be a good wife.

That was how she would defend herself. When Bastion called her to stand before him as an accused witch, it wasn't her past that he would be judging. No one knew of it. She would insist that he judge her based on only one piece of evidence: Had she been a good wife to Bjorn? Had she not concerned herself, day and night, with being the wife all men taught as ideal?

That was the truth, and they would all see it. If they did not, if the truth did not save her, then Bastion would.

Chapter Twenty-three

Stefan tried to cry out as the hand forced against his mouth to silence him pressed harder. Another hand went around his ribs, dragging him out of the cell. His feet left troughs in the filth of the floor, and the jailer watched with amused interest. Outside the jail, Stefan saw the stars winking down on them all. He was flung to the ground and turned over on his back. Bjorn stood over him.

"What are you doing, Bjorn?"

"Let's go."

"Why? Where?"

"Where all good priests go."

Bjorn's boot came down on his ribs, then pinned him at the neck. "Get up."

"Your boot seems to be in the way."

Bjorn scraped his boot off Stefan's neck. Stefan stood, in small increments, waiting for the boot again. Bjorn stepped back, motioning for Stefan to lead the way into the church.

"Why? Why now?"

"I did as you said. I found Mia. At the home of a witch. She had not run away at all. And you thought I should save her. Do you understand what you almost did to me?"

By the faint light falling in the familiar path across the altar's edge, Stefan knew it to be about 3:00 a.m. No one else was there.

"What do you want me to do now, Bjorn?"

Bjorn sat on the first row bench. "Pray. Pray as if your life depended on it. Decide to join Bastion and me. Because we're right. I do not want any more mistakes made." Bjorn lifted his bag away from his belt, and Stefan saw the blade beneath it.

Stefan cleared his throat and knelt at the altar, his back to Bjorn. Years ago, the church fathers had moved the altar away from the people and turned it so the priest would work with his back to the people. If they'd had a parishioner like Bjorn, they would have been more cautious.

Stefan took a breath to begin a prayer, waiting for inspiration. He had no idea what to pray with a knife in the church and innocent women in the jail. Bjorn groaned behind him. Feeling a strong light piercing the darkness above, Stefan looked up and fell to his knees. A bright image of a man in blinding white robes—a vision from his imagination, surely—towered above them both.

Bjorn crouched down, shaking. The image grew brighter, and Stefan covered his face with his hands.

Wind blew past them, knocking over the candlesticks on the altar, and then the room fell into darkness.

The moonlight on the altar moved over the course of the night. Stefan watched it, dumbfounded by the hours, unable to use human language to describe what he had seen. Bjorn remained facedown for a long time too, and when he rose, he would not look at Stefan.

Stefan noticed the shadows had moved down the altar steps as dawn approached. "Bastion intends to try the women today," he said.

Bjorn nodded.

"Let them go, Bjorn. God is not happy with this work. Resign as sheriff and confess to the people. Send Bastion away."

"It's too much to believe in all at once. That all of this is my fault, not God's."

Stefan reached for Bjorn's shoulder, resting a hand on it. "That is a step toward true faith."

Bjorn stared at him, a lost, blank stare. Whatever hope those women had, it was not in Bjorn. Stefan had to end what he should never have begun.

"How could you not see Bjorn for who he was?"

The women were talking to Mia now. Why had she ever wished for that? Their words were painful.

"How could you not see me?" she could only reply. "I was lost. If you had befriended me, it could have changed everything. I did not know what had happened. I was caring for a sick child."

"If we had spoken to you, even hinted at what we knew, Bjorn would have hurt you. Or us, for telling you."

"Shut up," the jailer bawled at them. "You're a bunch of clucking hens. A man can't get any relief."

"Oh, I don't know. For a drink and a bite of bread, maybe he could." Mia recognized Dame Alice's voice.

One woman stifled a giggle, but the hysteria caught. All the women began giggling. The jailer cursed the day of his birth, which made the women laugh harder. A sigh swept through them before silence returned.

"Mia?" Dame Alice asked in the darkness.

"Yes?"

"Why would you never come in and eat with me? Why did you hate me so?"

"I never hated you!"

"You ran. You refused to hear my voice. You knew I called your name."

"I was afraid."

"Of me?"

Mia could not answer. The answer floated in the darkness above her, too big to put into words.

"I was afraid. But I am not afraid anymore. I am sorry."

"How many hours now?" someone asked. Mia could not tell who was in each cell around her; she could only judge the distance between them as near or far. She wondered if horses in a stable felt this disoriented.

She looked out her window into the hall, trying to judge by the light. "It's not quite noon, I'd guess. They'll be coming for us in a few hours."

"Do you think we'll die fast or slow?" someone asked.

"Do not give up hope," Mia said. "We don't know what might happen." Mia had courage to say this. She believed in miracles now, and in strange and wonderful timing.

"I know what will happen, They will torture you." The voice sounded like Mary, the girl from the village with the dry cow. "They'll tell you that the Devil puts a spell on his witches so they can't reveal his secrets. He erases their memory, makes them go mute. That's when Bastion takes a hot poker to your body, or tears out your fingernails, or pulls your shoulders out of their sockets. Innocence is the worst thing you can claim when you go before them. It's a trap."

Mia sat back on her bench next to Alma, covering Alma's ears.

She heard the jailer thanking someone. A hooded figure appeared at her jail window in profile. She could see nothing of the face, just shadows where the robe fell forward. Alma began to squirm in her arms, and she pressed her face into Mia's stomach.

Mia's jail door opened, its hinges grinding, giving Mia a cold shudder. Bastion pushed the robe off his face and came to sit next to her.

He put one hand on her neck and pulled her ear to his mouth.

"When you stand before me, say nothing, and I will save you," he whispered.

Mia tried to say something, but he pressed a hand against her mouth.

"Do not try to thank me. It would give us away."

She shook her head. He eased the pressure against her mouth, and she whispered. "Do you have any food? For Alma?"

Bastion released her, pushing back and standing as if he had never seen the child before, a shocked look on his face. He began patting the bag on his belt, bringing up a nibbled rind from a bit of cured pork. Alma turned her back to him, refusing it.

Mia took the rind and forced it to Alma's lips. "You will eat this, Alma."

The jailer appeared in the square window, tapping his keys on the door. Bastion threw the hood back over his face.

Mia used her sternest voice. "I said to eat this, Alma. Keep your strength. We do not know what will come. To starve is to die."

"I know what will come," Bastion whispered before he stood to leave. "Remain silent. I will save you."

⸙

If deception had damned them, just as it had Eve, Stefan knew the one true cure. He led Bjorn to kneel at the altar, telling him it would be wise to pray for wisdom and strength. If Bjorn prayed for anything other than his own desires, Stefan could not guess. But it gave him time to slip to the cupboard where the Bible was kept. He had no time for anyone to teach or interpret.

"I cannot wait for help to arrive, Lord," he whispered, bringing the book out and laying it across the top of the cupboard. A wind blew through the hall, flipping the pages of the Bible, and Stefan turned, expecting to see the mother cat, come round to beg for food. The door leading outside was still closed. Stefan turned, slower this time, back to the Bible. It was open to the book of John. Jesus was speaking:

> I am come that they might have life and have it more abundantly. I am the good shepherd. The good shepherd giveth his life for the sheep. A hired servant sees the wolfe coming and leaveth the sheep. The wolfe catches them. The hired servant runs because he is a hired servant and careth not for the sheep.

Stefan served as a priest, but he had chosen; he was no hired servant. He would be a shepherd. He would not leave his sheep, not while a wolf was here. Whatever happened, Stefan would never leave them.

Bjorn was done praying. He called for Stefan. Stefan left the book open and out. He would not hide it again.

Bastion's face registered shock when he saw Stefan and Bjorn sitting on the church steps in the morning sun. Stefan held his breath, waiting to see what Bjorn would do.

"Are you joining us, Stefan?" Bastion asked, watching Bjorn. "Did Bjorn finally win you over?"

Stefan could not stay close to the women, but he could stay close to Bastion, which might prove of greater benefit to them. "Yes. I am looking forward to today. That may sound strange. But it was a strange night."

People began approaching from the square, most walking straight to Bjorn or Bastion with beaming faces.

"Not a one of my hens' eggs have broken since Dame Alice's arrest," one said.

"My stomach hasn't gone sour in days. Praise be to God for your good work here, Bjorn."

Stefan watched the two men receive the praise, his own stomach taking on an infirmity. More people came into the square, craning their necks to get a view of the condemned women waiting for their trial. Ava sat in her cage, watching the other women with a look of great envy.

Bastion took Stefan by the elbow, surprising him. "So there will be no trouble out of you today?"

Stefan tried to catch Bjorn's eye before answering. "Not from me. I won't even say a word."

"As priest, you will, actually. If the women are found guilty of witchcraft, you must concur with death by burning. A formality, but it must be indulged."

"I will not fail to do my duty today." Stefan rested his arm on Bastion's, as if to confirm his resolve.

"It is good for a man to love his work. Isn't that what the Bible says?"

Stefan shook his head. "I don't know. I don't know it as I should."

"But you preach from it. You demand the people build their lives around it. And you don't know everything it says?"

"I preach what I was taught. I'm afraid I'm not a very good priest."

"You're a fine priest. You're just an odd man. I gave you the chance to win their hearts," Bastion said, gesturing to the crowd, "to be their savior, and you rejected it."

"There is still time."

Bastion's face brightened at that thought. "Yes, Stefan, there is still time. Come and join me, won't you?"

He led Stefan up through the crowd to the chairs set at the top of the church steps.

There was time indeed for a savior.

Chapter Twenty-four

The women had been led out to stand below the church steps. Mia stood just below the spot where Catarina and Cronwall's bodies had been dumped. The women said it had been Bjorn's doing, but she still could not believe that, not with her whole heart. She had lived with him, and, while she knew he hid secrets, she never suspected he could hide something quite so terrible. Could anyone really be so depraved and yet appear so normal? Didn't all devils look frightening?

Mia searched the faces of the gathering crowd. She saw some of the men of the village and a few of the women brave enough to leave their homes, but mostly she saw strangers. Word must be spreading about the so-called witches of Dinfoil. A man she did not know pointed her out to his wife. Mia wondered what her reputation would become if she did not live—the witch who was married to the sheriff. She decided to ignore the crowd as she kissed Alma, willing herself to soak in every bit of her child, the softness of her cheek, the rough edges of her dress, her nose a tiny, perfect version of her own.

"You are beautiful, Alma," she whispered. "I see God in your face. It is a fallen world, Alma. But you have been God's grace to me, my reason for believing that good was still possible. Pray hard,

Alma. Pray for God to save you once more. Pray He will grant you one more miracle. He alone healed you, Alma, I believe that now. While everyone chased devils, while I slept and dreamed of these strange days, God walked right into our home and healed you. Do you understand? He didn't need me to be perfect. He doesn't want our perfection, Alma. He just wants our hearts."

Alma reached up her hands and touched Mia's face. Mia closed her eyes. She would remember Alma's soft touch. She would think of that no matter what happened.

Mia handed Alma to Erick, who stood behind the condemned women. She met his eyes and tried to communicate the worth of her little girl. But Erick nodded, solemn. He understood.

"Who shall be tried first?" Bastion called out.

"I will." Mia nodded at the three men seated above the church steps just in front of the doors: Stefan, Bastion, and Bjorn. Bastion shook his head at her, his back straight in his tall, unforgiving chair. No one sat in a trial except the judges, and they sat in high, stiff chairs, a sign to those not wise enough to attain such a position.

"We are not ready to hear your case. The court would like to begin with another woman. Bring us Dame Alice."

Murmurs rippled through the crowd, but Mia took another step forward. "No. Try me first, or do not try me at all."

She saw the anger on Bastion's face. Some would think him ready to burn her right there for her sins.

"Mia, step back. I could have you flogged."

"Then flog me, but I will speak. This court accuses me of witchcraft. I stand before you to proclaim there is no power in me, save the power of God's love. I have not the power to cast spells or make charms by magical means. But the power within me is far greater. I have the power to love the unlovable, to endure scorn and disdain, to abide hunger and loneliness." Mia looked directly at Bastion. She wanted him to understand. She was not powerless. She did not need him, even if she was unloved.

Mia realized she had never heard a woman speak in public to a crowd. Her knees turned soft from her boldness as she continued, facing the people. "Does a witch love? Does a witch tend the elderly and wipe the brow of the infirm? Does a witch bear beatings and scoldings and return for them love and good service? I tell you, that is who I am, and that I what I have done.

"The women of this village say I blinded myself to my husband's evil. Bjorn is accused of terrible things. If this be true, I cannot say. I only know what he has told me. I was wrong to not look deeper, to be so afraid of darkness that I had to pretend it was not there. The darkness in us, the darkness around us, is real. But we are not alone in it. I wish I had believed that much earlier. I wish I had never doubted that the power of love is far greater. I read it once, long ago, but I did not believe it for many years. Only now, when I may lose everything, have I come to embrace that as truth."

"An eloquent defense," Bastion said, his fingers digging into the arms of his chair. "The court will set your case aside until we can consider it in depth."

"We should hear from her husband," Stefan said, gesturing for Bjorn to speak.

"Move on from this case," Bastion said. "Bjorn is not on trial."

Mia watched as a look passed between Stefan and Bjorn.

"Stefan is right," Bjorn said. "My wife is accused. I should speak."

A round of applause broke out as Bjorn stepped down from his chair, walking down two steps to speak with the people. Stefan frowned, lifting his hands for the people to quiet. Mia watched Bjorn searching the faces in the crowd as if for an answer. He looked white, all the blood drained from his face.

"We are proud of you, Bjorn," someone called. "You are the reason we sleep in peace now."

"I did not want an Inquisitor brought to our village," Bjorn said. "But much has changed."

At his words, the crowd fell silent. Stefan lowered his hands. Mia kept her eyes from meeting Bastion's.

"Mia," Bjorn addressed her. He pulled the green vial from his belt bag.

Mia had forgotten that vial. So much had happened, so fast. "No! Bjorn, do not drink it! It can't save you. If you are bewitched, it is by nothing more than evil, the same evil that whispers to us all. And its curse has already been broken."

Bjorn looked like he had been slapped. He must have been stunned by Mia's boldness. He looked at the women standing with Mia, the faces of his victims and the women who knew his secrets. Mia had thought he would be relieved to know he was no different than any other man, but he looked stricken.

"I have struggled to know who and what to believe," he said to the crowd. "I did not want an Inquisitor because I thought my own secrets would be discovered. But Bastion arrived and told me my sins were not my fault. Now my wife, even my priest, says Bastion is wrong. Who can a man believe?"

The crowd murmured and nudged each other.

His expression changed suddenly, as if someone had just whispered in his ear, and Mia recognized the set jaw and cold gaze that came into his eyes. He had made a decision. He pulled the vial and tipped his head back, drinking the contents. He grimaced as he wiped his mouth on his sleeve, then continued.

"My wife was discovered at the home of a known witch. I believe that because I discovered her there myself, where she gave me this vial. It is a witch's counterspell. She said it would set me free from all the evils I have suffered. She urged me to drink it. Now, standing as a condemned woman before you, she begs me not to drink it. Why? Because she hates me. She knows now what I did. She wants me to suffer, just as she surely will. But I have chosen what and whom to believe." At this, he turned and nodded to Bastion. "I will live a good long life, and many will hear of me. Everyone will know my story."

Mia hung her head, shaking it with her eyes closed. She had been a fool to trust in Hilda, even for a moment. Charms and potions had no saving power against this madness. The old wound ached in her heart. Bjorn would not be saved, and he would know that she had failed him. Again.

People began gasping, murmuring all at once. Mia opened her eyes. Bjorn had fallen to his knees, clutching his stomach. He began retching, eyes opened wide, his face in a tight grimace.

"Mia?" he screamed, trying to crawl to her. "What did you give me?"

Mia scrambled back, afraid to touch him, but someone in the crowd caught her, forcing her to face Bjorn, who fell onto his back, writhing, his face turning green.

He looked up at her. "You said I would be free."

He arched his back one more time then collapsed, lying still. Mia could not see his chest rise or fall.

Hilda's words pierced her heart: *It is the only way to set him free from his evil.*

Bastion jumped to his feet, his mouth opening and closing in his shock. Stefan ran to Mia, pushing her back from the crowd. "Get away from here, now."

"Witch!" someone screamed.

"No. You did not understand what Bjorn was saying." Stefan cried, trying to push Mia and face the crowd, too. "He wanted to confess."

"Witch! Burn her!"

"Mia!" Stefan screamed to her. "Run!"

But the villagers caught her, pinching and hitting. She tried to hold her breath after they began spitting in her face. She was shoved at Bastion's feet, the crowd in chaos. Bastion grabbed her by the hair and pulled her up, turning her to face the crowd, his breath on her neck like a burst of steam.

"Look at them, Mia. Look in their faces. They want you dead. There is no future for you here."

Mia could not see Alma in the crowd.

"Friends and good Christians, patience." Bastion called. "You do not know the law. We cannot burn Mia. Not yet."

"I'm offering you a chance to live," he whispered in her ear. "I'll give them my witch Ava to burn. I'll put a sack over her head and tie it at the neck. No one will know it is not you. Come with me and live."

"Make her die in my place? Crawl inside her cage?"

"It is the only way out."

Mia searched the crowd again for Alma. She couldn't see Erick, either.

"I forgive you for disobeying me, Mia. We can still be happy."

Mia looked down at the angry, spitting crowd, her body starting to bleed from her wounds, her scalp burning as Bastion held her. She turned her head, wincing, to face Bastion. "I have lived my whole life in a cage. The bars were my own, made by my own hands from my fears, and all the lies in the world held it together. But I have been made free. I will never be caged again."

"You will die."

"But I will die free."

Bastion pushed her, and she tumbled down several steps, trying to catch herself.

"What says the law?" someone yelled. "Why can we not burn her right now?"

"A woman cannot burn until she has confessed," Bastion said. "Do you want Mia to confess? Shall we know all her secrets?"

Someone hit her on the back of the knees, and Mia fell to the ground.

Bastion glared down at her. "We will break her. We will get what we want."

A hand shoved bread at her mouth. Mia spit at it as she came to, accidentally spitting on Dame Alice's face. Her mind cleared, and she tried to sit up, reaching for Dame Alice, apologizing.

"'Tis all right, Mia. I shouldn't have tried to feed you so soon. But you asked for bread."

"Alma? Where is she?"

"I cannot tell you."

"Please."

"You didn't confess. Bastion will put you to the question again in a few hours. 'Tis better if you do not know about Alma."

Mia tried to press one hand down against the wooden bench she sat on to make the room stop spinning. She tried to move forward but her hand was limp. Pain screamed through her shoulder.

"Why can't I move my arms?"

Dame Alice stroked her cheek. "Bastion tied them behind your back and lifted you off the ground by them. He did this three times, making all of us watch. Still, you confessed to nothing."

Mia lowered her eyes to look at her shoulder, swelling underneath her shirt.

"Whose clothes?"

"Mine," Dame Alice whispered. "I won't get cold in here like you. You've always been too thin."

Mia tried to focus on her. Dame Alice looked like she had tied herself up in rags.

"Alma?" Mia asked again.

Dame Alice stroked her cheek. "I cannot tell you. Not if you love her. You might confess, if the pain becomes too great."

"Please. I won't survive this. Tell me."

"I will tell you this and no more: I have not seen Alma since the crowd stripped and beat you and the interrogation began. But neither have I seen Erick."

Mia groaned. She knew Dame Alice was right. "I killed Bjorn, didn't I? Hilda tricked me."

"Then why did you go into the forest? Didn't you know there were witches about?"

The jailer's voice cut her off. How he must have enjoyed eavesdropping on these women. "But I forget, you are one, aren't you?"

"Leave her alone," Dame Alice called back. "She did what none of us had the nerve to do."

"I didn't mean to kill him."

"Don't tell us that. We're just starting to like you," Dame Alice said.

"She said it would set Bjorn free."

"It did," Dame Alice said. "In its own way."

"But I'm going to burn for it! There is no one now who can prove my innocence."

"There is no way to prove your innocence," Dame Alice told her.

"But why? Why will truth not be accepted?"

"My dear, we'll all be dead in a few hours," Dame Alice said. "It makes no sense to worry about it now." She put her arms around Mia. "I do not want to die with a stranger. Tell us your story, Mia."

"No. I am ashamed."

"Why?"

"You have been so kind to me. I hated it when you called my name in the market. It was not because I did not want to know you. I did not want you to know me."

"Well, that is all in the past now. There is still time."

"Time for what?"

"Time to love each other," Dame Alice said. "Tell me, Mia, of your story. Tell us all who you are."

Mia closed her eyes for strength, exhaling. She was free to tell her story. The burning days were not over, but Mia would not burn for reading the Bible. If she died, it was because more people had not read it, and lies passed as truth so easily. Mia wanted Dame Alice, and all these women, to know where the truth could be found. If she would die, she would die telling anyone who listened about the only source of truth and the only hope for this age.

Chapter Twenty-five

Stefan directed the boys dragging two wooden stakes to the church steps. The largest and heaviest of stakes went in the ground first. It took three boys to lift it into place. When it stood, Stefan regarded it. The structure looked incomplete.

He rubbed his eyes, clearing the dust. He hadn't slept at all last night.

With the uproar over Bjorn, Bastion had suggested it best to dispatch Mia the next day. He said Mia needed one more night to consider her crimes and repent. He had not asked where Alma was. He seemed to have no interest in the little one. Not that it mattered now.

Stefan looked over his stretching shadow. Morning sped along too fast. He had much to do. He walked through the square, empty except for a stray rooster pecking about. Even the dogs were not at the windows this morning, pushed aside by their masters. Stefan saw faces, human faces, popping up and then withdrawing, spying on the two stakes set in front of the church steps.

Stefan stepped into the baker's shop, buying honey syrup. It would do fine. He would return home and mix it with the preparation from his own garden. Stefan rarely had a chance to make this recipe. Rarely had he need, except when some white-haired old man needed a broken leg set, or a frightened child needed a rotted tooth out.

Bastion was sitting on the steps, watching the boys work, when Stefan returned. Ava's cage was covered. At the sight of it, Stefan patted the bag hanging from his belt, as if to remind himself what he must do.

Bastion sighed, frowning at the stakes.

Stefan sat beside him. "Mia did not confess, I heard. Is this what is troubling you?"

"Mia is troubling me, yes."

"Tell me something, Bastion. When did you first understand what you were to do with your life?"

Bastion looked in the distance. "I was a child."

"Go on. It's a good day for stories. Let's sit and have a drink while the boys work." Stefan offered him a flask. Bastion eyed it, then stared at Stefan, who smiled.

"Come, Bastion. I would like peace."

Bastion sat on the steps and reached for the flask. He took a long draught and wiped his mouth. He shook his head before starting. "I was a child. Maybe seven or eight. I thought my mother a good woman. She could be very industrious. She fed me sweets all the time, little raisins soaked in honey or wine. She'd give me a pile of sweets and then leave me for an hour or so. Oh, I'd stuff myself. But she did not dote on my father that way. We both knew he did not love her. I didn't even think he saw her. He traveled often. When he returned, he ate and slept. Then left again. One morning I woke up, alone in the house, except for him. He had been away. He must have returned in the night while I slept. He asked me where my mother was. I had not realized she was gone. I did not know what women did."

Bastion's voice faded.

"And then?" Stefan prodded him.

Bastion shrugged. "I told him. There was a neighbor she often visited. I pointed toward the man's house, and my father left me. A few minutes later, the neighbor came stumbling out of his house, blood spurting from his throat. He had been sliced clean. I never saw my mother again. I am grateful my father spared me that sorrow. He must have killed her."

Stefan sat, silent. There was nothing he could say.

"That is when I knew how I would live, although years passed before I knew there was a name for this work. I wanted to save women from their sin. Women must not repeat her mistake." He sat quiet for a moment, thoughtful. "But perhaps I am getting too old for this," he finally continued, "or growing careless in my work. It seems that some women cannot be saved. But I must not trouble myself. There are other towns that need me. I will go to a new town after this."

"Yes. Once a man sees what must be done, he should think of nothing else."

Bastion took another swig and grinned, casting off the memories. "I've never known a priest like you. *Inconstant* is the word I would use. I cannot predict a word you will say."

Bastion yawned. He had not slept last night either. Stefan had heard him, sitting against the wall instead of lying in his bed, banging his head against it. Whatever Bastion wanted here, it eluded Stefan. Stefan decided not to dwell on it. It would not matter soon.

"Come with me inside, Bastion. You should rest."

Bastion spit on the ground. "I don't want to sleep. I want to watch these boys work. I want Mia to see these stakes and consider what she has done." Bastion drained the last of the flask and stifled another yawn again.

"You were up all night. I heard you."

Bastion looked away, so Stefan pressed further. "I'll not doubt you again about your work. Only recently have I begun to understand mine. But you should lie down in the dormitory. The day ahead of us is a long one."

Bastion needed help standing. Stefan led him to the dormitory, feeling Bastion become heavier with every step, leaning against Stefan. He began murmuring like a child, speaking about strange things like his generous nature and women's inconstant temperaments. Stefan deposited him onto a bed, lifting his legs onto the straw mattress, resting his arms at his sides.

He leaned down and called Bastion's name but heard no reply. Stefan slapped Bastion, hard. He did not move. The flask had done its job.

Stefan reached into Bastion's bag and removed a key, placing it in his own bag.

"Good-bye, Bastion."

Ava pried his fingers off the lock, then bent her head down and tried to bite them.

"Stop!" Stefan said.

"What are you doing? I'm going to die today. Bastion promised."

"You don't want to die."

"Yes, I do."

"You want your son back. Dying won't do it. Dying is no assurance you'll see him again in heaven, either."

Stefan swung the cage door open. Ava pushed herself against the back bars of the cage, cowering.

"Don't do this to me, Father Stefan. You don't have a child. You don't understand."

"I am beginning to understand, Ava. That is why I cannot leave you caged."

"No, please, I would die a thousand deaths for my son. Please don't stop me."

"Only one death was ever needed. And it is not yours." Stefan's heart ached for her. He had learned so much about God since reading from the Bible, but there was no time to tell her of everything. He said a silent prayer that wherever she went next, someone in that village would have a Bible. And read it.

He stepped back away from the open door. "I should have done this a long time ago. Come out of there, Ava." He extended his hand. "If God intended for you to suffer for your sins, why did He send His own Son to die for them? You must never again punish yourself. That is the only blasphemy you are guilty of, not witchcraft. This punishment, the condemnation you have heaped on your own head, these are the true blasphemies. Jesus died, and your sins are no more.

You are beloved. Take your freedom, Ava, today. Do not wait. You are beloved."

"You're wrong!"

"I cannot force freedom on you. And you are still His beloved, even if you remain in this cage. Because you are forgiven, only you should have this." He held out the key to the cage door. "I want you to come inside the church."

Ava stared in horror at it, transfixed. She did not move. Stefan threw it inside the cage, getting it close to her feet.

"Good-bye, Ava. I cannot express how you have helped me. You were presented to me as a witch, but I saw a woman. I thank God for that." He could think of nothing else to say and grinned at the irony of words failing him now. They had failed from the moment he took the priesthood, and this was as it should have been. He had learned so late the ways of the Shepherd. If only he had read the Book so much sooner.

As he walked away, he heard the slam of metal on metal and glanced back. Ava had pulled the cage door closed, crouching down in it, glaring at him. He bit his lip and kept walking. He hoped that the next time he opened the door for a prisoner, there would be less resistance.

Chapter Twenty-six

"Father."

Mia heard the jailer greet Father Stefan, his chair scratching against the polished wood floor as he did.

"Would you do a priest a kindness?" Stefan asked.

"Yes, of course," the jailer replied. "You made quite a sight sitting up there with Bastion. I rejoiced to see you join our cause."

"Yes, well, there are more changes to come. Now, for my favor?"

"Anything."

"Leave."

"What?"

"You can return tomorrow. I haven't thought through all the details of what will happen after the burning, but that should be right."

"I don't understand, Father. The burnings are in a few hours. I can't leave the witches here without guard."

"Please, son."

"I can't just—"

Mia heard a wet snap and a loud collapse, then Stefan's voice. "Well. Throwing a punch is as easy as it looks."

Father Stefan stood at Mia's cell a moment later, peering in at her. He twisted and slid the lock across itself, pulling the door open.

Mia sat, unable to move. Dame Alice didn't rise either.

"Are you able to walk?" he asked them.

Both women nodded.

"Good."

"Where is Alma?" Mia said.

"Erick has her hidden. She will be safe with him."

Stefan dragged the jailer into Mia's cell. He deposited the man on the filthy floor. The jail was silent except for Stefan's movements.

"He'll wake within the hour, I think," Stefan said, loud enough so all the jailed women could hear him. "It would be better if you were gone when he came to."

Dame Alice stood, lifting Mia up, helping her to the door.

Stefan followed and locked it behind them. The women were in the corridor of the jail, all out of their cells, confused and anxious. Stefan counted eight women.

"My friends," he said. He began to speak but broke off. There was no other sound. Mia looked at all their filthy faces streaked with blood and dirt. She could tell them apart more by the skirts they wore than their faces.

Stefan coughed to free the words. "The church. It's your best hope. The law cannot touch you once you are inside. When I open the door to the jail, those of you who can run, do. If you can help one another, do that. But we must be fast. I cannot protect you if you are not in the church. Are you ready?"

"But where is Bastion?" Dame Alice asked. "He will stop us if he can."

The women glanced at each other, nodding.

"He is asleep in the dormitory, and for a long time. Once you are inside the church, he can do nothing to you."

Mia's face looked pale and drawn; she would be too weak to get across to the church in her own power. Dame Alice did not appear much better. Stefan walked to Mia, his arms extended. Dame Alice began releasing her grip on Mia. Mia's chin began trembling as Father Stefan wrapped one arm around her shoulders and one around the back of her knees, carrying her like a child.

Stefan nodded at Dame Alice and took a deep breath.

"Open the doors."

The women and Stefan ran from the jail, startling people in the square. Shock froze their faces. Not one of them would move in time to stop them. His legs pounded the earth, making the world shake in his vision as he ran with Mia in his arms.

Stefan could see Erick move to the doors from the window where he had been standing as soon as he saw Stefan and the women running. He threw the doors open. They made it to the steps before the townspeople could get their bearings and attempt to detain the group. Stefan was last to enter the church. He stumbled across the threshold, collapsing onto the floor near Mia. Erick slammed the doors on the approaching crowd. Stefan had seen how the men were furious. They gnashed their teeth and called down curses.

Stefan scanned the women, counting quickly. They had all made it, every last one. He looked up at Erick and began laughing as tears welled up in his eyes. Mia reached up for Stefan's face, turning him to look at her.

"Why are you so happy?"

Stefan smiled, peace flooding through his soul faster than the adrenaline could drown it. He exhaled and softened his grip on her.

"This is a sanctuary, Mia. Once inside the church, the law has no more power over you. You are safe from condemnation. You will not die."

The women looked at each other, reaching for each other's hands, embracing, weeping. Erick bowed his head in prayer, and Stefan gave thanks as he sighed, trying to catch his breath.

Stefan waited for Erick to lift his head before speaking.

"There is a story. I found it in a book." Stefan smirked, catching himself still afraid to admit that one secret. "I have a Bible. One of the forbidden ones. A Tyndale."

"You never told me," Erick said.

"A man left it here, long ago. I never found out his name."

Stefan saw Mia trying to sit up and listen.

"There is a story about a grain of wheat, a seed of what could become a harvest, food for many hungry people. But it was only a seed when our story opens. The seed must choose between life and death. Is it better to remain whole and avoid death? Or is it better to allow the farmer to cast it to the ground, to force it under the earth, where it will be subject to heat, and flood, and the pain of its hard outer shell splitting?"

Erick frowned. "The answer depends on who is listening to the story. If someone is hungry, they want a harvest."

Stefan nodded and wiped his brow. Although the room was cold, heat was creeping up from his chest, making his cheeks burn. "And the seed has no reason to desire its own death. Unless it desires a harvest that others will eat more than its own life."

Erick shook his head. "I do not understand."

"Neither did I. You will, in time. But run now, and bring Alma to Mia. We still have work to do."

Erick brought Alma from the cellar, where he had hidden her. Alma ran for her mother at once, kissing her face and stroking her hair while Mia tried to hold back her sobs.

Stefan could not watch without tearing up himself, and he needed a clear mind. Looking at the plain window of the church, he saw the gray sky pressed down in a long, single layer over the last of the afternoon's white clouds, streaming pink rays to the earth below. Stefan looked out the window from inside the church, grateful now he had never had the prestige and money to afford stained glass treatments for every window. He only had one stained glass window, and he had not been thankful for even that back then.

He wondered what color the sky had been in Gethsemane, what Jesus thought as He looked up. Jesus knew what hid behind the dull, gray clouds of earth. Jesus knew the splendor of a raging sun. Stefan wondered if that made Gethsemane harder, or easier, to bear.

He returned to caring for the women. Erick stayed near his side, diligent in his attentions, not minding the stains that smeared across his clothes, the sweat that rose along his hairline as he lifted the weak to help them drink. Stefan realized then that Erick had always known the Shepherd's secret. He watched as Erick continued, carrying water for washing faces, fetching vinegar for the wounds. He tore apart his linen belt, using it to hold up Mary's arm, which looked broken.

His tenderness surprised Stefan. He had never taught him that, never done that himself. But he was grateful. Erick had been listening for God all those long years while Stefan slept. Erick had grown into more than a man. He had become a shepherd. The thought brought Stefan another outpouring of peace.

Mia nuzzled Alma with her cheek, clearly thankful Erick had washed her face. She still couldn't move her arms. Alma looked up at Stefan, a curious expression on her face. She did not look afraid, though her mother was in pain and had been abused, though angry villagers waited outside the church. Alma just smiled at the image of Jesus in a painting hanging from a wall near the altar. Alma looked at it as if it was a holy relic, a shy awe on her little face.

"The women are hungry," Erick told him. "What should we feed them?"

"Give them what we have with us. Do not go to the dormitory for fresh supplies. Do not leave them again."

"We have nothing left, save the bread and wine for the Sacrament."

"There must be something else. Check in the cupboards."

"Already did."

"Ah, Lord," Stefan muttered. "I had hoped you would make this easier on me." He could preserve his proper office or give life.

He motioned to the altar. "Fetch the Host and wine. We will give them the Sacrament."

Stefan fetched a clean white linen and laid it across the altar, waiting for Erick to bring the bread. He opened the wine, inhaling the aroma of earth and grapes and sun.

The women smelled the bread as it went past, reaching for it, groaning in pangs of hunger. Stefan watched Erick pick his way through the women, gently removing the grasping fingers that caught him by his shirt hem.

"Almighty God," Stefan began, "the body of Christ, broken for our sins."

He motioned for Erick to begin tearing the bread. There was not enough to feed these starving women. Stefan had counted eight when he left the jail, and until their faces had been washed, he had struggled to remember each as she truly was. Now with the others, he saw they were all his women, the women who had sat through many Masses and sermons and lectures, the women who probably knew his words by heart and had profited none.

"Divide it between them," he whispered. "The body of our Lord Jesus Christ, given for thee," he said for the women to hear.

Erick began circulating the bread among the women, trying to hold his legs steady as they reached for bread. Dame Alice took a larger share but dumped it in her lap and began feeding it to Mia. Mia only took one bite, turning her head to resist more.

"Feed Alma first," she whispered.

Stefan knelt in front of her. "Alma has been well fed by Erick. Do not worry any longer about her. It is time for you to regain your strength." He took a piece of bread from Dame Alice's hand and pressed it to Mia's mouth. She did not raise her eyes to look at him, so he stroked her cheek with the back of his hand as he spoke. She looked exhausted, and he worried she had no more strength to eat.

"Eat, Mia."

He fed her, then stroked Dame Alice's arm before he stood to attend to the others.

All the other women ate with ferocity. They kept reaching for more, making the panic rise in Stefan's belly. He had nothing else to feed them. With nothing else to do, he moved on to the cup.

"The blood of our Lord Jesus Christ, shed for thee."

Erick offered the cup to each woman, running back to Stefan for it to be refilled. Stefan prayed the wine would hold out. The women gulped, wine running down their chins, drinking and gasping for air, not enough wine in the world to satisfy their thirst. Erick ran back one last time to have the cup refilled, and Stefan obliged.

Stefan heard people gathering outside for the burning. Stefan looked down at his altar, crumbs of bread and drops of wine making it an improper mess. He once would have been ashamed to let the bishop see his altar like this. He looked out at the women, who were rubbing their stomachs in awe, having been filled beyond measure after their great hunger. Stefan looked down at the mess and understood.

It was enough. God had always been enough to satisfy all their hungers and all their questions. He had been enough, even when prayers seemed unanswered and lies grew in power.

He nodded, chuckling in reply. Little arms wrapped around his legs. He bent down and hugged Alma back as she kissed his cheek.

"I must do something for you now," he told her. "Whatever happens, take good care of your mother for me."

Alma stood, walking to the picture of Jesus, her upraised face illuminated in the flickering torchlight. She looked as if she belonged to another world. Love radiated from her face as she took in the image of her Lord.

Stefan smiled as he watched her, washing his hands and face in the water bowl behind him, straightening his robe. He took off his belt and bag and laid them on the steps beneath the altar. More torchlights floated into view, fuzzy yellow orbs illuminating the windows. The crowd outside grew.

He went to Erick's side, whispering in his ear so none of the women would hear. "I am going out there. Lock the door behind me. Let no one in until it is over. Do you understand?"

"You can't go out there."

"Do not unlock the doors until it is safe. No matter what happens. Do you understand?"

"Burn the witches!" came a cry. "Let the burnings begin with Mia and her cursed child!"

The women inside did not move. Stefan watched their terrified faces, like foxes caught in a trap at the sound of a hunter's footfall. He could not make them understand, not with their fear. He did not even try to speak. He walked to the church doors and threw them open to wild cheers from the people, the crowd of a size he would expect for an Easter Mass. They were hungry, their lean faces menacing in the torchlight.

"Come on, then," someone called.

Stefan walked down two steps, holding his palms out, motioning for patience. He heard the doors slam behind him, the heavy bolts sliding into place. *Good boy.*

"Do you want a death?" he called, and they answered with screams of encouragement. "Do you want curses broken? Debts settled? Justice paid in blood?"

"Yes!" the people yelled, their torches dripping, their eyes dark pools.

"Sin demands blood; in this you are right. But you are wrong to demand it of those poor women. God has already given you the blood that washes away all sins."

"Come down here, Father." Bastion lurched through the crowd, still drunk from the sleeping tincture Stefan had given him, his eyelids swollen and half lowered, pushing aside the people in his way. "Come and join your people, you frightened little worm." Stefan marveled at the man's strength to overcome the tincture Stefan had given him. Bastion was here for blood, and Stefan had nothing else to stop him.

"No."

"Bring us Mia!" Bastion called. "We want her first!"

"No."

Bastion staggered up the steps, his strength punching through the stupor. He grabbed Stefan by the collar, throwing him against the doors. The handles gouged Stefan's back, expelling his breath. He pushed to the side, away from them.

"Open your church. Bring out Mia."

"Never." Stefan saw flecks of black swimming in the sides of his vision.

Bastion turned to the crowd. "Father Stefan called for me, begging my help, and now he will not let me have a witch to burn. Why is that?"

No one had answers. Stefan did not recognize many of the faces. Most were not his people. But they were anxious for blood or the amusement of another's suffering.

"What if?" Bastion called. Stefan thought he had not heard correctly, so he shook his head, careful to keep his back to the church doors.

The crowd leaned in.

"What if … the Devil has made a disciple of this priest?"

Gasps raised up from the crowd. Some nodded, eager to believe, eager to know what punishment would be inflicted.

"Prove yourself to us, Father Stefan. Who is your god? Who do you worship? Bring me the witches, and we will know you are a good Christian."

"No." Stefan would not debate him. Bastion's fury did not disturb him as much as the fear of Bastion's slippery words. Stefan dug his feet in, bracing his back against the wood, his legs straddling both doors.

"Is he one of them?" a woman called out from the crowd. "Is he tainted?"

Bastion held up his hands for silence. "This is a serious accusation. We must let Stefan reveal the truth by himself. By his own actions, he will decide if he lives or dies. As you are all my witnesses, I will do nothing until Stefan tells us who he really is."

Everyone's faces turned to stare at Stefan, eagerly devouring every little twitch and bead of sweat on his forehead. They were all he ever could have wanted in a congregation. The irony of the moment made the corner of his mouth twitch.

"I could tell you who I am," Stefan said. "But of late, I have discovered someone more interesting. He is the Good Shepherd, and He chooses to protect His sheep with His life. He offers forgiveness for sins and grace, which is a far greater wonder than any magic you could imagine."

Bastion pointed at Stefan and cried out, "Either open those doors and bring out those women, or you will stand convicted of witchcraft. You will be the first to die."

"Do you know the difference between you and me?" Stefan whispered. "At first, I thought it was education, or study. Or wisdom. But now I know. You are compelled to do things you should not do. I am invited to do what I must."

Bastion whipped around, grabbing a torch from a man standing below. Pointing it at Stefan's face, he waved it side to side.

Stefan turned away from its searing heat, his eyes watering. He heard the silence sweep over the crowd. He heard only the sound of the torch snapping and popping and the hiss of flame. Bastion's leering face, distorted by the flame, shimmered in its waves. Stefan stretched himself further across the doors, the wood digging into his back as he wrapped his arm through the handles. He prayed Erick would stay strong and resist coming after Stefan. Stefan had to do this. He had to keep those doors closed until Bastion was gone and the women were safe.

Bastion moved the torch closer, burning Stefan's cheek. "If you are a good shepherd, save yourself. Your people will need you."

"You don't want Mia to burn. You want her for yourself. She will never have you. She has seen through your lies and your promises. It seems that you are the only one left who is deceived."

Stefan saw a light breaking through the clouds above. Never had the moon and stars burned through a dark sky with such force. The heavens opened in hundreds of glimmering points, the glorious white moon holding back the night. Stefan turned his gaze from the promise of the moon and looked through the flames to face his enemy.

"Have you not read?" Stefan asked. "The good shepherd gives his life for just one sheep."

The crowd was motionless. Father Stefan looked at them, their horror plain, piercing through their deception. Bastion had all control now, over life and death, and they realized they did not know this man.

"You are condemned!" Bastion screamed, plunging the torch into Stefan's abdomen, oil and flame spilling across his robes, incinerating the dry linen. Flames shot from all directions as they caught his robes on fire. Stefan saw a flame leap across his arm and lick against the wood door of the church.

Bastion turned on the crowd. "You are my witnesses! He condemned himself by his actions!" He came down the steps, still carrying the torch. "And I will kill any one of you who does not tell the story this way. If you want to live, if you want your children to live, then when you are asked, you will say he was an admitted witch who would not let me burn his consorts."

Bastion threw the torch at their feet, making the crowd scream and scatter as he walked into the night. Stefan cried out against his will. The flames moved to his legs and arms. His mind began to seize and tumble. He saw Bastion leaving. He did not want the last thing he saw on earth to be that man. He turned to look at Ava instead.

Her cage door hung open. She was gone.

Stefan's legs gave out. He stumbled toward the church steps and fell down them, landing on his back. He lifted his eyes to the stars as he died.

Chapter Twenty-seven

Stefan was dead, Mary had said. His body was at the bottom of the steps.

Bastion was gone—he had ridden away on his horse, no one knew in which direction—and the streets were empty. Smoke settled in the church, stinging their eyes. Alma closed hers for relief and slept.

Mia couldn't help the tears that flowed, and when Dame Alice wrapped her arms around Mia and spoke soft words, Mia embraced them. Eventually, she fell asleep.

When she woke, strong daylight illuminated the windows of the church. Alma sat with Erick. Mia watched as Erick tore a linen shirt in his lap into strips, braiding them, then tying them off, making a little rag-doll figure. Alma held her hand out, looking down. Erick lifted her face up, gently, with his fingers, and tapped her on the nose. He stared at the doors, still bolted, as if looking beyond them. He rose, surveying the women. Seeing Mia awake, he nudged Alma and pointed to her. Mia nodded, still too weak to move first.

Erick turned to the doors. He pushed back the bolt and swung the doors open to the day. Brilliant sunlight flooded the church. The women looked away, squinting, murmuring, some just awakening. Mia saw the empty town square, the abandoned church steps, and the stakes. She looked away from the spot where Father Stefan's remains rested.

Erick walked out, returning after a few minutes with a shovel. Mia and the women watched him choose a spot at the front of the church steps and begin to dig. He was digging a grave, she realized. No one would be able to enter this church again without thinking of Father Stefan. He would be its constant gate, its conscience.

Erick finished digging the grave, then laid the body inside. He moved to remove the largest stake first, and Mia shuddered.

Erick wrapped his arms around the larger stake, grunting and heaving, doing the work of three men. Mia saw it move, rising from the cold ground, teetering, before Erick let it fall. He went to the smaller stake next, lifting it, letting it fall, then dragging it to the first. Laying the smaller stake across the taller one, he fetched rope from the sheep pen and returned, fastening the stake together. He dug again, another grave perhaps, Mia thought. But it was deeper, and round.

Villagers had begun to come out of their houses, watching from the lanes, some getting the courage to walk out into the square. None seemed angry. Mia knew the expression they wore. It was shame and confusion. Her heart opened to them, forgiveness surprising her in its sudden birth, and, like a newborn, its lack of logic or principle.

Erick lifted the stakes, dragging them to the smaller hole, and dropped them in. Mia heard her own gasp at what Erick had built, echoing among the others who watched.

Erick had built a cross. When his work was finished, he looked up into the church and caught Mia's eye. A feeling passed between them, clean and pure, like a sacrament.

Alma left Mia, walking to the painting of Jesus above the altar, straining on the tip of her toes to point to His face. The women watched as she ran her little hands over the altar below, then held her hands up to the light. Her fingertips were dirty with soot. She looked at Mia, a question on her face.

"Yes, we will clean this church, Alma."

Alma turned back to stare at the painting, a single tear rolling down her face.

Chapter Twenty-eight

A year later

Mia felt satisfied as she walked. Dame Alice cooked such heavy meals, even in this warm weather. Spring had come early this year, but Dame Alice still insisted on feeding Mia thick roasts and dark breads. She still thought Mia was too thin, though Mia had put on weight. Everything about Mia was different this spring. Her face had softened, she slept without worries, and she was not afraid to talk of the Bible. She was not afraid to read it either, although the new priest the bishop had sent needed convincing that this was a proper thing for a woman to do. Erick had helped convince him, she recalled with a grin. She hoped he had been kind.

Alma ran ahead of Mia as they made their way toward home with surprising energy after hours of playing with little Marie from the village. Alma skipped and hopped as she tried to flush out the spring rabbits for a good chase.

When they arrived at home, Erick stood in the doorway. "What did you bring me?" Alma squealed, running at him with full speed.

Erick wiped his hands on the side of his trousers, grinning at them both. "Brought you some fresh milk. From Mary."

Alma ran to him, and he caught her under the arms, swinging her in an arc around himself, spinning in a circle. Mia watched as Alma threw back her head in laughter.

"Not from her cow, surely?" Mia said with a smile.

"She finally traded it for three goats. The goats are at least giving her milk." Erick set Alma down, and she immediately opened the bag at his side, plunging her hand in.

"Alma! Stop that!" Mia laughed and smoothed out her skirt to busy herself. Her exhortation was futile. Alma pretended not to hear. And Erick himself had created this ritual.

Alma held her prize up to the light. A plain, round stone, but when she turned it, Mia saw it held inside jagged purple fingers, sparkling like gems. She smiled at Alma, whose sweet face glowed with wonder.

Erick took a step forward to leave, and Mia stepped to the side to make room, to avoid coming too close or touching him by accident.

He emptied the bag into his palm as he approached, nodding at Mia to hold out her hand. She did. Erick poured dark, firm black seeds into the folds of her palm. She did not recognize them.

"For flowers. I want you to have something beautiful to look at out your window while you tend to Alma."

Mia's breath caught in her chest. She forced herself to look up, into his eyes. She wanted him to know what she felt. She would keep her promise to herself never to run again.

"You are so kind to us. I do not know what to say," she replied. She truly didn't. She wanted to put it all into words, but they did not seem enough, after all he had done, after all they had survived together.

"You don't need to say anything." Erick smiled at her.

She found it hard to think with him so close. "Well, I thank you. But tell me, what are these seeds called?"

"Bride's flowers."

She knew the blush was rising in her cheeks.

His smile widened as he reached for her hand. "We mustn't waste another spring."

after
words

... a little more ...

When a delightful concert comes to an end,

the orchestra might offer an encore.

When a fine meal comes to an end,

it's always nice to savor a bit of dessert.

When a great story comes to an end,

we think you may want to linger.

And so, we offer ...

AfterWords—just a little something more after you

have finished a David C Cook novel.

We invite you to stay awhile in the story.

Thanks for reading!

Turn the page for ...

- **Bonus Chapter (for readers of the Chronicles of the Scribe series)**
- **Author's Note**
- **Discussion Questions**
- **Supernatural Housekeeping**

Bonus Chapter

For readers of the Chronicles of the Scribe series

Reporters spilled out onto the sidewalk as satellite trucks jockeyed for parking. Everyone scrambled to be the first to the door and into the building. Seasoned pros waved large bills in the air.

Amber-Marie held the foul bag away from her body as she waited in the alley across from the hotel. Her driver, Jim, would start the car as soon as he saw her. Until the press disappeared inside the building, chasing down the story she just gave them, she'd stay hidden.

A greasy stench from the manuscript Amber-Marie just stole nauseated her. The author she represented, Mariskka, had lost her mind writing a sequel to her surprise best seller. She was up there now. Those reporters would get a good dose of crazy. Let them have Mariskka. Amber-Marie had gotten what she wanted. She peered around the corner. Jim watched for her, the engine already running. *Good man.*

She had to get rid of the source of this smell first. One fast breath and she opened the bag. A violent blast of burned hair and skin stung her nostrils as something sharp latched onto her ribs from behind. She flew backward so fast her stomach lurched forward. She tried to scream.

Shoved into darkness and dropped, she recognized the sound of a bolt sliding into a lock. She could not detect walls around her or anything else—just a dark void. Then the smell hit her again, stronger now. She put her hand over her mouth, trying not to breathe.

Something burned in here, a combination like fast-food grease and melting vacuum belts.

"Is anyone here?" she whispered.

A torch burst into flames near her head.

"Take this," a man's voice said.

Her whole body went cold. She couldn't move her arms. The light was brilliant yellow against the black void.

"Take this."

A hand grabbed hers and forced the handle of the torch into her palm. Her fingers closed around it out of instinct.

"Start it," he said.

His hand grabbed hers again, forcing it down, pointing the torch at the ground.

The flames lit a narrow stream of fluid, flames shooting down a straight line before bursting into a starburst of rivers.

At the end of each river of flames, women stood chained upright to wooden posts. They screamed when they saw Amber-Marie holding the torch. Flames shot along the rivers, igniting the pyres of wood beneath their feet.

"Why?" they howled, hair blowing straight up, carried above their heads by the smoke. The flames ate up the pyres, igniting their long skirts. They would die, all of them.

Amber-Marie had killed them. The vision of the burning women grew brighter, and she shielded her eyes, looking for the man in the shadows. He stepped into the light, and she sank to her knees in terror. His face was more beautiful than she expected, smooth like a newborn's, with dead, dull gray eyes. He lowered his face to hers as he spoke.

"What do I love more than innuendo, rumor, half-truth? Do you even remember the feel, the smell, of real truth? Or do all your words stink of burning flesh?"

"I don't understand."

He patted her head. "Of course you don't. I just love you for that."

ﻋﻟ

When Amber-Marie opened her eyes, Mariskka was sitting beside her. Amber-Marie was lying on a hard board, with tubes and strange hoses dangling from the ceiling of the vehicle. She understood. She was in an ambulance, but Mariskka was not the patient. Amber-Marie was. "I didn't see an angel," Amber-Marie said. "Or I did. But not like yours. I don't want to go back."

The paramedic shook his head. He missed as he tried to land the IV needle in her veins. A different paramedic shoved a clipboard to Mariskka, who took it and signed where he had scrawled an X next to the waivers and permissions.

"What did you see?" Mariskka asked.

"I saw … words. What words have done."

The heart rate monitor flat-lined, and paramedics shoved Mariskka away. One straddled Amber-Marie and began chest compressions.

Mariskka sat with her back against the side of the ambulance, the men and the tubes and wires blending into a whirlpool of motion. At her feet, Amber-Marie's bag flopped open. Inside was Mariskka's manuscript.

She released the bolt holding the ambulance doors closed. The doors swung open as the ambulance took a corner. She didn't listen to the screams as she reached for the manuscript, flinging it out into the streets, watching the pages scatter. Some floated in unexpected directions; others sank and landed without any air to move them. No one in the streets moved to gather them. It was just more litter in this city of accidents and betrayals. The heart monitor registered a return to life for Amber-Marie.

Mariskka shut the doors and sat back, waiting for whatever would come next.

Author's Note

Based on conservative estimates, we can say that for every word on these pages you just read, one woman was chained to a stake and set on fire. In Germany alone it is estimated that twenty-four thousand women were burned alive for witchcraft. These witch hunts were fueled in large part by the textbook for witch hunters, the *Malleus Maleficarum*, written by two monks. The *Malleus* could be considered one of the first best-selling books. What can explain the infamous "success" of the *Malleus*?

- Women were excluded from leadership in church.

- There was no readily available translation of the Bible in a commoner's language (until William Tyndale risked his life to produce one).

- Commoners couldn't read anyway.

- Women were often specifically banned from reading the Scripture.

- Denied a voice in the church and persecuted for their distinct gender differences, women frequently turned to folk magic for help.

- The attraction between men and women is a powerful, mysterious chemistry that every generation continually seeks to understand and control.

Gender Roles and the Church

According to medieval religious belief, evil existed outside of men and inside of women. This theory was the backbone of witch hunts. When the Age of Enlightenment swept through Europe, these theories about witchcraft and women's nature were discredited—and the church lost its credibility too. This is why teaching about gender differences and gender roles must be undertaken with extreme care and extreme attention to the Scriptures. We must be careful never to put words into God's mouth.

The reality is that no one understands the complete truth about men and women, our chemistry together, and how each gender is a unique reflection of the divine nature of God. But we do know this—when we finally see God's face in heaven, we will fully understand ourselves, each other, and God: "Now we see but a poor reflection as in a mirror; then we shall see face to face. Now I know in part; then I shall know fully, even as I am fully known" (1 Cor. 13:12).

When half-truths, incomplete truths, or our best guesses are taught from the pulpit as if they are Scripture, we wreck the credibility of the church. We also shame both men and women into believing they are not normal. One expert on gender roles and sexuality told me that young girls raised in church sometimes believe they are abnormal if they have strong desires. After all, the modern church often teaches that women are more emotional than carnal and don't tend to have strong sexual urges like men. A woman or girl who doesn't agree is subtly labeled abnormal. If men, on the other hand, are emotional, they are labeled as "feminine." Church leaders decry the "feminization of the church" as if femininity were a bad thing, as if the church was meant to be a strictly masculine organization, reflecting a strictly masculine God. Such half-truths leave us little room to discover God in ourselves or one another.

I had a chance to chat over email about these issues with one of my favorite nonfiction authors, Jonalyn Grace Fincher. I'll close this section of our discussion with her thoughts:

> Gender differences come in handy when we find ourselves baffled by those closest to us. Isn't it so much easier to blame something we can't control for our problems? For instance, when a man and woman get close (this is especially true in marriage), they discover those annoying differences about each other. Wouldn't we rather locate these irreconcilable differences in gender or sex instead of personal growth?
>
> I've often heard married couples give up understanding or intimacy by discounting the baffling differences in the opposite sex—"Oh, men are all like that," or, "Maybe this is just a woman thing." Instead we could push into knowing one another and realize most of the gender differences are due to culture, family of origin, personality, or unique life experiences.

I wouldn't say the church at large leads the charge in defining gender roles because our Eastern Orthodox and Catholic brothers and sisters do not clamor to put the hard lines down around the differences. However, many churches where men (and their women) fear losing their power tend to define what women and men can and cannot do. The more fear, the more strictly the roles are delineated. For instance, I've been saddened how many gender-defining books are fueled by a misunderstanding and fear of feminism.

Lingering Effects

One other issue of particular interest to historians about the medieval witch hunts was the lurid connection between women's sexuality and their prosecution for witchcraft. Not only were many of the accused women molested in the name of "interrogation," but the witch hunts blamed women for sexual crimes in a way that still permeates our culture today. The prevailing medieval social theory was that women "made" men sin. According to the theory, if women weren't so carnal and tempting, men would have no trouble staying pure. Today women are still held responsible for sexual crime in many of the same ways. The shame of reporting a rape and the fear of being accused of tempting a man beyond what he can bear still keeps women silent and rapists free. Our justice system continues to operate with a double standard when prostitution is involved too. Women are arrested for prostitution at nearly three times the rate that men are arrested for solicitation.

But why should you and I care about prostitution arrests or subtle slurs on "femininity" within the church? Because history has shown us, time and again, that even little twists on truth can end with plenty of destruction. From the garden of Eden to the witch hunts of the Inquisition, to the persecution of Jews, to cults and suicide pacts, half-truths and best guesses leave a wake of pain.

The issues of gender roles and religious thought are so much more complex than I can cover here. If you want a beautiful, thoughtful exploration of gender roles and differences, I recommend you read Jonalyn Grace Fincher's excellent book *Ruby Slippers: How the Soul of a Woman Brings Her Home*. You can also learn more about her work at Soulation.org. Jonalyn writes about these issues with passion and searing intellect.

Which Witch?

The vast majority of witch-hunt victims were not witches, but true witchcraft has always played a role in history. Throughout history, many women have practiced folk magic because they were denied access to education, medicine, and the courts. Women relied on the promise of magic to fight disease, keep their children alive, and bring justice to the afflicted. Wherever women were powerless and excluded, magic seemed to offer help.

Today, you and I live in an age of unprecedented abundance and access to law, medicine, and education. So why is witchcraft often cited as the fastest growing religion in America?

I decided to find out.

I contacted a local New Age bookstore, and they invited me to sit in on a regular meeting of local witches. I was given free rein to ask any question. I came to the meeting with a notebook, a pen, and plenty of prayer. I worried that the witches would be strange, hostile, or want to hurt me because I was a Christian.

I left the meeting burdened with sorrow and with a tender spot in my heart for these women. The women I met—these witches—were just like the women I knew in church. Lovely, wounded, searching, fascinated by a world beyond our own, generous, and open. These women were my neighbors, fellow taxpayers, and part of my larger community. We were much more alike than I would have guessed.

In fact, all the women I spoke with that day grew up in church. Each expressed a strong awareness, early on, of the hypocrisy rampant in churches. (This is, of course, a plague affecting every church across the world. I don't think Christian hypocrisy disproves the validity of Christ and Christianity. Rather, it proves it.)

At my meeting with the witches, the women said something else that shocked me. Most of the women had experienced a strange supernatural event as a child. One woman saw spirits. One was plagued by bad visions. Each had sought help, or information, from others in the church and church leaders. Each received no help, no counseling, no information. So the women turned to the only people willing to listen, explain, and help: the local occult bookstore.

Many of these witches now say that persecution, especially from Christians, is part of their everyday lives. One woman received death threats that included Scripture. Stories of hostility from Christians toward these witches broke my heart. If you want to reach out to a practicing witch or Wiccan, know that they most likely have been abused or

berated in the name of Christianity. As with any opportunity to evange-
lize, we must *earn* the right to tell others of our experiences or opinions.

As I sat with the witches and we discussed Jesus, one woman
sighed and said, "I'd like to think that if Jesus were here on earth,
He'd walk right into our meeting. He'd want to know us."

Knowing that Jesus lives within my heart, I smiled at her. "He is
here," I said. I saw myself in a new way that day: as a physical body
with the spirit of Jesus living within. My job was to take His Spirit out
into the world so that He could tend to the wounded and reach out to
the hurting. I'm just His physical chauffeur. I wasn't given this body
so I could run my own errands. Those women belonged to Him, and
He wanted to be there, sitting in that meeting, listening to their stories,
looking into their eyes, and hearing their hearts. I know that He longs
for them, for us all, to know Him and to know His truth expressed in
love. This truth and this love are the source of all true hope and salvation.

As I close this book, you may like to know that much of the book
is based on fact, including the baptizing of the cat. Bastion's arguments and theology and some anecdotes are taken from the *Malleus*.
Stefan's story of ministering to Ava the witch is based on a true story
too. During the witch hunts, a witch was kept in a cage and used
like a circus animal to scare people. One wise and courageous priest
developed a relationship with her and taught her the truth of who
Jesus was and how she could find true peace and love only in Him.
This priest led her to Christ, and the woman escaped her captivity.

Thankful for this freedom,
Ginger Garrett

Discussion Questions

1. Read these three statements:

   • "All witchcraft comes from carnal lust, which is in women insatiable."—the *Malleus Maleficarum*

   • "This [theory of the insatiability of women, which I teach,] comes out of some social research which suggests that some women are insatiable or never satisfied. From that, I point out that Eve had paradise but wanted more. She lacked satisfaction with paradise!"—best-selling Christian author who teaches on marriage and gender roles

   • "The temptation to give in to evil comes from us and only us. We have no one to blame but the leering, seducing flare-up of our own lust."—God, as recorded in James 1:13 (MSG)

   The *Malleus's* false theories are still being repeated today, often under the guise of "Christian marriage teaching." What does the Bible say about the root of lust and temptation? Is it a particularly male or female problem? If lust is a male problem, what can explain the actions of Potiphar's wife? (See Gen. 39.)

2. Jesus said, "Watch out for false prophets. They come to you in sheep's clothing, but inwardly they are ferocious wolves.

By their fruit you will recognize them" (Matt. 7:15–16). Not everyone who uses God's name speaks for God. What are some of the signs that a person is truly doing God's work? Is success always a sign God is endorsing them?

3. Throughout the story, Mia is hungry. She presses her hand into her stomach to keep it from growling. In your opinion, what is this hunger symbolic of? Why was Mia always so hungry? Did she need anything more than food?

4. Deuteronomy 8:3 says, "He humbled you, causing you to hunger and then feeding you with manna, which neither you nor your fathers had known, to teach you that man does not live on bread alone but on every word that comes from the mouth of the LORD." In our culture of abundance and instant access, do we experience hunger of any kind? Is there a connection between humility and hunger? What interferes with the experience of hunger, especially spiritual hunger, in our lives and culture?

5. Bastion knew Scripture very well and twisted it just slightly to make a convincing case for evil. Did you find any of Bastion's arguments persuasive? How can we recognize the actual truth of Scripture versus a false little twist someone puts on it?

6. Why was Bastion able to come in and swiftly turn the villagers to evil? Are you safe from the Bastions of our age? What are your defenses?

after
words

7. Father Stefan knew many prayers and rituals, most of them in Latin, a language few understood or spoke. Did he have true spiritual authority in his village? What is the true source of spiritual authority? Did he ever acquire it?

8. Mia made a decision to honor God by avoiding temptation. She recognized that Bjorn was not worthy of her faithfulness, but God was. Have you ever seen a broken marriage healed when one partner commits his or her life fully to God?

9. Mia is afraid of the darkness in the world and the darkness in her heart. But toward the end of the novel, she realizes she has never been alone in either one. Which is harder for you to feel and trust in: God's presence in the darkness outside your door or God's presence with you in the darkness you have in your heart?

10. Which is more important: experiential truth (deciding that what I experience is also a universal truth) or Scriptural truth (deciding that Scripture is true, regardless of my experience)?

11. The witch hunts were a volatile combination of religious half-truths and public imagination. Do you think the church teaches any half-truths today? What has our culture's imagination right now? What do we seem to be fantasizing about, obsessing about, and fearful of? How can we apply the antidote of truth and love to these issues?

Supernatural Housekeeping

In my research, women told me that they became involved in the occult after experiencing a strange supernatural event. They were often unable to get help from their Christian church, so they turned to the occult or witchcraft for answers. If you believe you are being plagued by a demon, spirit, or any other supernatural phenomenon, you can find relief and restoration.

1. Start by reading these verses about Jesus:
   - Salvation is found in no one else, for there is no other name under heaven given to men by which we must be saved. (Acts 4:12)

   - All the people were amazed and said to each other, "What is this teaching? With authority and power he gives orders to evil spirits and they come out!" (Luke 4:36)

   These verses give you a bedrock, a firm foundation to work from. Jesus is the sole source of salvation, both in the eternal sense and in the earthly sense. He alone can save you from a supernatural affliction. His name is the only name with the power to save us from ourselves or anything else. While on earth, Jesus ordered evil spirits around, and they obeyed. He can handle whatever problem you may have, whether mundane or supernatural.

2. If you have a spirit in your home, don't talk to it. Don't attempt to engage it in conversation. (If you need to understand why, read the story of Adam, Eve, and the serpent.)

3. Pray over your home, room by room, speaking aloud the verses above. In Jesus' name, command any evil spirits to leave. I'd like to suggest that a Christian should do this, since Christians have Jesus' spirit within and have His authority to drive spirits out. If you're not a Christian, you can consider asking a Christian friend to do this with you. You can also contact a nearby Christian bookstore or church. Many larger churches have counselors with training in what is frequently called "spiritual warfare."

4. Satisfy your curiosity about the supernatural by going straight to the source: God. In the Bible you'll find plenty of frank conversation about spirits, ghosts, psychics, and supernatural phenomenon. If you don't know where to start, you can use BibleGateway.com. Search by keyword to see any verse that addresses that topic, in almost any translation. For example, I can enter the word *demon,* select my favorite translation, *The Message,* and see every verse in the Bible that talks about demons. It's a good place to start your research, but you will still want to read the Scriptures in depth so you get the proper context.

5. I also recommend the books *The Invisible War* by Chip Ingram and *Victory Over the Darkness: Realizing the Power of Your Identity in Christ* by Neil T. Anderson.

My research told me that experiencing a supernatural occurrence presents you with a choice. You must decide who to listen to, and which path to follow. I pray you choose to listen to Jesus: "A thief is only there to steal and kill and destroy. I came so they can have real and eternal life, more and better life than they ever dreamed of" (John 10:10 MSG).